PRAISE
FOR
A
NEW MASTER
OF
SUSPENSE!

"His stories of international intrigue belong on that too-small shelf which contains the works of Eric Ambler and Geoffrey Household!"
—*The New York Times*

"For heady, breath-taking storytelling at its best, mark as a must THE MOST DANGEROUS GAME!"
—*Book Week*

GAVIN LYALL

the most dangerous game

AVON
PUBLISHERS OF
DISCUS · CAMELOT · BARD

AVON BOOKS
A division of
The Hearst Corporation
959 Eighth Avenue
New York, New York 10019

First Avon Edition, September, 1969

DISCUS BOOKS TRADEMARK REG. U.S. PAT. OFF. AND
FOREIGN COUNTRIES, REGISTERED TRADEMARK—
MARCA REGISTRADA, HECHO EN CHICAGO, U.S.A.

Printed in the U.S.A.

the most
dangerous
game

CHAPTER 1

THEY were ripping up Rovaniemi airport, as they were almost every airport in Finland that summer, into big piles of rock and sandy soil. It was all part of some grand rebuilding design ready for the day when they had enough tourist traffic to justify putting the jets onto the internal air routes. In the meantime, it was just turning perfectly good airports into sandpits.

In some rush of enthusiasm they'd even gone and torn up the area between the aircraft park and the airport building, a long low wooden affair with the control tower in one corner and the coffee *baari* in the middle. To reach it now, you had to walk along fifty yards of plank path laid across the muddy sand. He was waiting for me at the near end of the path.

Then, I didn't know him from the angel Gabriel, except that he was perhaps a little short for that. I just got an impression of somebody looking smart in a light-coloured raincoat and hat and with a lot of snazzy luggage laid out neatly along the planking to keep itself dry and me wet.

The cut and colour of his clothes had marked him as not being Finnish, so I said in English: "You wouldn't be offended if I broke my neck falling over your luggage, would you?"

He said: "Mr Cary?"

I said: "Yes, I'm Bill Cary," and cranked my eyes around until I could look him over more carefully. My first idea was that he looked blurred, but then that was true of everything else I'd looked at that day.

He was shortish without being small, and slightly tubby. His raincoat was a single-breasted beltless job of that ivory white colour that looks a lot more expensive than plain soap-commercial white. And it managed to look clean and crisp without looking new. His hat was of the same material, the American golfing version of the Cockney peaked cap. He had small, brown shoes with punched patterns and a rich deep gloss in them. He looked expensive, in a quiet way, and he looked used to it.

With all this, and with standing on a torn-up airfield just

inside the Arctic Circle, his face seemed off-key. It was round and smooth, with a baby-angel gentleness in his big grey eyes. But if he was a softie, at least he didn't think he was. Among the luggage laid out on the path there were four worn gun cases.

He said: "Pardon me, sir—Frederick Wells Homer," and held out his hand. He had a watered-down American accent and he said his name as if he always said it that way, not as if he was trying to impress me.

I shook his hand. It was small and well-kept, but firm.

"Mr Cary, sir—I wonder if you could fly me somewhere?"

The thought landed in my brain with a soggy thud. I waved a hand at him. "Later—later. Say, after breakfast."

"Breakfast, sir? Today? You breakfast rather late." He raised a polite pair of eyebrows at me. The slow, controlled movement of his face gave him his age: around thirty-five. A few years younger than me and about a century younger than I felt.

He had a point there, though. It was about four in the afternoon.

"I've just got in from Stockholm with a hangover," I said carefully. "I didn't feel like eating and drinking anything before I left and to tell the truth I don't feel like it now, either. But if I'm going to live, I'd better try at least a cup of coffee."

The thought of coffee made him get fuzzy again. Through it came a new thought. I asked: "How did you know who I was?"

He smiled gently. "I was told to look for a tall, thin Englishman, flying a Beaver amphibian and—and dressed as you are." Whatever else he had, the man had manners. 'Dressed as you are' was a baseball-style cap, a pair of oily khaki drill trousers, a leather jacket that looked as if I'd decoked an engine onto it (probably because I had) and American paratroop boots with a Fairbairn commando knife clipped to the right one.

I smiled knowingly more or less in his direction and said: "You can't fool me. You're Robert E. Lee, the well-known Southern Gentleman."

He smiled gravely back. "I hate to disappoint you, sir. But at least we come from the same state."

I said: "Virginia." And he nodded and I nodded, and then floundered over his luggage towards the *baari*.

I got my coffee, large and black and hot, and went away to fight it alone in a quiet corner. But long before I was ready for loud, close noises, somebody had rasped out the chair opposite, flopped into it and rasped it back up to the table. Robert E. Lee would never have done that to a sick man. And in fact, he hadn't. It was Veikko.

He said: "How soon can you finish the Kaaja company work?"

He said it in English, which, even to me in my state, suggested he wanted something from me. When we spoke to each other, we usually spoke Swedish. Finnish is one of the toughest languages in the world and I'd never got fluent in it. But I speak Swedish all right, and most Finns have it as a second language.

But normally Veikko and I didn't speak anything. He was Lapland's biggest crook. I've nothing against talking to crooks, only against those who are well known to be crooks. Also, I didn't know what particular crookery he was up to this year.

I said: "Go away. I'm busy dying."

He leant across the table at me. "I have a job for you, if you finish off the Kaaja work quick. Not here—in Sweden."

I focussed on him. He didn't look like Father Christmas. He still looked like Lapland's biggest crook: a shortish, very solid man in a double-breasted suit of snappy green-and-black stripes that looked as appropriate to Lapland as a Tiger Lily. A good deal of flesh on his face—which isn't untypical in a country which likes its potatoes—but very smooth and unweathered.

I took a long swallow of coffee. "Who's the company on this job?" Then I thought of a better question: "What's your cut?"

He spread his hands and smiled the happy, open smile of a second hand car salesman. "Just a few per cent."

"When does the job start?"

"How soon can you get the Kaaja company work finished?"

I went back to my coffee. "I can't. I'm contracted to them until the first snow."

"No." He smiled some more. "Kaaja does not give contracts like that. When can you finish?"

I swallowed more coffee. It was beginning to do its work. By now, I could think out that perhaps his whole approach was some way of finding out what area I was surveying for Kaaja. You don't know about nosiness until you've seen one mineral company's interest in the areas where another company thinks there might be minerals. And Veikko would be the ideal man to hire to find out what I was up to.

Except, of course, that everybody except the reindeer knew he was a crook, and even they must be getting suspicious by now.

"What's the job itself?" I asked. "Survey? Transport?"

"The company will tell you. When can you start?"

"I can't. I'm contracted to Kaaja. Why don't you give the job to Oskar Adler?"

He was the only other floatplane pilot working in Lapland that summer.

"Hell." He spread his hands again. "The work needs flying off both land and water. He doesn't have an amphibian; you have the only aeroplane with both floats and wheels up here."

At least that was true.

"Sorry," I said. "I'm contracted to Kaaja." I went to get myself another coffee.

When I looked back, he was just getting up. He didn't look as worried as he should have, not after missing his few per cent. Or not finding out something about the area I was surveying for Kaaja.

Perhaps I was a damn fool. My Kaaja contract didn't last until the first snow. It was just to survey an area, and I would probably finish that in two weeks.

But Veikko still didn't look like Father Christmas to me.

I finished my second coffee and my hands were still shaking like a battle flag. But at least I was awake enough to realise what I should have done in the first place: had a beer.

The only problem in buying a beer on a Finnish airport is that you can't. The Finns are roughly divided into those who take it, and go on taking it, and those who leave it alone and think it would be better if everyone else did. The last bunch made the drink laws. One law is that you can't buy a bottle in Lapland anywhere north of Rovaniemi, and can't even buy a glass except in the half-dozen tourist hotels. This makes for plenty of illegal home distilling and a good trade in imported crates of the real stuff. I'd flown in one or two myself when I had an unloaded flight from the south.

The second law is that you can't drink on airports. Not a bad idea for stopping pilots taking off drunk, but not much help to a pilot who knows by long experience that the only way to get a hangover roped and back in its cage is a beer. Or two.

Happily, there was a man down in the maintenance hangar who made half his living doctoring hungover pilots. I stood up to go and get some maintenance just as Frederick Wells Homer came in.

He smiled at me and came and sat down.

"I trust you're feeling recovered, sir?"

"Better, anyway." I sat down again and lit a cigarette. At least I owed this character an apology.

I said: "I'm sorry about the way I behaved outside."

"Think nothing of it, sir. You were not a well man." He smiled gravely. "It must have been quite an achievement to fly that distance from Stockholm—I believe it's about five hundred miles?—with such an affliction. I feel reassured in placing myself in your hands."

I squinted at him. That should have been sarcasm, but it was said dead straight, the way he said his name.

I said: "I'm not sure I follow your reasoning. If I met a pilot with a hangover like mine, I'd go by submarine."

He just smiled again. "Then you think you'll be able to transport me, sir?"

"Depends where and when." I didn't much want to take him anywhere at any time. I was contracted to the Kaaja company and I owed them an early night. But you don't often meet somebody with the manners of Robert E. Lee. I'd met a couple of Kaaja directors in Helsinki on my way to Stockholm and they hadn't had the manners of Billy the Kid. I'd been flying a survey for them for over five weeks and hadn't found a Finnmark's worth of nickel; therefore I was loafing on the job. Flying out to Stockholm for the weekend just proved it.

He said: "I was hoping you'd be able to advise me, sir, with your knowledge of the country. I'm looking for bear."

"Bears?" Then I remembered the gun cases outside. Then I shook my head anyway. "You hardly get any bear shooting. Then mostly in the spring. I read somewhere that they only shoot forty-odd a year."

He just nodded and waited.

I was stalling. I knew where there were bears. Flying a mineral survey means flying mostly no higher than 300 feet, and in a single-engined aircraft that means spending the time watching the ground, looking for landing places in case the single engine gets the sleeping sickness on you. In Finland, which is mostly woodland, this doesn't help much, but at least it means you know what's happening down there. And I'd seen five bears, or the same one five times, in the last fortnight.

There were a couple of snags. One was that putting him down in the only bit of bear country I could vouch for meant putting him down in the middle of my survey area. Not a good idea if he was a rival company's spy. Still, I didn't really think he was.

That left just snag number two. "Look," I said. "I can put you down near where I've seen some bears recently. The trouble is, I'd be breaking the law in doing so."

He gave his eyebrows a polite lift, and waited for me to explain.

I said: "It's a prohibited area. Prohibited to aircraft, anyway. It runs up and down the Russian frontier, anything up to forty-five miles wide. It's all Finnish territory, but they make it prohibited as a sort of peacemaker. So the Russians won't have any excuse for complaints about somebody spying on them. And the Finns take it seriously—if they catch you in it."

They hadn't caught me—yet. Which was partly because their radar net isn't complete and partly because at mineral-survey heights you're well under most radar coverage. But it was also partly luck, because the whole of the Kaaja survey area was in prohibited territory.

Kaaja had covered themselves by giving me a dummy contract for a legal area further west, and done something towards covering me—since I'd be the one to get jugged—by paying nearly double the normal rates. But I still had a better-than-usual reason for keeping my survey area secret.

But I didn't think Homer was a Finnish government agent, either.

"I don't mind flying you in there," I said. "And it's no offence for you to *be* there, on the ground. But I don't want anybody to know how you got there. While you're there, I'd rather nobody else knew where you are, and when you get back I'd rather nobody knew exactly where you'd been. That means pretty well stranding you there, you understand?"

He thought about this, then nodded. "That's quite agreeable to me, sir. Indeed—provided I'm not leading you into unnecessary risks—I'd prefer it that way. You're sure you're happy about this, sir?"

I waved a hand. "I'm sure. When d'you want to go?"

"Whenever you're ready to fly, sir."

I looked at my watch. It was nearly five o'clock, which left us over two hours of daylight, and a long twilight after that. We were on the edge of autumn, just crawling down from the days of the midnight sun to the long, long night of the Lapland winter.

"Okay," I said. "There's an old cabin up near the place I'm thinking about. I don't know what it's like, since I've only flown over it, but it's probably better than a tent. I suppose you've got supplies?"

"I think I have everything, sir, including a fortnight's food. Perhaps, after that, you could fly me in some more?"

"No trouble." Then I began to wonder how long he'd reckoned it would take to shoot a bear. "How long were you planning to stay?"

"I'd thought of five or six weeks—to begin with, anyhow. Were you going to be in these parts that long?" He said it with a kindly—and honest—anxiety, as if he might accidentally detain me on the wrong side of the world.

"I'll stay as long as there's work. It can be a damn long winter for a pilot." I must have sounded sincere, because he glanced at me quickly, then looked politely away again.

I stood up. "I'll see you outside in a quarter of an hour. I've got a man to see down at the hangar. All right?"

"Perfectly, sir. I'll start loading my baggage, if your airplane's not locked."

I smiled at the idea. "Not in a long time." Then I nodded, which was a mistake with my head feeling as it did, and went on out, thinking of the sort of life where you can take five or six weeks off to go and shoot a bear.

The maintenance man knew me; he had a bottle in one hand and an opener in the other before I was within shouting distance.

I drank half the bottle of beer in one gulp, then started slowly on the second half.

After a time he asked: "How was Stockholm?" He spoke Swedish, for my benefit.

I said: "Fine, as far as I can remember."

"What did the de Havilland's man say?"

I'd flown over primarily to see what the manufacturer's agent thought needed doing to the Beaver to keep it going another season.

"He was very polite and kind. At least he didn't laugh."

"Did he say you needed a new engine?"

"He said I needed a new aeroplane."

He nodded gloomily. "I could have told you that myself.
Only I thought it would worry you."

Beavers are among the toughest aircraft built these days
—they were designed for the Canadian bush jobs—but even
Beavers grow old. This one had grown old inside a few seconds, when some Finn Air Force pilot had tried to make a
long landing on a short lake. They'd picked it out of the
trees and sold it off cheap—to me. I'd done what essential
work I could afford, such as putting on a propeller, but one
of the floats was slightly out of line, the fuselage was
twisted so that none of the doors fitted properly, and the
engine bearings were waggling like a film star's bottom.

"Did he give you a price for an engine overhaul?"

"He said if the engine was giving full power the whole
aeroplane would pull apart in the air."

He nodded again. "Maybe you'll get work this winter."

That was always the problem. Most charter flying and all
mineral survey work stops with the first snow. Up to a few
years ago, I'd been able to find winter work in Norway or
Germany or Austria; by now, they've got too many aircraft
of their own. Last winter I'd laid the Beaver up in Helsinki;
it looked like the same this year.

But even steady winter work wouldn't buy me a new
Beaver; what I needed was to find nickel. Under the bonus
clause with Kaaja, that might just do it.

I asked: "Mikko about?"

He nodded his head at the back of the hangar. I walked
down there. Mikko was leaning against the wall, watching
a man working on a piece of electronic equipment on another
bench.

According to the salary I paid him, Mikko was my assistant. He sat behind me and watched the magnetometer recorder and scintillometer, and got them repaired when they
blew up. As it had turned out, soon after I'd hired him, he
was somebody with a brand-new pilot's license looking for
real work and not sitting watching a bunch of electric nonsense.

I tapped him on the shoulder and he jerked out of his day-
dream of being Finnair's chief jet pilot.

"Recorder fixed yet?" I asked.

He pointed at the bits and pieces on the bench. "They had

to make a couple of new parts," he explained disinterestedly. "Did you have a big party in Stockholm?"

"When'll it be ready?"

He shrugged. "Tonight, sometime."

I said: "I've got to fly a hunter up a few miles. I should be back in a couple of hours. If it's not ready before then, get us a couple of rooms somewhere—and *not* at the Polar." Leave him without clear instructions and he'd book us the best rooms in town. Pilots, he thought, had a front to keep up.

He shrugged and went back to leaning against the wall.

"All right," I said. "I've got to go and earn our keep. Don't strain your eyes watching somebody else work."

Homer had got most of his luggage onto the Beaver by the time I got there, and even got it into a sensible position relative to the centre of gravity. He'd flown in small planes before. I dumped a cargo net over his cases, tied it down at the corners, and we were ready to go.

CHAPTER 2

I FLEW due north until we were well out of sight of Rovaniemi. In the righthand seat, Homer had his raincoat and cap off by now. He had very fine, limp, near-blonde hair that added to his baby-angel impersonation, and grey Venetian-cloth slacks and a brown-and-black cashmere sports jacket that added to the impression of money in the bank. He caught my eye and loosened his seat straps. The seats in a Beaver aren't exactly club armchairs, but he fitted in easily enough.

I lit a cigarette; he refused one. After a while he asked: "Just where are you putting me down, sir?" He had to say it fairly loud over the blast of air that was leaking in around the pilots' doors.

I passed him a map and tapped where I was heading for. "There. Small lake just off the Värriöjoki river. You've got the old cabin about a mile north, and a few miles beyond that there should be bear."

He studied the map for a while, but it was too small scale for him to make any deductions about bears from it—except to see that it was one of the emptiest bits of Finland there is.

Then he asked: "Is the country the same as it is here, sir?"

I looked down out of the window. "Pretty much. Bit rougher, perhaps. You don't get much change in the land around here." We were drifting across a series of low east-west ridges. The trees—spruce, mostly—were widespaced and lean trying to find a living down there. A spruce will put down roots into a bit of carpet fluff if there's nothing better, but the tops of some of these ridges were bare rock. Among the trees there were the scattered grey bones of other trees that had gone down in the winter storms. We were inside the Arctic Circle.

Homer asked: "You think I'll be fairly much alone up there?"

"You should be. There probably isn't a soul within twenty-five miles." The Kemijoki-Värriöjoki lies in what looks, on the map, to be a big eastward bulge of Finland into Russia. In fact it's the other way round: after the war the Russians moved in north and south of the bulge. Among the things they moved in on was the nickel mine near Petsamo; that was why finding more nickel was such a high-priority job.

They didn't grab the bulge because it wasn't worth having. The timber's too thin to be worth cutting, and the ground's too rough to haul it out anyway. And nobody's found any minerals in it—yet. The only reason for going there is if you're a rock or a bear, or somebody looking for either.

We flew for a while with just the sound of the Beaver growing old around us. Then I asked: "You come just to shoot bears? I'd've thought there were plenty of bears in the States and Canada."

"There are, sir, and I've shot some myself. Now I want to try to get a European brown bear."

I picked my words, and tone, carefully, and asked: "What d'you do the rest of the time? Got your own business?"

He smiled gently ahead at the windscreen. "No, sir. I just hunt. I spend my life hunting—and travelling to hunt. It's what I like doing."

I managed just to nod and keep my eyes on the oil pressure gauge. You meet all kinds of unemployment.

I looked across at him and said: "You really are hunting, are you? You're not after the Volkof?"

He seemed genuinely puzzled. "I don't think I follow, sir."

I nodded. "Sorry. I suppose not. The Volkof's our buried-treasure legend, up here in Lapland. We usually get one or two people looking for it every summer."

"Really, sir?" He looked interested, but only politely so. "I didn't know you had buried treasure up here."

"Well, in my opinion, we don't have. If it was ever there, I should think it's gone by now, and I don't believe it was ever there. But it's the sort of story people like to believe."

"Perhaps you'd tell me the story some time."

"Hell, there's as many stories as people looking for it—they all have some new angle. Basically, Volkof was supposed to be some White Russian, a rich engineer or something, up in Murmansk, on the north coast. When the Revolution came— some time in the winter of 1917–18—he tried to skip out and head for Finland. Finland had just become an independent country then. Him, his wife, and his treasure. His wife made it, he and his treasure didn't. So somewhere up here—" I waved a hand through an arc of about 270 degrees "—lies his whitened skeleton, clutching a handful of doubloons and the Czar's second-best cufflinks to its bony bosom."

"The treasure consists of that, sir?"

"God knows what it consists of—nobody who comes looking seems very sure. They assume they'll know it when they find it."

"And Mrs Volkof—what happened to her?"

"Volkova," I said automatically. "Russian uses feminine endings on proper nouns. Yes—that's a good question. Nobody's ever found her, either. She's supposed to have left Finland. Each new rumour is supposed to be something she once revealed. Remember, this is all forty years ago, now. She's probably dead long since."

I dropped my cigarette on the floor and ground it out with the toe of my boot. One of these days I was going to fit an ashtray in the Beaver—probably on the day the floor fell out, and I really needed it.

"Me," I said, "I don't see why—if the treasure was ever there—she didn't come back some time in the twenties and collect it. Come to that, if the treasure was jewels or gold, why didn't she stick a bit in her pocket when old man Volkof lay down to die?"

He nodded sympathetically. "Do you get employed to try and find it, sir?"

"Every now and then. I don't like the job: they hate paying up at the end when they haven't found any treasure."

He smiled. Soon after that, I turned east and started to lose height so as to be under the radar net before I hit the prohibited area.

The lake I was heading for lay just over twenty miles inside the area. It was nearly 400 yards long, running roughly east-west, and mostly about 50 yards wide. The snag came with a small island about two-thirds the way from the western end, which gave a bottleneck of water only twenty yards wide and made landing on it look a shaky idea.

For a green pilot it might have been. But I'd grown old and brown and curled at the edges landing floatplanes in shaky places. And looking an unlikely spot was one of its advantages: I had a pile of petrol tins under the branches on that island so that I could refuel without going back to Ivalo or Rovaniemi. From the length of my flights Veikko or Oskar Adler must have known I had a dump somewhere, but I hoped the sight of that lake wouldn't help them guess where.

I circled over the cabin in the woods to show Homer where it lay from the lake, then landed. There was a small beach at the eastern end of the lake, and I let down the wheels under water and ran the Beaver up onto that so that we could unload without getting our feet wet.

The first thing he did was open one of his gun cases and take out a slender, single-barrelled bolt-action rifle with protective metal petals around the foresight. He got out a box of rounds, loaded five into the magazine, then slung the thing from his shoulder. Then he caught me staring.

He smiled and said: "You said there were bear in these parts, sir. I wouldn't doubt you."

Fair enough. Why should the bears wait until tomorrow, even if he was ready to?

I started handing down the rest of his luggage. "What guns d'you use?" I asked.

"All Purdeys, from London. I don't think I'd use anything else, now. For bear I have the .300 Magnum." He touched the gun on his shoulder. "Then a 7-millimetre in case I try for moose. And a pair of guns."

"A what?"

"Maybe you'd call them shotguns, sir."

I said: "I'd've thought a .300 was a bit light to use on bear," just to keep the conversation going. I knew hunters liked arguing about bullet weights. The only idea I had about what to use on a bear was a fast takeoff.

He nodded gravely. "There is a school of thought that agrees with you, sir. And if you were planning to shoot any tough-skinned animal with the same gun, then I'd agree. But a bear's soft-skinned and you'll recall it's a Magnum cartridge. And, of course, you're fairly close."

"Close?"

He looked around at the thin grey-green trees and heavy boulders knitted together with a mess of undergrowth and fallen branches that hadn't been cleared since the year One.

"In this sort of country," he said, "about twenty yards would be normal."

I said: "Jesus." I couldn't quite see Frederick Wells Homer and his baby-angel face, even with his Purdey .300 Magnum, up within twenty yards of a bear. But then, when I thought about it, perhaps his sort of calmness was exactly what you'd need at in-fighting with a bear.

He said, almost apologetically: "You'll understand, sir, that the whole sport with dangerous game is in getting up close."

I said: "Yes," just as if I did understand, and went on hauling down luggage.

Then I remembered an idea I'd been thinking about for a couple of years. "Maybe you can advise me," I said. "I've been thinking of getting some sort of gun, just in case I have to force-land up here some time. Just to knock down a bird for supper, but I'd rather like it to be some use if a bear tried to knock me down for supper. Can I do that with just one gun?"

He said promptly: "A 12-bore."

"A shotgun? Would that do anything to a bear?"

He smiled. "You might be surprised, sir. In the right place, close up, a 12-bore would certainly kill a bear."

"If I'm given the choice, I won't be close up."

He smiled again. "But you can also get a solid bullet for a 12-bore. That'll kill bear at sixty yards or more. With one of those in one barrel and birdshot in the other, you'll be as versatile as you can be with one gun. Perhaps you'd let me write to Purdey's on your behalf, sir? Then, the next time you're in London—"

I said: "Hold on a minute. These things cost money, don't they?"

He looked slightly pained. "It depends on your choice of decoration, but I'd say about one thousand dollars apiece."

I grinned at him. "I'm just a bush pilot. All I want is something to go bang in emergencies. I can probably pick up a 12-bore in Rovaniemi or Ivalo, but I haven't heard of solid slugs up here. So if you'd tell me where to write for some, I'd be grateful."

He was sunny again. "If you'd permit me, sir, I'd be happy

to get them for you. I believe you'd need an import license, and as I already have one . . . ?"

"Thanks." We got the last of his luggage stacked up on the shore. If I'd been a Virginia gentleman myself, I'd probably have offered to help carry them up to the cabin. But it was over half a mile and the time was getting on to sundown: I didn't want to pay night landing charges back at Rovaniemi if I could help it.

Certainly he didn't expect any help, because he pulled out what looked like a chequebook in a dark snakeskin cover and said: "I owe you for transportation, sir. Would one hundred dollars cover it, sir?"

I did a little quick currency conversion in my head—you don't often meet dollars in Lapland—then said: "About twice too much."

He nodded and filled in a cheque and handed it over. It was a Bank of America traveller's cheque for one hundred dollars. "Can you cash that, sir?"

"I can, and for rather more than you could. It's still twice too much."

"You not only transported me, sir, but did it without notice and, I believe, in your off-duty time. You've been very kind." He dug in his pocket. "And perhaps, sir, you could call back in two weeks or so, if you could find some of those things?" He handed me a piece of paper.

It was just a straightforward list of tinned stuff and other supplies I could pick up by just crossing the street in Rovaniemi or Ivalo. It was on a piece of notepaper with 'Frederick Wells Homer' engraved in small copperplate script up in one corner, and under it a Washington bank address.

I tucked it away. He was scribbling on a small pad of the same notepaper. When he handed it me, I saw the Purdey's address in London at the bottom.

He said: "And if you'll put that in an envelope to that address, I'm sure the solid cartridges will turn up soon."

"Thanks. I'll drop back in about twelve days' time. You should be completely alone here, you're over twenty miles from the nearest road, and it's very rough country in between. So if you shoot your own foot off or get nibbled by a bear, nobody'll know until it's too late. You appreciate that?"

He smiled. "I've been alone in the wilds before, sir."

"Good. But this place is a lot wilder than it looks. And don't get caught here by the snow. We shouldn't have it for another month, but when it comes, you can't move in these woods. Then the lakes start to freeze and I can't land.

"So if it starts to snow, be down on the beach the next morning and I'll get you out."

"I'll do that, sir."

I felt awkward and schoolmasterish lecturing this character, but there was one thing left to be said. "The Russian frontier's about twenty-five miles that way." I nodded east. "Don't get too near it."

He just nodded and said: "Thank you for reminding me, sir."

We didn't shake hands, which was odd for an American but not so odd for him. He'd picked up a lot that was a certain sort of English along with his glossy brown shoes and Purdey guns. And along with blowing the bejasus out of the wild life in faraway places. If I had my social history right, that was originally an English idea, too.

CHAPTER 3

MIKKO had got rooms for us in—for once—a cheap boarding house. Supper was a choice of boiled beef or staying hungry, but that's true of most Finnish boarding houses. We lived through it, but the thirst afterwards began to worry me.

Mikko had a girl he wanted to look up, so I walked over to the Polar and had a couple of glasses of cloudberry by myself, then walked back. The streets were empty; Rovaniemi doesn't have much night life until the boys off the military end of the airfield come in on a Saturday night.

I was just coming around the last corner before the house when they jumped me. Three of them. One stepped out behind me and hooked an arm around my neck and yelled for the other two to get started on me. I caught the glint of *puukot*, those nasty little hook-ended Finnish knives, as they came.

If they'd been good, it would have been over before I'd known it had started. They'd been standing too spaced out, trying to look unsuspicious. But if they weren't good, they looked eager for practice.

The one behind me was a bit shorter than me. I gave as much of a pull forward as I could, to get him pulling back,

then threw myself backwards. He landed on the pavement
and I landed on him. His breath went out past my ear in a
long hoot like a ship's siren. His arm turned to chewed
string. I rolled off him as the first *puukko* merchant dodged
round his feet to get at me.

I had my Fairbairn knife clipped to my right boot, but no
time to get at it. I stayed where I was, down, and stab-kicked
at his knee. I missed, but it made him dodge. He slashed
downwards at my foot. He missed.

The third one was coming round to get me from behind.
I still had my cap on my head; I yanked it off with my left
hand and swiped it at the first knife as I came up kneeling.
The knife went straight through the cap but caught on the
edge seam, and the drag of my swipe yanked his knife arm
out sideways. I hit him in the stomach as I came off the
ground, cannoned off his shoulder and ended up behind him,
with him bent over gurgling between me and the third party.

Now I had time. I pulled the knife off my boot and waved
it around in front of me, so that he'd know about it. He
stopped. I moved forward. Just to maintain the odds, I booted
the first knifer on the ankle as I went past. Hard. He dropped
with a thump that raised dust.

The third lad was young, with long fair hair and a dark
leather jacket and not much idea about knife fighting. But
he hadn't been counting on a fight—just a nice easy massacre.

He held his knife too high. I went in crouching, and offered
him my left hand to take a stab at. He tried it—and I lunged
my knife in a low upward thrust at his crotch.

It didn't get within two feet of him, but the thought went
all the way. He let out a squeal and jumped a clear yard
backwards.

I gave a low, nasty laugh that wasn't entirely acting: I
felt low and nasty. The shock of being jumped was wearing
off into a cold angry blood-hunger. I crabbed in towards
him, holding the knife low and pointing straight at him.

He cracked. He made one vast hammer stroke that would
have taken off my hand if it had come anywhere near my
hand—then he ran.

I suddenly remembered the other two, and whipped
around. There was only one left—the lad whose ankle I'd
kicked. He was climbing off the ground and it was a long
steep climb. I'd have liked to have had a quiet word with
him about why the whole business, but a Rovaniemi street
wasn't the best place for that.

I picked my cap off the end of his *puukko*, said: "Good night," and went on to the boarding house. I was nearly there before I realised I was wearing a cap with a six-inch rent in the crown and holding a knife out in front of me.

I put the cap in my pocket and the knife back on my boot and went straight in up to my room and the bottle of Scotch I'd brought home from Stockholm.

Two stiff snifters later, I hadn't deduced any more than I knew already: that three young thugs had jumped me. They might have been a roving gang, except that they'd seemed to be waiting in ambush. But why? Bill Cary might be known for a lot of things, but carrying large sums of money certainly wasn't one. It looked as if they'd been hired.

But again—why? Veikko was the obvious suspect, but another consultation with the Scotch didn't suggest a motive. Him apart, it could have been anybody who knew my address —and I'd left that with the airport control tower along with instructions to tell anybody who asked. I like clients to be able to find me.

I went to bed with the creepy feeling you get when you know the aeroplane isn't quite right, but you can't put a finger on it and find an excuse for scrubbing the flight. If somebody had really started something, that fight down in the street hadn't ended it.

CHAPTER 4

THE WEATHER stayed good for the next eleven days and we surveyed nearly 600 square miles of the area before the magnetometer recorder blew up again and started trying to draw dirty pictures. I flew it and Mikko down to Rovaniemi and left him to try and sort it out while I spent an evening with the magnetometer and scintillometer graphs trying to work out whether we'd discovered nickel.

I'm no laboratory miner, but I can read a magnetometer graph well enough to know when I've flown over a mountain of ninety per cent nickel, or when I've flown over absolutely nothing at all. And that was what we'd found: nothing. I packed up the graphs and a large-scale map locating them to go out on the 6:45 southbound Dakota the next morning for the Kaaja company to worry about. I spent the morning shopping.

I picked up a fifteenth-hand 12-bore shotgun for 27,500 Finnmarks—just over £30. It was London made and the assistant tried to tell me it had once belonged to an English sporting lord. He was wasting his salesmanship: it was simply the cheapest double-barrelled gun in the shop. Apart from that, all I could tell about it was that the barrels looked straight and the hammers clicked when I pulled the triggers. What reassured me that it wouldn't blow up in my face was that it had probably been in recent use. The Finns don't own guns—or anything else—unless they intend to use them.

Then I did Homer's shopping, and flew out to see him at about noon.

I hadn't seen him, or a sign of him, in the last eleven days, although I'd put down on the lake five times. I hadn't gone looking—most of my unsurveyed area was south of the Värriöjoki by now—and I hadn't mentioned him to Mikko. No particular reason, except a vague feeling that I'd entrusted him with my secret and I was prepared to keep his. Again, there wasn't any particular reason for feeling he had any secrets, except another feeling that he might have come to the emptiest part of Finland as much to be away from people as to be near bears. I'd checked with the post office in Rovaniemi before I took off. Nothing for Frederick Wells Homer.

I did a beat-up of the cabin and he was at the lake about ten minutes after I'd landed.

He came out of the pines wearing a suede hunting jacket with plain leather insets on the shoulders to take the rub of a gun, cavalry twill trousers, hunting boots—and his Purdey .300.

I waved and called: "How's business? D'you mind if I stay to lunch?"

He smiled as if he were genuinely glad to see me and said: "I'd be delighted, sir. Come on up to my residence."

"How *is* that cabin?"

"In very fair condition, sir. A few places I had to plug it with moss to keep out the draughts—and rain—but otherwise very solid. They build well in this country."

"Good." I had the boxes of food out on the beach already; he opened them and sorted them around and repacked two.

"We'll take these, if you don't mind carrying one, sir."

"Happily." Then I remembered my new toy. I climbed back into the Beaver and brought it out. "What d'you think of this thing?—bearing in mind it's for emergency use only."

"Have you fired it yet?"

I shook my head. He took the gun and opened it without seeming to bother to find out how it opened. He squinted down the barrels, snapped it shut, played with it in his hands a moment, then swung it into his shoulder. He tried that again, then nodded. "A fair enough gun, sir. A trifle long in the barrel for me and built for a man with broader shoulders, but I'd say it was about right for your build. You can't really tell until you've fired it—but I'd think it would meet your requirements."

"It's met the important one already." I took it back and shoved it in the cockpit. We picked up a box each and started carrying.

I said: "I should have asked before: how's the anti-bear movement? I'll fly you somewhere else if I was wrong about this place."

"You brought me to the right place, sir. I've seen three and got one."

"What happened to the other two?"

"One was a female, sir, and I couldn't get close enough up to the other to make it a sporting shot."

After that I shut up and carried my box. We got to the cabin in about twenty minutes.

It must have been at least sixty years old: a simple square box of half-smoothed pine logs notched and overlapped at the corners like interlaced fingers. The roof was the same unfinished logs laid down the slope and well plugged with moss. The stuff was growing there of its own accord by now.

There was a window at the back and a door at the front and the rest was up to you. Homer went off into one corner and started routing around in a box and coming up with plates and cutlery and a primus stove. Along the right-hand wall there was a rolled up quilted green nylon sleeping bag and ground sheet and under the window there were four suitcases stacked up to make a table. The only other thing he'd done in the eleven days he'd been in the cabin was ram pegs into the wall over the sleeping bag to rest his guns on.

"I don't see any sign of your bear," I said. "Did you want me to fly the skin back for curing or whatever?" I'd done that for other hunters a couple of times.

"I don't keep trophies, sir. A peculiarity of mine. I believe an animal—particularly a noble one like the bear—is entitled to a fair burial."

"You buried it?"

"Yes, sir. Did you know that the Lapps, when they kill a bear, do so in the form of a ceremonial intended to apologise to its departing soul? They kill for food and clothing, of course. I don't do that, but I feel I needn't go to the further extreme of crowing over it. Forgive me—you must know far more about Lapp customs than I do, sir." He went out with his arms full of plates, knives and forks.

I hadn't known that about the Lapps—they don't need to hire me when it comes to killing a bear. Homer had obviously been reading up on his Lapland.

But how the hell do you convince the boys at the club that you've knocked off a bear unless you've got it spread out in front of the fireplace? Maybe he didn't care—or maybe they didn't need convincing. When I thought about it, I found I still believed he'd shot one.

I took another look around the cabin. The stacked luggage was a matching set of deep green-brown handstitched horsehide, with stainless steel fittings. It could only have been custom-made for him—and he'd stacked it up to shave off. On top were a dark pigskin toilet box and a case holding a pair of what they call 'military' hairbrushes—probably because it involves exactly twice as much equipment and effort as you really need.

Out of long habit of nosiness I lifted the lid of the toilet box. An ordinary safety razor worth about three shillings, shaving cream, toothbrush, toothpaste, and a shaving brush whose handle was so uneven and yellow it could only have been ivory. With two thick silver bands.

Did silver go sour in water? Probably not—not if this character used it on his shaving brush. I was beginning to build up a background to Homer from his luggage. You can learn a lot that way—if you know what to give significance to.

Partly the picture was just a mixture of St. James's Street and the backwoods. But it got more complicated than that. He had the best of everything that it was worth having the best of—but all you could say about it was that it was the best. There was nothing personal about any of it. He was a man the women hadn't got at and individualised; and he wasn't so self-consciously a bachelor that he'd stuck his initials on everything.

I went outside. He had started up a primus and was opening tins into square mess tins.

"I hope you don't mind eating in the open, sir?" he asked.

"I'm wearing my mosquito paste." I was, too. They don't carry malaria in that part of the world, but they still like the taste of blood.

"One thing you didn't mention," I said, "but I brought anyway." And I hauled out a hip-shaped bottle of Scotch from my hip pocket.

He smiled and shook his head. "I'm afraid I don't drink, sir—but you go ahead, if you don't mind a tin mug." He handed me one. I shrugged and poured myself a lunch-time dose.

He cooked up a stew of corned beef, baked beans and red peppers, followed by tinned peaches and coffee from a pot that had survived Pompeii.

We ate without saying anything.

I had finished and was lighting a cigarette and trying to think of something to say that fell somewhere between what nice weather it was and how the hell did you get so rich, when he said: "I believe you said you hadn't yet fired your gun?"

"Right."

"It seems a fine afternoon. Would you care to stroll down to the lake and we'll try it?"

"Happy to." I emptied the mug. He dumped the pots and plates in a canvas bucket of water and fetched out his rifle, a cartridge belt of shotgun shells, and a box of empty tins. I took the box and we strolled.

I got the gun out of the Beaver while he picked a flat outcrop of rock that stuck into the water at the corner of the beach. I had some shells of my own and had loaded up before he could offer his own—which was all he could have brought them for.

He held up a stub of dead branch. "Would you care to fire at this, sir? Or would you prefer me to try it first?"

"I picked it. We'll let it blow up in my face."

He nodded and heaved the wood about thirty yards out into the water.

I said: "I told ya to be outa town by sundown, din' I?" to the branch, and swung up the gun and pulled the first trigger.

It was some time since I'd fired anything. I caught myself watching the jump of the muzzle instead of the target. When I looked at the piece of wood there was a long smear of shattered water over and beyond it.

I snook a sideways glance at Homer. He was staring at the piece of water I'd massacred as if he was trying to calculate something.

I swung the gun up and fired again. Spray straddled the wood, leaving the water fore and aft of it pocked with fading rings.

Homer nodded and said: "A slightly spread pattern, but I believe it's quite an even one. It should be effective at the ranges I expect you'll want. Of course, you've shot before, sir. I can see that."

"Long ago and far away and at something rather different."

He asked: "May I?" and I passed him the gun, remembering to leave it broken open. He reloaded and I threw a tin in the air and he blew it out of the air. Just that. There was nothing fancy about the way he did it, nothing you could call a style of shooting. Styles are for the fairground. The people who hit things just aim and shoot.

I threw another tin and he got that, too. I asked: "Where did you get interested in shooting? Back in Virginia?"

"That's so, sir." He gave me the gun, then threw a tin for me and I put a blast within easy commuting distance of it. "I happened to come of a family which owned a certain amount of land."

I gave him the gun. "They don't now?"

"My parents are dead, sir. It belongs to me now."

"You said you spent your life hunting and travelling between hunting," I said. "D'you write books about it or something?"

"No, sir, I don't write books. I just like hunting." He fired a couple of shots.

"Fair enough," I said. "I don't see the big attraction, but it must be there."

"Are you opposed to hunting, sir?"

I jerked a look at him. He'd spoken quite sharply—at least for him.

"Me? No. I haven't really thought about it."

He nodded quickly. "Of course not. Anybody would have better things to think about. A life spent hunting isn't a very important life."

I said: "I'm sorry—I didn't mean—" But he wasn't listening. He wasn't being angry or sarcastic or anything. He was just standing, staring across the lake.

It was very quiet between our shots. There was no wind, and the water just swayed gently against the foot of our rock without lapping. The trees around the shore were stiff gaunt spruces finding it a hungry life living off almost bare rock, and the occasional lighter grey-green dead one, hung with a sort of fungus that looked like bundles of horsehair, waiting for the winter to topple it over.

Homer said quietly: "I rather envy you, sir. I don't imagine you inherited the task of being a pilot; I presume it was your choice. I never got offered a choice. I found I was born into the expectation that I would continue to manage a large piece of Virginia and a number of investments."

I may have chosen being a pilot, but nobody offered me the alternative of owning half Virginia. I managed not to say it.

Homer said: "I found the life had no appeal for me—nor I any talent for it. So when my parents died I saw no further need even to pretend an interest."

"You sold out?"

"No, sir, I was lucky in that my sister married a man who —of his own choice—was an expert in such things. I let him run it all."

"And went hunting."

"That's right, sir." He smiled suddenly. "I think I'd be more trouble to them at home."

"Where've you been to so far?"

"Just the ordinary places for big game. Africa for the lion and rhino and water buffalo and elephant. And a few crocodiles. Then India and Nepal, for tiger. Alaska for the Kodiak bear. South America. I've spent quite a little time in England, of course."

"Anything you *haven't* shot yet?"

He smiled wanly. "None of the so-called dangerous game —except snakes and so on."

"Shooting the bear wraps it up, then? What now?"

He wasn't smiling now. "I don't quite know, sir," he said softly. "I seem to have completed my life's work."

He gave me back the gun.

"Get the rifle," I said, "and join in on this round." He looked half interested, half dubious—probably because it might seem like boasting. For anybody else it might be. But if he was good enough, I was ready to watch.

"Go ahead," I said. I lit a cigarette while he fetched a rifle and a couple more tins.

"I'll throw," I suggested, "and you take the first shot." Hitting a flying tin with a heavy rifle isn't as easy as the cowboy

films make out. Hitting it on a suddenly changed trajectory
—such as after I'd blasted it with the shotgun—would be
several times more difficult. Riflemen like that are one in a
million.

I glanced at him to make sure he understood. He gave me a
blank, innocent look and snick-snacked the rifle bolt.

I threw a tin—and he said suddenly: "Your shot."

I said: "Hell," and fired and got it. The tin jumped out of
its arc. He swung up the rifle, tracked for a half second, and
fired—and the tin jerked away again. One in a million.

I had the shotgun lowered. I fired from the waist. The tin
stopped in the air, hung, and fell wearily into the water.

The echoes slammed away down the lake like distant doors
in a barracks corridor. Little shreds of gunsmoke hung in the
air between us. We grinned at each other through it. Shooting has something nice and simple and schoolboyish about
it. You hit or miss. *Bad luck old boy* or *Jolly good shot* and
you too can take tea with the Duchess.

Life would be that way.

I said: "Damn good shooting."

He said: "I don't believe I've seen a shot from the waist
like that before."

"My party trick." We both grinned again. The echoes died;
and smoke shuddered and melted; the ripples from the tin
smoothed out on the lake.

I said: "Well, you're good at it. Not many people devote
their lives to something and get that good at it."

He said, quite seriously: "I often wonder, sir, how good
I'd be under fire myself. If some lion or bear suddenly started
shooting back. I understand it tends to throw a man's aim
off; he fires too hastily."

I stared at him. "You probably get the same effect letting
a bear up within twenty yards."

"I don't think so, sir. You still have those twenty yards'
margin; you wouldn't have that with a bullet." He flipped
the rifle bolt and let it spring back into the crotch of his
thumb. The cartridge case jumped out and rang on the rock.

"Well, I wouldn't try finding out," I advised.

"You've been under fire, sir?" he asked quickly.

"Me?" I said harshly. "Why should I have been?"

"I'd imagined you'd been in the Royal Air Force, sir. And
I'd gotten the impression—from the way you'd fired from
the waist like that—that you'd learnt to shoot on military
small arms."

I said: "You wouldn't get that sort of training in the R.A.F. Just a party trick."

He said: "Ah," and nodded again, just as if that explained it all and he could suddenly remember the sort of party where you learnt that particular trick.

CHAPTER 5

THE SCHOOL holiday atmosphere had seeped away by now. With our banging and chattering stopped, the lake had grown to its full size again. The loneliness of the North had crept back around us like a small cold wind. The trees had troubles of their own to think of; we were just small whispers at the bottom of a well nobody had heard of.

I walked to the edge of the rock and pitched the empty shells down into the lake. I watched them flicker down through the water like goldfish, fading as they went— Then I saw it.

It was a cross. A square-ended cross edged in white. Then ripples broke across it, and I shifted my head, trying to see through the glint on the water. Slowly it reformed again: the old Luftwaffe cross.

I climbed down off the rock and went along to the Beaver and dug out the rubber dinghy. Homer wandered up, carrying the rifle and my shotgun. "Can I be of any help, sir?"

"I think there's an aeroplane down there. You can help balance the boat, if you like."

I launched it off the beach and paddled round to within a few yards of the rock, then let her drift. I lay down carefully and peered down over the side. Homer picked up the paddle.

I saw a straight, unnatural line on the lake bed, faintly crinkled by small weeds.

Then a skull without a jaw smiled up at me.

He was bald, white, clean—unlike the casual dirtiness of everything else down there. His teeth were young and even, except at one side where a sudden emptiness gave the wry sideways smile. Maybe he'd just been down there long enough to start seeing the funny side of it.

The dinghy drifted. I saw the close walls of the cockpit, the faint dusty circles of the instruments on the panel in front of him, the shapeless hump of the rest of his body, with a gleam of white bone down inside the jacket. He was wearing his head in his lap.

You would, of course. You'd sit there for a few weeks or months or years, without much minding which, until the fish got familiar enough to come in and start to nibble. And because the fish aren't hasty but are very, very thorough, after a time there wouldn't be any reason for your head to stay where it had always been before. And after another time the same gentle quiet dirtiness of the lake bed would touch you and you'd become part of it.

I lifted my head away from the water. The rock we'd been shooting from was a few yards ahead and to one side. The cross I'd first seen must be on one wingtip. I estimated the lay of the plane, then peered down again.

We'd drifted a few feet off to one side. I could make out the long straight line of the fuselage, the big hump of the greenhouse-style cockpit canopy and just behind the canopy, very faint, another cross bracketed by the letters J O.

I waved to Homer to bring us back and he paddled back over the cockpit. The rear hatch was open and the tattered leather straps swayed like reeds. As we drifted away again, the white sideways smile looked up again. But not at me. Only at the sky, where there are no fish.

I sat up again and wiped my hand over my face. It was cold and wet. "I should have known," I said. "I should have known it." Then I remembered Homer was staring at me patiently. I waved a hand and grabbed the paddle. "Take a look."

I paddled him backwards and forwards until he sat up again, then headed us for the shore.

He said tentatively: "I presume, sir, that it's a German airplane, so it'll have been there more than eighteen years."

"Must have landed on the ice," I said. "When the lake was frozen. It'd slide most of the length of it, bump into the rock. Then, when the ice melted, down she'd go."

Homer raised a polite eyebrow. "You can tell that, sir, from what you saw?"

"That plane is a Messerschmitt 410. The man down there is sergeant pilot Kleber. He took off from the Luftwaffe airstrip at Ivalo on March the 26th 1944 and I presume we're the first people he's met since then."

Homer was watching me, his face a perfect polite blank. If he thought the woodworm had got at my head, it wouldn't be his sort of manners to say so.

I ran the dinghy onto the beach. "I met a man who has the old Luftwaffe arrivals-and-departures book from Ivalo airport. Somebody must have pinched it when the Germans were pulling out. I remember seeing this flight logged: aircraft type, identification letters, pilot's name. It was marked 'missing.'"

We climbed ashore. Homer said: "You happened to remember this particular flight?"

"I was looking it up. I thought a man I knew had been flown out as passenger about that time. This flight was the only one near the time with an unnamed passenger on it."

"I didn't see any signs of a second person—"

"They were there. The rear hatch was open and the straps undone. No pilot would have flown the plane like that. And the pilot himself—he wouldn't have killed himself on that sort of landing, not without smashing the plane up a lot more. You saw he was missing a piece of jaw?"

Homer nodded.

"You'd get that effect if the rear-seat passenger had shoved a pistol in the back of his neck and pulled the trigger. And that sounds like the passenger I'm thinking of."

Homer said thoughtfully: "Hardly a sporting shot." My turn to stare, and I probably didn't do it as politely as he had. But he wasn't looking at me; he was standing looking over the lake, probably thinking about what had happened there on the ice nineteen years before.

"No," I said slowly. "Not really a sporting shot."

Homer came back to life and smiled and said: "You'd been thinking your man—the passenger—was dead?"

"Yes. For nineteen years. I should have known better."

"He may still be alive, then?"

"I hope so."

"He was a wartime friend of yours, sir?"

"No. It's just that I'd always rather wanted to kill him myself."

Homer just nodded quietly to himself and didn't push the subject. I unscrewed the valve on the dinghy and squashed the air out and bundled it up.

"Well," I said, "I'll be rolling. I'll come back in another ten–twelve days with another load of the same. Is that all right?"

"That would be very kind, sir. I'll give you a cheque." He reached for his chequebook.

"Never mind; next time'll do." But I ended up with another hundred-dollar traveller's cheque.

I thanked him and tucked it away. "Any messages for anybody?"

"I don't think so, sir. And thank you for wasting an afternoon with me; I've enjoyed it very much."

"Pleasure." I turned away, then turned back. "Does anybody know where you are?"

"They usually find me, sir." He gave a wry little smile.

"Well, supposing somebody comes looking: they'll find *me* —what do I say?"

"Why do you ask, sir?"

I wasn't sure myself. Perhaps it was that I couldn't see how anybody who owned a sizable piece of the world could escape from the world for long. And perhaps, also, the way he seemed to want to stay hidden itself suggested somebody might come looking.

I shook my head. "I don't really know. But what should I say?"

"I'd rather stay unknown, sir. Unless it's a real emergency. I'll let you judge."

I said: "Ye-es," rather doubtfully. That left the bomb in my pocket. There wasn't much I could do about it, though. I nodded and lifted a hand and walked down to the Beaver.

As I slammed the cabin door, I had an odd feeling of coming back to a familiar world without having realised I'd left it. I looked back: he was just a tubby figure moving away into the trees with the rifle on one shoulder and carrying one of the remaining food boxes.

I knew then that a dozen other bush pilots—and maybe a couple of dozen white hunters and guides the world over— must have had the same conversation with him. Perhaps it was the only conversation you could have. Perhaps they had stood and swapped shots with him and blown down empty tins into quiet lakes—and then come away with the odd feeling of returning to reality and watching him fade into the trees a few yards, and another world, away.

Partly the other world was him being rich. But it was more than that: he was a very lonely man.

Still, everybody in the Arctic is a lonely man. That's one of the reasons you come to it.

CHAPTER 6

I LANDED in Rovaniemi at about half past four. I parked near the maintenance hangar and went in to find Mikko and the magnetometer recorder. Instead, I found Oskar Adler.

Although he was the only other pilot doing small-plane charter work in Lapland that year, you didn't often find him on airports: he owned a Cessna 195 floatplane, which meant he had to park on water. At Rovaniemi that meant parking on the river almost in the town itself, three miles south of the airport.

He saw me, jumped at me and grabbed my arm. At first I thought we were in for a fight; then I found it was just his idea of how to start a confidential, unsuspicious conversation.

"You may be in trouble, Bill," he said in a hoarse whisper that carried the length of the airport. "Have you been flying into the prohibited area?"

"I may have cut a corner." We were speaking Swedish: Oskar was one of the small and—so they themselves tell you —select bunch of Finns who are mostly Swedish blood. He was built a little shorter than me, with a sharp face and lank mousey hair that's far more typically Swedish than the pure blondes they cast in the movies.

"Look, I'm telling you this only to help you. You understand?"

"No."

"Have you been doing any smuggling? A case of whisky? A bit of out-of-season moose meat, or birds?"

I took his hand off my arm and gave it him back. "No. I've spent the summer knitting socks for the Ivalo Old Folks' Home. What's all this about?"

"*Suopo's* here." He gave a sharp V of a smile, and settled back to watch the result.

I tried to look a lot less worried than I felt. *Suopo* meant *Suojelupoliisi*—the internal security police. Flying a prohibited zone, which could cause an international incident, might well be a *Suopo* affair.

I nodded as calmly as I could and asked: "What's that got to do with me?"

His thin sharp face got disappointed. "He's questioning all

35

the pilots. I thought you'd want to know—so that we can make our stories the same. He's already seen me."

I leant against a work-bench and lit a cigarette. "There's no stories to get the same, Oskar. Where's the trouble?"

"Look," and his face was serious now. "I told him I don't know who you're flying for this year. You tell him you don't know who I'm flying for. All right?"

Perfect. Just the answer to make an experienced spy-catcher realise he's made a blunder and go quietly home again. It sounded as if Oskar had done exactly his best to make my Kaaja work sound as suspicious as possible.

I shrugged. "Well, I *don't* know who you're flying for. Who is it?"

"It doesn't matter." Then he realised this wouldn't quite wash. "I'm just flying hunters and people. Not much work at all. It's a bad year."

It would be, if he hadn't got a mineral-survey contract, and I certainly hadn't heard that he'd got one.

"All right," I said. "Where do I find this *Suopo* character?" This time his whisper was real. "Right behind you."

I turned and managed not to turn fast. He was standing at the hangar entrance, just a black figure against the light with a hat and briefcase.

"Pilot Cary?" he asked in Finnish: they always give you the courtesy title of your profession.

"Yes?"

He came up, holding out a hand, and I shook it. Away from the light, I could see he was tall, though not quite my height, and a few years older. He had a long, oval face without as many potatoes on it as most Finns, a hefty beak of a nose, and grey eyes. He was wearing a smooth dark grey suit and a light grey homburg, both a lot too cityfied for the streets of Rovaniemi. He hadn't got the tan you pick up in the long Lapland summer days, either.

To me, that meant he'd been sent up from Helsinki on this job, which threw out any idea of it being a routine enquiry.

"Do you speak Finnish well?" he asked politely, still in Finnish.

"Not well enough for speaking to policemen." I said it in English. He seemed to follow easily enough, nodded pleasantly, and said in good English: "Very good—we will speak English. I am Aarne Nikkanen, of *Suopo*. Shall we talk outside?"

He smiled over my shoulder at Oskar, and then drifted out of the hangar with me following.

"You have been flying this afternoon?" he asked.

"Taking some supplies up to an American hunter."

"Mr Homer?"

"Yes."

"Ah. We wondered if he had engaged you." He stopped by a set of wheeled air-steps and dumped his briefcase on the top step. The upper side—the side he'd been holding against his leg—had a bulge in it. The size of a packet of sandwiches. Or a pistol.

He took off his homburg and placed it on top of the bulge. He was almost bald on top, but wasn't trying to hide it with the long grey-blonde tufts above his ears.

He asked: "And where did you land him?"

"About eighty miles north-west of here. On the edge of the prohibited zone."

"But not actually in it?"

"No." He couldn't have expected me to say anything else. But at least he now had a denial of something he might, without too much trouble, be able to prove. If that was what he wanted.

He said: "And the area you are surveying for the Kaaja company—that is not in the prohibited area?"

"No."

He stared at me with a friendly, sad smile.

I said: "I can show you on a map. I've got one in the plane."

I had, too: one carefully marked out with a dummy survey area just for an occasion like this. I did the real work using a celluloid overlay with wax-pencil marks that I wiped off after each flight.

"Forgive me—" his smile got a little sadder. "I have already seen the maps in your aeroplane. I am afraid I cannot know if somebody is telling the truth just by listening. So I looked in your aeroplane."

I just nodded. This man was no fool. No reason why he should be. But I still couldn't see why they would send up a Helsinki man to worry about a possible prohibited area infringement.

He brought out a packet of cigarettes, a brand with hollow cardboard mouthpieces built on. He lit one and took it out of his mouth and looked it over and said a little sadly: "There is a theory that it is only those parts of tobacco which turn into

smoke at very high temperatures which cause lung cancer.
Have you heard that? This is supposed to cool the smoke before it reaches your mouth." He shrugged and put it back in
his mouth and asked: "Have you ever flown across the border?"

"The Russian border? Christ, no."

He nodded, then fumbled in his lefthand trouser pocket.
"But that is not exactly what I want to speak about. This is."
He leant across and with the precise gesture of a poker player
raising the stakes dropped a little stack of gold coins on the
step near my elbow.

Sovereigns. About eight of them. Funny how when you
haven't seen any for a time they always look smaller than
you'd remember them. Something to do with their being
gold, perhaps.

I looked up at him. "And—?"

"They were found in Rovaniemi, on a man."

"Yes? It isn't illegal to have them, is it?"

"No—but the man himself was very illegal. A small crimi-
nal—a dealer in anything." He gave me a slight smile. "Naturally he himself could not remember who had given them to
him, or what for. But we are interested."

"So you come to the nearest Briton? Britain's about the one
place you can't get sovereigns."

"No." He shook his head. "Not because they are British
coins. But because they are smugglers' coins."

A small dry wind shuffled dust around our feet. Away to
the south, a Finnforce Pembroke trainer was droning in on
the approach. The only other sound was my breath pushing
out a long broadside of cigarette smoke.

He was watching me carefully with the small, half-sad
smile that was as much a part of his stock in trade as the
bulge in his briefcase.

I said: "Smugglers' coins?—how so?"

He reached out and tapped his cigarette neatly on the edge
of the stacked coins. "They are gold—so they have a value
of their own. About 3,100 marks, I believe. Also, they are
recognised everywhere. They are the one truly international
coin. So—they are the perfect smugglers' payment. These are
not yours, then?"

"No."

He nodded. "Yes. Please show me what is in your pockets.
I still cannot tell from the voice what is true. It is very
stupid." It wasn't. You can spend a lot of time trying to read

secrets in a man's eyes and still miss the pistol in his pocket. I started dumping handfuls of stuff on the steps.

It didn't add up to much: cigarettes, matches, a wallet, a passport, a keyring, some Finnish coins, a handkerchief, a couple of papers about the Beaver's engine, and a sparkplug that didn't spark any more.

He didn't touch any of it. He just said: "You have a lonely life, I think, Mr Cary."

At first I didn't get it. Then, when I looked over my own stuff, I did: no letters, and only two keys and a bottle opener on the key ring. You can tell a lot about a man from the things in his pockets.

I said: "Yes. But no sovereigns. You want to search the plane?" Then I remembered he'd already searched the plane.

I was beginning to get angry. That could have been just what he wanted, but I got angry anyway. After he'd turned out my aircraft and my pockets there wasn't much left of my life that didn't have the smell of policeman about it. I started shoving things back into my pockets without asking permission to do so.

"Happy now?" I asked him. "I could always fly you up to look over my room in Ivalo. Except probably you'd rather wait until I'm not there."

He heard me out without looking as if he was listening. Then he said: "But what is there in Rovaniemi that is worth smuggling in—or out? Where would they come from?"

"Stand facing east," I said. "That's where most of Finland's troubles have come from, if I've got my history right."

"Russia? Yes, quite right. That, of course, is why I am talking to those who have the means of crossing the border easily."

I stared at him. "In a plane? You're crazy."

"Oh no." He smiled a little more widely and sadly, as if I'd forgotten something very simple. "Please, Mr Cary. We are not either of us young any more."

I looked at him carefully. He was right: the border could be flown all right—if the Russians wanted it done. The Finns didn't have a complete radar net along it, and most pilots knew just where the Finnish radar stations were and what their coverage was. I knew myself, anyway. I also knew that most of the convictions for flying in prohibited areas had started from Russian complaints after *their* radar sightings. If they wanted a flight to come across, all they had to do was not complain and the only risk would be being spotted by a Finnish border guard. And with a throttled-back engine on a windy night a small aeroplane can make surprisingly little noise.

"It could be done," I said slowly, "but it would be strictly a spring and autumn sport." The midnight sun and the clear summer skies would see to that. "There'd be simpler ways."

"Undoubtedly there are those also. But not quicker."

The Pembroke waddled down onto the runway, its engines making dry husking noises.

I made agreeing noises at Nikkanen and picked the top sovereign off the stack. It was dated 1928 and was showing hardly any sign of wear. Without much thinking about it I held it up so that the light caught on the relief, and down at the hind hooves of St. George's horse there was a very small letter I.

"Minted in Bombay," I said. "And India has a Russian frontier—almost."

He was looking at me intently. He said softly: "And I had to look up what that little mark meant. I think you know about sovereigns, Mr Cary?"

"We come from the same Empire, remember?" I held the second one up to the light.

He said: "About half come from India—there are more than this. The rest have no mark. From London, I think. Not that it matters where they come from; they move all over the world." He dropped his cigarette end and crunched the hollow mouthpiece under his foot. "But we almost never see them in Finland. Because what have we to smuggle here?"

I shrugged and shoved across the stack of sovereigns. He picked them up, chinked them once in his hand, and dropped them into his pocket. As part of the same movement he brought out his cigarettes and lit one.

"Do they work?" I asked. "They really keep you from getting cancer?"

He glanced at me, surprised, then took the cigarette out of his mouth and stared at it as if he couldn't remember how it got there.

"They help keep my wife from complaining about how much I smoke," he said. "You could say they work." He picked his briefcase up off the top step and held it bulge side against his leg. "If you hear of anything worth smuggling —or anything that may be connected—I would like to be told of it."

"I got jumped by three young thugs with *puukot* in Rova-niemi the other night."

He paused with his homburg in his hand, and looked at me oddly. "And why do you mention that? Does it have any connection with sovereigns?"

I hadn't quite known why I'd mentioned it, except that it helped make me sound like an innocent party—and in case he could suggest any reason for it.

I shrugged.

He asked: "Did you report it to the police?"

"No."

"Why not?"

"Well . . . I won."

"And had you thought that if you had lost, you would not have been able to report it, either?"

I didn't say anything. He smiled another small, sad smile, and said: "I am happy to see that your training as a mineral survey pilot included how to deal with three young thugs."

He put on his hat and walked away to the airport *baari*. He didn't say 'Good-bye.' Policemen almost never do. It's a polite way of saying 'See you again.'

CHAPTER 7

IVALO is just a bridge on the Arctic Highway and the sort of village that grows up around a bridge, filled with the sort of people who live in that sort of village. There are a few local government offices, a new tourist hotel, a filling station, a few shops—and in the summer a few reindeer. The Lapp herders let them wander in so that the tourists can hand out a bit of biscuit and cake: it saves money on pasture. But even the reindeer don't make it Monte Carlo; the most important thing in Ivalo is still the bridge.

By now the tourists were mostly gone and the reindeer were having to eat grass. The rowing boats were all pulled well up on the river bank just behind the hotel, and the only life in the streets was a couple of taxis that hadn't yet gone south for the winter and the two cops who sit in an old American car up in the sandy square just south of the bridge.

I had a room in a bungalow cabin just east of the hotel that year, and walked up the street to eat eggs in the Mainio

baari every morning. After that I went up to the square to
meet Mikko and hope to meet an airport employee who
would give us a lift in a car. The airport lies a good quarter
of an hour's drive south.

I was waiting up in the square feeling the autumn chill
blowing up the river off the lake and betting a taxi driver I
wouldn't have to hire him today, when the trailer arrived.

The front end of it flowed around a bend in the road south
of the square and the rest just kept on flowing. It was a clear
sixty feet long by ten broad and whoever had hauled that
thing up the Arctic Highway was very fond of his home
comforts. 'Arctic Highway' sounds pretty grand, but it's just
graded gravel. Six months of frost would crumble an asphalt
road to dust.

The trailer stopped in the middle of the square. It was
square-edged, made of aluminum ridged to look like planking, and painted duck-egg blue below and white above. Down
my side of it were two doors and four windows. Just parked
there, it was one of the biggest buildings in Ivalo, and it
even made the car pulling it insignificant—which doesn't
often happen to a Facel Vega II. Painted scarlet, with Swiss
number plates.

The taxi driver climbed out and said: "I want to watch
this."

The driver of the Facel Vega got out leisurely and lit a
cigarette, which he'd have had room to do inside the car.
You can throw a party in the front seat of a Facel II. Then
he sauntered up to look at the bridge.

He was dressed about how you'd expect a man who drove
that trailer with that car to be dressed: a leather jacket cut
like a sports coat, a very white shirt with a yellow silk
scarf at the neck, slim dark trousers and white moccasin
driving shoes.

He glanced at the width of the bridge, then walked halfway across—it had a slight hump—to look at the other side.
Then he took his second puff at the cigarette and threw the
rest of it into the river. He pulled a pair of bright yellow
pigskin gloves out of a hip pocket, tugged them on,
and sauntered back to the car. Then he drove the whole lot
over like a runaway rocket.

The taxi driver jumped as if I'd stuck a pin in him. One of
the cops hopped out of the car and ran up to the bridge to
look over. On the far side there was a cloud of sandy dust
heading north. It faded and the trailer had gone.

The cop walked back past us. He said to the taxi driver: "I've never seen *you* tow a load over a bridge as fast as that."

"Let him try towing a wife and four children if he wants to try something difficult." He got into his taxi and slammed the door angrily.

The cop grinned at me. "He must have special gears in that Facel, to get up that speed that quick."

I nodded.

He said: "I've seen it up here before—the trailer anyway. Couple of years ago. You weren't here that summer?"

"I was based in Rovaniemi that year."

"Come down in the world, hey?"

I shrugged. "D'you know the man who drives it?"

"Him? Don't remember. But it's the car I like: American engine, French body. That's the way to build a car."

I said: "Maybe women, too."

I went back to leaning against the bridge and waiting for Mikko. The whole episode seemed vaguely unreal and meaningless. A man who had enough worldliness to own a car and trailer and clothes like that would have checked his bridges in advance. Anyway, he'd been over this one before, two years ago. So the bridge inspection had all been an act—put on for us, although he'd pretended not to notice us.

As it was, the act—plus the clothes and the car and the trailer—had almost made me miss noticing that the man underneath was a tall, solid dark-haired party with a calm expressionless face that could stare a hole in armour plate.

The cop *had* missed it. Maybe he was supposed to.

Soon after that, Mikko turned up and we got started on the day's work.

CHAPTER 8

WHEN we got back that evening, the tower had a message for me. I was to ring the Kaaja company's Helsinki number if it was before six o'clock, or a residential number after half past. It was seven o'clock by the time we got into town, so we went into the tourist hotel for a schnapps and to put in the call.

When the call went through, it was one of the company's directors. He didn't bother to tell me his name; he was the Kaaja company, a well-known sub-division of God.

He wanted to know how far I was from finishing the survey.

I told him I had about half a day's work to do—unless, of course, he wanted to extend the area to keep me going as long as surveying weather lasted.

He didn't like the idea. Was I sure I hadn't missed anything?

I said: "You've seen my recordings and survey pattern, haven't you?" He hadn't—I could tell that from the pause and cough at the other end. All he must have seen was the laboratory analysis on the recordings.

I said: "What made you think there was nickel there in the first place? The recordings weren't giving anything like the sort of pattern that would give nickel. You usually get nickel along with iron and copper—like up at Petsamo and out at Sudbury, Canada. The recordings didn't give a sniff of either."

He gave another cough, then said: "We don't want to broadcast this knowledge—you understand? But many years ago a mining engineer did a lot of exploring in south-eastern Lapland. Most of his reports are lost, but we have one that says there is nickel near the Kemijoki valley."

Only an area of a hundred miles long and fifty miles wide; say 5,000 square miles, even if 'near' really meant 'near.'

I said some of this. Also: "You only gave me about a third of that area to cover. Who picked this particular part of it?"

"Our experts decided it was the most likely part of the area."

"Wrong, weren't they?"

He coughed his way around that one.

I said: "Well, why not try and get some of the rest done before the snow?"

The company had decided not. Unfortunate, but there it is. The contract would be completed once I'd delivered the magnetometer recordings for the last square miles of the original area. Glad to hear of me if I happened to be in Lapland again next year—but no promises, of course. Thanks for my good work. Certain I'd done my best.

I came away from the phone knowing two things: that the first thing the Kaaja company did next summer would be get somebody better known and more expensive to re-survey the area I'd just done. And also that if I happened to be contemplating suicide, they wouldn't talk me out of it.

I went back to the dining room and Mikko and the schnapps.

"Well," I said, "by tomorrow lunch, the Kaaja job should be over."

"No extension?"

"No extension."

Mikko stared into his schnapps. "You could say there's bits you want to do again."

"Why? D'you think we missed anything?"

"No-o. But is work."

"For this year. There's next year's work to think of. They won't be impressed by me shoving up the price and still not finding anything." It probably wouldn't make much difference; whatever I did, they wouldn't want me next year.

Mikko drained his schnapps and stared at me defiantly. "So now you want to pay me off, yes?"

"We agreed to a week's notice. Sorry, Mikko, but you've just got it."

"And what do you do now?"

"I'll stay up here another week or two, just to pick up what hunters I can. There won't be anything more."

"I'm no good any more?"

"Listen, Mikko. The summer's over. In two–three weeks there won't be any flying at all, just as soon as the first snow. The sooner you go south, the better chance you've got of a good winter job. I'll pay you for the week, but you're free the moment we've got the last bit of surveying done. That's the best I can do."

He just glowered at me.

I said: "And we'll have a big dinner tonight, here in the hotel. On me. Salmon and steak and the best hock they've got. Just to celebrate the end of another summer when I didn't become a millionaire."

Mikko stood up and shrugged his shoulders, more expressively than I thought he knew how. "No. I get something at the Mainio and go to bed. See you in the morning."

"Mikko," I said, "take the dinner. It'll happen again; summers are always ending. Just remember that a pilot's a luxury item. We're people with expensive skills using expensive bits of machinery; not many people can afford us. We can't do anything that wasn't done before except fly, and that's no damn use unless we're going somewhere for some reason. Take the dinner and forget it."

He shook his head and muttered something and went

away. I whistled up the waitress and ordered the dinner I'd planned, plus a schnapps to keep me on the boil until then.

It wouldn't help much; I'd still be out of work by the next night. All you learn in all the years is ways to forget about it until he happens.

I was through the dinner and into the second glass of cloudberry liqueur when Oskar Adler came in. I waved cheerfully at him; I'd reached the stage when you know the world will end at midnight but have forgotten it will start again at seven the next morning. Everybody was my friend.

Oskar already had a friend: the dark, solid character from the trailer that morning. Oskar hadn't wasted any time finding where the big money was.

They came across. Oskar said in careful, slow English: "Monsieur Claude, this is Bill Cary. Cary, is Monsieur Claude. What do you drink?"

I said: "Cloudberry," fast, just in case the invitation hadn't been meant for me.

Claude shook my hand and sat down in the same movement. His hand was warm and firm; his face stayed cold and firm. It was one of those square well-fed French faces that aren't giving anything away; he had no more expression than a stopped clock. But his movements were balanced and wary.

He was dressed more quietly than in the morning: a lightweight blue mac over a dark grey suit, white shirt, black knitted tie.

Oskar ordered drinks all round: two Scotches and a cloudberry. Then he asked: "You have finished with Kaaja yet?"

"Getting near it." That was true, all right.

"Soon you are free?"

"Soon. Why?"

"There perhaps is a job. Are you wanting it?"

The waitress brought the drinks. While she was issuing them, I studied Oskar. His style of dress had sobered down a little: usually he wore jeans, a tartan shirt and a denim flying jacket. Tonight he was in a fairly smart pair of brown trousers and a shaggy cream sports coat buttoned all the way up.

He was leaning his left arm on the table in a slightly awkward way and his face was tense. I looked at Claude; his face was tense, too—blank but tense. He lifted his glass and said: *"Kippis,"* showing he knew his Finnish customs.

I said: *"Kippis.* Yes, I'd like a job—providing somebody tells me what, when, where and how much."

Oskar seemed to relax a little and glanced at Claude.

Claude said: "You will understand this is a secret, Mr Cary. Mr Adler is doing some work for me, and I may want you to help." He didn't put on any expression as he spoke: he just opened his mouth and the words walked out. But he spoke good English, with just a trace of a French—or perhaps Geneva—accent.

He said: "I want to find the Volkof treasure."

Two drinks earlier I'd have thought of Oskar's feelings and just made polite agreeing noises. But now it was two drinks later.

"No," I said. "Absolutely not. Not that. It doesn't exist. It isn't there. It never happened. No, no, no."

"You don't believe in it, then, Mr Cary?" Claude asked.

"You could put it that way."

"And if I had definite information about it?"

"I still wouldn't believe it." I poured cloudberry down my throat and started giving him the benefit of my expert opinion. "In the first place, if the original story about Volkof coming out with it is true, why hasn't somebody found it in the last forty years? The legend must have been around as long as the treasure. And if anybody *had* found it they wouldn't have boasted about it: they'd have had to split it with the state and Volkof's heirs and God-knows-who.

"In the second place, I don't believe a man like Volkof would have had any treasure in the first place. He was supposed to be an engineer—a bourgeois, wasn't he? That sort of Russian never went in for jewelry, gold and so on. Nobody but the Church and the Court did. If he'd had any money, he'd have bought land, summer residences and so on. He wouldn't have owned jewelry any more than Chekhov's characters did. Just cherry orchards."

I looked at my glass: empty. I waved to the waitress. Then I looked at Oskar. He didn't seem as worried as I'd expected; he was just sitting there, his left arm in the same awkward position and a faint smile on his sharp face.

Claude said: "That sounds logical reasoning, Mr Cary. But it is my hobby to look for such things, and if you are paid for your time I hope you will have no objection to helping me."

I shrugged. "All right. As long as you know what I think. What d'you want me to do?"

"When are you free, Mr Cary?"

"Any time, provided I'm given a few hours notice."

"Very good. And how can I find you?"

"Oskar may know where I am. If not, Ivalo control tower will know."

The waitress put down another round. I said: *"Kippis,"* and got started. After a while I said: "Well, what is the job?"

Claude sipped his Scotch. "I will tell you exactly when I get in touch with you again."

I turned to Oskar and said very deliberately: "Are you finding that, this season, people keep offering you secret jobs at an uncertain date for an unspecified amount? Almost you might think they were just fooling you."

Oskar had gone very tense and serious again. He started to say something in English, then lapsed into fast Swedish. "Shut up, you stupid fool. I'm doing you a good turn; you don't know how good. Just keep quiet."

Claude glanced at him with as near a real expression as he'd had. He didn't like not understanding something.

"The hell with you, Oskar," I said, in Swedish. "If you don't tell me what game we're playing, don't expect me to stick to the rules."

The way he held his left arm still bothered me. He might have had a stiff shoulder, except he wouldn't be flying with a stiff shoulder. Ordinarily, I would have let it go on bothering me. But tonight I had just enough schnapps and hock and cloudberry inside me to get annoyed at mysteries.

I emptied my glass, banged it down, and reached across and yanked open his sports coat. He had a revolver slung under his arm.

He grabbed at my hand, missed, then shrugged the coat shut again. He gave me a look that should have been pure hate, but had something else in it; fright, perhaps.

Claude was watching, looking as interested as if I'd offered to show him a picture of my favourite dog.

I said to Oskar: "Are you any good with that thing?"

"Go to hell."

"If you aren't any good, I should stop wearing it."

"Go to hell."

"Carrying guns has a way of increasing your chance of getting shot. You may always shoot yourself, and it also makes other people a bit faster in shooting you. They have to assume you *do* know how to use it."

Oskar finished buttoning up his jacket and stood up. He turned to Claude. "I am sorry for that behaviour." Then he told me to go to hell in Swedish again. Then he stalked off, stiff and outraged and managing to look oddly dignified with it.

Claude stood up, a flowing, balanced movement. "Do you wish to see under my coat, Mr Cary?" If he had anything there, he didn't look like somebody who'd let it show. Nor like somebody who'd let you look.

I shook my head. Claude turned and walked out after Oskar.

After a time I stopped wondering exactly how stupid I'd been, and waved at the waitress again.

CHAPTER 9

THE MORNING MIST crawled away into the trees around the airport. I just sat there, watching my hands wander around the cockpit, checking and setting, and hoping they were doing the right things. That morning I had grit in my veins and broken glass in my brain. I felt like something from the south end of the swamp. But my hands knew the job better than I could remember it. Trimmers to take-off, throttle nut tensioned, mixture rich, air filter in . . . They could do it, dark or light, hungover or not.

For how much longer, Cary? Until your hands miss for the first time. Just a small, unimportant slip—to begin with. But then you know you're living on borrowed time. How much longer to then? I was forty next year; already I had more flying hours behind me than I could hope for ahead. I was over the hill, like the year. Just the long slope down to winter.

How much longer?

Just another summer. That's all you need. Because next summer's the one when you fly over a mountain of nickel. And you make the bonus and a big name and you can pull out and hire a couple of nice, safe twin-engined survey planes and bright-eyed sober young pilots to fly them. And Bill Cary can sit behind a big bleached-oak desk in Helsinki or London or Toronto and drink himself paralytic from breakfast on-wards.

It was that sort of morning. It had started with my head and worked down through Mikko not turning up, to a fore-cast of strong north winds. I staggered the Beaver off the ground and headed south.

Surveying by yourself isn't much fun. There's no auto-pilot in the Beaver, so you have to set the trimmer for nose-heavy flight, then clamber down the back of the cabin hoping your own shift of weight will balance the whole thing out. Then all you have to do is switch on the scintillometer and magnetometer recorders, unwind the winch that lowers the magnetometer through the cargo drop hatch so that it's well away from the metal influences of the plane itself, make sure the recorders have warmed up and are working properly, then fight your way forward to stop the plane stalling or spiralling in.

All with a hangover like the gardens of Babylon.

Then you get to the area, make a check pass over a point of known magnetic value, fly back and climb a bit, go aft to make sure there's no exceptional variation—and find the readings are way off what they should be. A storm some-where east across the Russian border is giving electrical in-terference. The strong north winds would have told you that if you'd been awake.

I climbed out of the area and was just about to turn north when Rovaniemi tower came on the air, asking for me. I was instinctively wary of radio calls: it took me a moment or two to remember that I was in an area where I could answer without giving away an illegal position.

Rovaniemi said there was a job waiting for me there.

I asked Who wants me to do what?

Rovaniemi said there was a young lady wanting to be flown somewhere.

I asked Does she know how much it'll cost her?

There was a pause, then they said: "She doesn't care how much it costs."

That's my sort of young lady. I hauled around and headed south-west.

The airfield was still mostly heaps of rock and sand, with the same plank path across the mud to the airport building. She was waiting for me at the end of it, with a stack of snappy white leather luggage piled up on the path behind her.

It all seemed somehow familiar, right down to the state of my health, and I should have guessed then, but I didn't.

She was smallish, but the right shape—as far as I could judge through a straight three-quarter-length coat in light blue leather. She was thirty plus a year or two, with a face that would never grow fat: she had strong cheekbones and a mouth just a bit too wide and big grey eyes and silky fair hair pulled back and coiled in a French pleat.

She shoved a small strong chin up at me as I got to the end of the plank path and asked: "Mr Bill Cary?"

"Yes." The accent sounded familiar, too.

She said: "I believe you know where my brother is. I think you flew him somewhere. I want you to take me there."

I stayed a couple of paces away, down in the muddy sand, and studied her. She had a silver-white silk scarf filling in the neck of her coat, pinned with what looked like a pearl-topped Victorian hatpin. Small single pearls in her ears.

She looked rich, in the same way that he had, and, like him, she looked used to it. She also looked like a problem. *They usually find me,* he'd said. He might have told me who usually found him, and perhaps how: by picking on the pilot involved.

"You'll be Miss Homer, is it?" I asked, leading a low card.

"I was Miss Homer. I'm Mrs Alice Beekman."

"I'm sorry. Your husband will be the one who runs the estate these days?" That question went right on past her and died all alone in the mud.

"Well, can you get me there today?" she asked.

I have engine trouble; I have airframe trouble; I have magnetometer recorder trouble. I also have trouble not finding nickel or enough money for a new aeroplane. On top of this I have to have family trouble—and not even my own.

"Mrs Beekman," I said, "I have a feeling you'll have played this scene before. What do I say next?"

The grey eyes got a glint of machined steel behind them. "They usually say: 'It's none of my business,'—and they're exactly damned right."

"Right. We'll skip that line. And then I'll bet they say: 'I'll go and find him and ask him if he wants to see you.' Am I right?"

"Something like that." It came out with an edge that would have cut diamond.

"Then that's what I'll do, Mrs Beekman. Meanwhile I'll

fly you up to Ivalo if you want to go. I'm usually based there."

"And just how much will this cost me?"

"The flight to see him—if he wants it—will cost you 15,000 Finnmarks. Say fifty dollars. Up to Ivalo it's on the house."

"You're forgetting your lines," she said. "I usually get run around for at least a hundred dollars' worth first."

"Your brother's already paid for this flight, Mrs Beekman. Partly in change he wouldn't let me give him, but mostly in other things."

For the first time she looked away from me. "Yes—he can do that." Her voice had lost its edge.

"We'll fly up there as soon as I've been into town to see if there's any mail for him."

"You needn't bother. I already did that: one of them was a letter from me telling him I was coming over."

Her luggage took up all of the baggage compartment and a good bit of the space behind the second row of seats. She took up the righthand front seat and strapped herself in neatly and without fuss, which suggested she knew as much about light aeroplanes as her brother.

She looked around the cockpit. "This is a pretty old airplane, isn't it?"

"Not as old as it looks. It crashed."

She gave me a look. "Is this part of your technique for making passengers relax?"

"I didn't crash it, Mrs Beekman. I bought it afterwards and put it together again."

She looked around again. "Somehow I just don't get the same assurance from a hand-made airplane as I do from a hand-made coat. Still, I guess you know what you're doing."

"I've always tried to believe that."

The Beaver and I put on a display of mutual confidence and got each other off the ground. I climbed to three thousand and headed up the airlane to Ivalo.

After a while she said: "When will you go see my brother?"

"I can drop in this afternoon." I lit a cigarette; she refused one, but brought out a packet of Chesterfields and shook one loose with a quick snap of her wrist. Then she lit it with a chromium-plated bonfire.

We flew a bit more, then I asked: "When I see him, Mrs Beekman, what d'you want me to tell him?"

"Just that I'm here and want to see him."

"Not why you want to see him?"

She turned and looked me over coolly. "I can tell him that for myself. Like I said, I don't see it's any of your business."

I nodded. "I'd just thought—in case you were trying to take him home again—that all American citizens were entitled to life, liberty and the pursuit of bears."

"*Thank* you. And for an encore, do you get out and walk on the wings?"

"I like your brother, Mrs Beekman. I'm probably no judge, because we don't get much Virginia society up here, but he struck me as having charm and manners, which aren't at all the same thing. They don't even usually go together. He also struck me as not wanting to involve others in his life and not wanting to be involved with them. It seemed to me a fair bargain."

"He seems to have involved you pretty well. D'you think that's what he wanted?"

"No—I'm sure he'd hate to think he'd got me involved on his behalf." Which left my argument facing firmly in both directions—although the bastard *had* said he'd leave me to judge.

She was looking at me with a small twist of amusement at the corners of her mouth.

I said feebly: "Let's just say I like him."

Also, I had perhaps a feeling about him. But I didn't know how to say that.

"Mr Cary—do you really believe I don't like him myself? Or that I don't maybe know something about him? D'you think I came all this way just to give myself the pleasure of nagging him?"

I stared sternly at the oil pressure.

"As it happens," she said, "all I want to do is try and persuade him to come home and make some important decisions about the estate—since he's still the legal owner of it."

"I thought your husband took the decisions."

She stared ahead through the oil smudges and mosquito-stains on the windscreen. "I don't see why I need tell you this, Mr Cary, but my husband and I are getting divorced."

"I'm sorry."

She glanced at me. "I'm not."

Time for Bill Cary, Your Family Problems Solved While You Wait, to shut up shop for lunch. I went back to worrying about oil pressures and temperatures.

CHAPTER 10

WE WERE just past Sodankylä when Rovaniemi Tower came on the air with my call-sign. They wanted to know my position. I did my usual double-take about giving it, then did.

Rovaniemi said, speaking clear slow English: "We have a distress call a few kilometres north-east of you. Can you investigate?"

I said: "Will do. Any more details?"

They paused a moment. Then: "It is an English aeroplane —an Auster floatplane. He said he had fire in the engine."

"Do you know any more about where?"

"He said he was trying to land in a big bend of a big river. We think the Luirojoki."

I thought so, too. It was the only big river near to but east of the airlane and its long westward bend was just on the horizon to me, about fifteen miles away. I turned towards it.

"We've got an emergency," I told Mrs Beekman. To Rovaniemi I said: "Is he still transmitting?"

"We have not heard from him for five minutes. Perhaps he went too low."

With an engine fire he'd be heading down as fast as he could go. Even if he'd managed to put it out and stop the engine, in a single-engine job like an Auster he wouldn't be flying any further than he could glide.

But he might still be working his radio, and he could be in range from me. I switched over to the distress frequency and called: "Auster with engine fire—do you read me?"

The earphones just hummed back at me. I tried again and didn't raise him.

I said to Mrs Beekman: "Keep a watch out that side. Look for black smoke."

I pushed on power and the Beaver gave a little twist and started a different tone of rattles and added a shade more speed.

When we were within gliding distance of the river ourselves I eased back on the throttle and started down, swaying from side to side to give myself a view over the nose. There wasn't any obvious column of smoke, as there would have been if the Auster had gone down burning only five minutes before. I started zig-zagging, to get a sight back

54

along our track in case it was behind trees from our approach path.

Mrs Beekman said: "I don't see anything in the river."

Then I had it: just a sharp glint among the pines half a mile west of the river. I put on power and went around in a tight diving turn.

It wasn't burning and it wasn't in small pieces, but that was about as much as you could say. The pilot must have seen he couldn't make the river against the north wind, and turned in to try for a cleared track through the trees. He'd been about a hundred yards short for that, but then he'd done the most sensible thing: dropped her on the short saplings and bushes just before a bunch of solid-looking pines.

Even then she'd flipped almost on her back. The floats had dug in and the tail had come up and over until it was caught in the tops of the first small trees. But it wasn't burning.

I did a wide turn about three hundred feet up and somebody stood up in the bushes and waved at me. I waggled my wings and started climbing up.

Mrs Beekman asked: "Can't you land?"

"Just about, I think. D'you want me to?"

"Well, of course." She actually looked indignant about it.

"All right. I just want to tell Rovaniemi what I'm doing; they can't hear me at this height."

I got through to them at about 2,500 feet and gave them as exact a fix as I could. They said they'd have a Finnforce plane overhead in half an hour: would I prefer to circle and mark the spot until he got there?

I looked at Mrs Beekman. She gave her head a sharp downwards jerk. I said to Rovaniemi: "I'll go down. He can act as radio relay. Over and out."

I spiralled down, lowering the wheels out of the floats for the landing.

On full flap and a burst of power to flatten the descent we slammed down between the line of tall trees on either side of the track, and pulled up in a cloud of dust and small stones within two hundred yards of the Auster.

A man waded out of the bushes to meet us just as we climbed down from the plane. He had a cut on the back of his right hand, and one trouser leg was torn just below the knee and his face wasn't very colourful, but he seemed to be moving pretty easily.

He said: "I think my pilot's broken his leg. I'm glad you got here so quickly."

"Just happened to be passing, so I thought we'd drop in," I said. "Are you English?"

"Yes. Are you?"

"We're a joint Anglo-American delegation. Did you get him out of the plane?"

"I'll show you." He led the way. The word for him was 'portly,' but he was moving through the undergrowth pretty well. And he wasn't caring much about what had been a nice grey mohair suit before the crash.

The pilot, a lengthy lad in his middle twenties, was stretched out where the tail of the Auster would have been if it hadn't been up in the treetops. His face was very white and I wasn't sure if he was conscious: his breath was coming out like a leaky exhaust.

His left leg below the knee was a nasty mess. The portly one had done some good to it, stopping the bleeding from a bad gash with a couple of handkerchiefs. But the leg was busted, all right.

There wasn't much I could do except keep the bleeding stopped, lash up the leg with branches as splints, and then haul him out before the shock started to wear him down. I pulled the Fairbairn knife off the clips on my boot, passed it to the portly one, and said: "Try and find a couple of straight branches about three feet long and fairly stiff."

"Right." He took the knife and chugged away into the pines, butting past the undergrowth.

Mrs Beekman leaned over my shoulder and asked: "Can I help at all?"

"You could lend him your coat. He's going to be cold when the shock starts to work."

She took it off and I spread it over him. He moved his head and opened his eyes.

"You're all right, son," I told him. "Just broken your leg. I'm flying you out in a minute."

He whispered: "Is he all right?"

"Hardly a scratch. You picked the best place."

"Couldn't make the river—or the road."

"You did all right. How did you get a fire?"

He closed his eyes and moved his head just a milimetre or two. "Just can't think."

"Oil pressure okay?"

"Bit low—and jumpy. But inside the limits. Until she started burning."

"Cylinder head temperatures?"

"Bit—bit lower than usual. I just—don't get it."

"Don't worry about it." But I was a bit worried about it myself. Engine fires just don't happen in these enlightened times.

Then the portly one came bulldozing back with the branches and we got to work.

We tied the branches to the leg with a couple more handkerchiefs, then wrapped his two legs together with a seat strap I cut out of the Auster. We shoved Mrs Beekman's coat underneath him and started lifting by the two sleeves and two bottom corners. We hauled him a hundred yards, then stopped for a breather.

The portly one said: "By the way, my name's Arthur Judd."

"I'm Bill Cary."

We shook hands—because he seemed to want to—across the spread-out pilot. Judd had a fat, pear-shaped face with his features grouped in a little oasis in the middle of it; in cheerier circumstances, it would have been a cheery face. His fair hair was beginning to thin out, and it was difficult to guess his age: anything between early and late thirties. He wore a club-striped tie in colours that were nasty enough to be genuine.

I said: "I'll be hauling him back to Rovaniemi. D'you want to go, too?"

"We'd been on our way to Ivalo—but I'd better go with him."

"Luggage?"

"About a hundred pounds."

He looked a good two hundred pounds himself. I was calculating take-off weights and distances as we hauled the last hundred yards to the Beaver.

When we got there I had it worked out: without Mrs Beekman's luggage, and preferably Mrs Beekman herself, the take-off wouldn't be too bad.

I put the idea to her. "You'll be in Ivalo as soon anyway," I said, "so the only worry is whether you feel like spending an hour and a half down here in the wilds alone."

"It doesn't bother me." She really sounded as if it didn't.

I started hauling out Mrs Beekman's luggage. For good luck

I unhitched and dumped the magnetometer as well.

We got the pilot, Judd and his luggage on board, pushed the Beaver round to face the way I'd come—we were taking off cross-wind either way, and what I wanted was the straightest bit of road—and I pushed on the power. We got off.

We got to cruising height and I called Rovaniemi and told them to have an ambulance down near the river: I'd land on that to save the journey time from the airport. They said will do.

I looked at Judd beside me. "Business trip?" I asked.

He nodded and smiled wryly. "And a bit of fishing—I'd hoped." There'd been two fishing rods among his luggage. "Looking for a bit of cheap timber up here—composition boarding stuff."

"You really need a plane for that?"

"Is this one for hire?"

"It's my job."

He thought about that, then said: "I'll think about that."

CHAPTER 11

I WAS BACK on the road near the Luirojoki just over an hour and a half after I'd left. I'd accidentally taken Mrs Beekman's coat with us, and she was sitting on an upended suitcase in a crisp dark grey suit looking like a gimmick fashion picture with the bedraggled wilderness behind her.

Except not quite. She actually managed to look as if she belonged in that piece of Lapland—or that it belonged to her. Either way, it's a touch not many women have.

I taxied up and stopped the prop about six feet before it knocked off her head. She didn't move an inch. I climbed down.

"Sorry I'm late."

"Is he all right?"

"The pilot? Yes, he should be okay." I started piling her luggage back aboard. Then I hitched the magnetometer—a streamlined bomb-shape—back onto the winch and rammed it into the retaining clips under the rear fuselage.

"Nearly ready to go," I said cheerfully. "D'you want to hop inside, away from the mosquitoes?"

"Where are you going?"

"I want to have a look at the crashed plane."

She frowned at me, but said: "I'll come, too. These nylons are all shot anyway." I led the way through the undergrowth.

It was an Autocar model, with a British registration; dark green letters on a duck-egg blue finish. The floats made it as rare as a vegetarian mosquito; nobody uses floatplanes in Britain nowadays, not with all the airfields they built during the war. Judd must have had this one built specially for him.

It was a sad sight: it would take a lot of work to get her floating or flying again. The floats had stubbed in their toes, then dragged as she flipped over, tearing the front struts loose so that the floats themselves were splayed out sideways like huge feet. The nose was almost resting on the ground. One blade of the wooden propeller had snapped off, but not shattered, which meant the pilot had stopped the engine in the air, before he hit.

The cockpit door was hanging open, at my shoulder level. There was a spatter of blood on the pilot's instrument panel, and the seat straps—those I hadn't chopped away—were hanging straight down, like jungle vines. I slammed the door shut against the weather.

Mrs Beekman said impatiently: "Well, what have you learned so far?"

"Don't tell anybody, but I think it's an aeroplane."

There wasn't much sign of the fire itself, apart from an intense blackening and blistering a few inches back from the engide cowlings, and a rich ripe smell of burnt oil, rubber, and carbon dioxide.

The engine was stone cold by now. I undid the press-screws with a coin, and the cowling flopped open. Inside, the engine looked like a side of beef that had stood for a month in the sun.

It was covered with dirty, hardened carbon dioxide foam from the extinguisher, threaded through with burnt-off wires like shrivelled tendons and veins. With the mess, and the whole plane being tipped over past the vertical, it took me a little time to find out where I was. Then I located the carburetor and traced the fuel line back through the bulkhead —and there was no break in it. I moved on to the oil lines.

The tank itself was inverted and most of what had been in it was a sticky patch on the ground below by now. I knocked away the dioxide crust and dug out the oil filter.

It had collected a lot of engine sludge and most of it was still on the outside edge of the filter grill. With the system open, there was a strong heady petrol smell.

I jammed the oil filter back in place, knocked bits of the crust off other parts of the engine to distract attention from it, then opened the oil tank cap to let the rest of the system drain out. The cap wasn't on properly anyway.

Mrs Beekman was peering over my shoulder. "Christ, but it smells," she said.

"I'll bet it smelt up there in the air. But they had other problems then." I slammed the cowling shut and screwed it down.

She said: "I'm sorry. I didn't mean anything; I was just finding something to say."

"Yes. Sorry I snapped."

"Does this sort of thing happen often?"

"No. I've known a few forced landings, never a fire in the air before. The pilot was new to this country."

She just nodded. She looked good, standing there in that Fifth Avenue suit with the sunlight catching in her hair. It crossed my mind that there probably wasn't anybody else within miles, certainly not within screaming distance.

The thought crossed and passed on, and I was sorry to see it go. But I hadn't finished with the Auster yet. There had to be something else about it. I didn't know what, but by now I knew there had to be something.

I found it under the instrument panel on the passenger side: a dangling electric plug and a couple of rubber-mounted clips that had once held something. The something wasn't around the cabin itself. I started searching in the undergrowth nearby.

Mrs Beekman said: "Now what?"

I went on looking. It took me nearly ten minutes to turn it up, and it would have taken a week in those woods if he'd really been hiding it. It was a box of electronics about the size of a big dictionary, with a length of wire leading from it to a piece of alloy tube with a handle and round plate marked in degrees at one end, and a small square-sided metal horn set square on the other.

I brought it out into the open and looked it over carefully. It didn't seem to have been damaged, although you can't be sure with electronics until you've tried them.

Mrs Beekman asked: "What've you found?"

I held it up for her to look. "Bit of stuff that fell off."

"Fell off? Just fell off and hid itself behind that tree?"

I smiled blandly at her. "Must have. Why would anybody hide this stuff—unless they thought some other pilot would pinch it?"

I led the way back to the Beaver with her thinking I was just some cheap crook looting a wreck. She was only half right. I planned to hang onto this stuff, all right—you can't get an import license for a radar receiver—a thing whose only use is to detect radar stations. Not if you're flying up near the Russian frontier, anyway.

There was also the question of why Judd thought such equipment worth carrying. And whether that had anything to do with why somebody had sabotaged his Auster.

We set down at Ivalo soon after three o'clock. I went into the tower to phone a taxi for Mrs Beekman and baggage, then ordered the Beaver refuelled.

"You won't have trouble getting a room at the hotel," I told her. "I'll see you there about dinner-time, when I've seen your brother. It may take a little time, if he's off blasting bears, but I'll be in by dark."

"Thank you, Mr Cary." She had her coat back on by now, with just a few blood smears on the lining that didn't show when she kept it buttoned. "I'm sorry I bitched at you earlier."

"Don't apologise yet. You'll probably be bitching at me again tonight."

She just nodded. "Perhaps you'll give him these when you see him?" She handed over an airmail letter and a well-wrapped packet about the size of a box of chocolates. "The packet seems to be for you, anyway."

I nearly dropped it: it was like a lead bar. When I looked at the labels, it was from Purdey's, London, addressed to F. W. Homer care of, and for the attention of, me. It could only be the solid 12-bore slugs he'd promised me.

She said: "The letter's the one I wrote him. It may help explain."

I stuffed it in my shirt pocket. "I'll do what I can, Mrs Beekman. I really will try and talk him into seeing you. But that's something you must know a lot more about than I do."

"Yes," she said. "Yes. A lot more."

She turned away and walked for the airport building.

CHAPTER 12

THERE was still no sign of Mikko, but the tower had a message from him: he was ill, hoped to be back tomorrow, but couldn't promise. While I was waiting for the refuelling to be finished, I broke open the package of cartridges and put one in the shotgun.

The cartridges were brass, about two-and-a-half inches long, with just the point of the lead bullet sticking out. I promised myself I'd pull one to pieces one day, just to see the size and weight of the bullet itself. It felt as if it might be fairly big and nasty.

I put the shotgun back; I'd meant to buy some straps or a canvas gun-case to fix it to the roof, out of the way but easy to get at. So far, all I'd done was slit the quilted sound-proofing over the passenger door and shove the gun down behind that.

The little cream van went hooting up and down the runway to scare off the reindeer, and I rolled out and took off at about half past three.

I did a beat-up of Homer's cabin and the surrounding area, deliberately throwing the plane around so that he'd know I was trying to attract his attention. Then I landed.

I'd got through two cigarettes and was beginning to wish I'd stopped in Ivalo for some lunch, when he marched out of the trees. He was dressed as before, hunting kit plus rifle.

I asked: "How's the hunting?"

"I've seen two more and got one of them, sir."

"Fine. Do you think you've had enough?"

"Why?" He sounded almost sharp—for him. "Are you wanting to leave Lapland?"

"I'll be leaving soon, anyway. But you've got a visitor. She's up at Ivalo." I gave him the airmail letter. "I think this explains it."

While he read it I wandered down to the Beaver and kicked its front wheel tires. Whatever else I did, they would need replacing before next summer. I walked around her looking pessimistically for other things wrong.

When I got back to Homer, he'd finished the letter. He

looked a little worried. "You've seen Alice?" he asked. "Is she well?"

"I took her up to Ivalo. Yes, she seemed fine, apart from the divorce."

"Divorce?" He seemed puzzled.

"Yes—doesn't she say? She's divorcing her husband, or he's divorcing her." I wrinkled my brain trying to remember if she'd said which. But anyway, how did I come to be carrying the bad news from Richmond to the Värriöjoki? "That's why she wants you to go back and do something about the estate, isn't it?"

He said: "Ah, yes, of course," and gave the thin airmail sheet another quick once-over. I lit another cigarette and wondered if I were still too hungover to appreciate the finer points of Homer family life.

After a while I said: "I told her I'd come and see you and ask if you—if you wanted to see her."

He said: "She wants me to go back to America."

"That seemed to be the rough idea."

"She told you why, sir?" Again, he was almost sharp.

"Well, the estate. Her husband won't be making the decisions about it, when he stops being her husband, I assume."

He nodded. Then he said: "No, sir, I don't think America is the place for me."

I dropped my cigarette in the sand and trod on it. I looked down the lake. The north wind was rippling it and swaying the tops of the trees. The sun was low and turning orange down above the far end of the lake. The wind had swept the air clear and had brought a chill with it.

I lit another cigarette and came reluctantly back to the Homer family. I said: "I don't suppose she wants you to go back forever. Can't you giver her power of attorney or something and let her lawyers handle the estate?"

He didn't seem to be listening very hard. "I don't want to go back to America yet, sir. I haven't finished here."

"Well, will you see your sister if I fly her in?"

He smiled wanly. "I'd rather not, sir. I'm planning to go on a little trip—hunting. I shall be sleeping out for two or three nights."

"She's come all the way from the States to see you. I can get her in here first thing tomorrow morning."

"I'd still rather not, sir."

Suddenly I got angry for no good reason except, perhaps, jealousy. "You came here because the only big game you

hadn't shot was the European bear. Now you've shot it—
two of it. I'm sorry if that leaves your life empty of purpose, but it was your choice of purpose. Personally, I don't
understand any of it anyway, but maybe that's because I've
never shot anything but people. Now why don't you go home
and do a day's work for once?"

If he'd slugged me with the rifle butt I'd have understood.
But he just frowned at me, puzzled. "You shot somebody,
sir?"

"Yes. That isn't the point. Will you see your sister?"

He nodded, and for a moment I thought I'd got through
to him. Then he said: "I *thought* you'd had military training
—from the way you handled that gun that afternoon."

I said: "Hell on square wheels," and took a short circular
walk to keep from stuffing the rifle down his throat.

Then I said: "All right. You don't want to see her. You're
in a democracy, so there's no compulsion. Will you give her
a message?"

He thought about this. "Perhaps I'll see her in a few days,
sir. And tell her she can have power of attorney if she
wishes it."

"Okay. I'll come back then." I turned, then turned back.
"But I still think you're running away from something,
Homer."

He pulled himself upright, a smallish, tubby—but calm
and dignified—man. "I can assure you I'm not running away,
sir. I'm a hunter. Perhaps you don't understand, sir."

"I'm damn sure I don't."

I stumped back to the Beaver and shoved it back into the
water and jumped aboard. I was still angry, but mostly at
myself. I'd done a wonderful job of trying to stay uninvolved
in the Homer family troubles.

I was back in the Mainio *baari* in Ivalo soon after sunset,
eating eggs again. I didn't feel like eggs; I felt like a couple
of fast glasses of schnapps, but I knew the eggs had better
come first.

I was feeling nervy and uncomfortable. Partly it was the
dying kicks of a hangover, partly it was knowing the message I'd got to pass to Mrs Beekman—but partly it was that
I'd had enough of prohibited zone flying. At the beginning of
the summer it had seemed worth it: I had a summer's flying
and a big nickel strike ahead. Now all I had ahead was half

a day's flying which wouldn't turn up a bent sardine tin. The risk didn't seem worth it.

But I knew I had to do it. Taking on a contract means finishing it. It was the same with the message for Mrs B.

I finished the eggs and a couple of cigarettes and finally there was nothing to do but go across to the hotel and tell my tale.

She was still in the dining room, sitting alone, taking fast angry puffs at a cigarette and sipping a big cup of coffee. The waitress wasn't anxious to let me and my flying jacket near their millionairess client, but I went anyway.

Mrs Beekman asked: "Did you see him?"

I sat down and ordered coffee and schnapps.

"Yes, I saw him." I took a deep breath. "He doesn't want to go back to the States, and he doesn't want to see you—yet. Maybe in a few days. He said he may be going on a hunting trip."

She had her chin up and her eyes were steady. "That's his answer?"

"In effect, yes."

"You gave him my letter?"

I nodded.

"And told him I'd come from the States to see him?"

"I told him that. Believe me, Mrs Beekman, I actually tried to persuade him. We ended up having a bit of a fight about it. I think he's probably in the wrong, but I also think that's his business."

The waitress brought my coffee and schnapps, and asked if Mrs Beekman required anything.

She said: "Not now." Then, to me: "I think you'd better just take me in to see him."

I gobbled at my schnapps and said: "Sorry."

She gave me a look that was like the big guns on a battleship swinging round at me. I grabbed for my schnapps again. She'd had far more experience telling people like me to say Yes than I'd had telling people like her to go climb a tree.

"So what would it cost me?" she asked grimly. "The flight in to see him?"

"I can set my own price?"

"Yes." The word was chipped out of hard, cold steel.

I thought about it for a while. Then I shook my head. "It's a nice idea, Mrs Beekman. But when he hired me, the agreement was that he was to be left alone. That still stands. He

said he'd see you in a few days. Meanwhile, he said you can
have power of attorney. Does that help?"

She pointed her chin at me and let loose the broadside:
"No-it-does-not-help-damn-you. I want to *see* him. Do you
understand *that*?"

I slammed my empty glass back on the table. "Then spend
a few millions hiring bears. They should know where he is."

I stood up.

She said, more quietly: "Just take it you don't understand,
Mr Cary."

"That makes it exactly one hundred per cent with the
Homer family, Mrs Beekman. *He* told me I didn't understand, either. You're both right. The whole family is a bit
above my head. But the big thing I don't understand is how
I came to be in the middle. Well—I'm resigning. If you're
still around in two or three days' time, I'll fly you in. Until
then you can forget about me."

I walked out.

I regretted it the moment I'd gone, and not just because
the dining room of the hotel was the only place in town that
sold liquor. I could have offered to spend the evening showing her the sights of Ivalo, one of which might have been
Bill Cary's cabin. If we could have stayed off the subject of her
brother.

But her brother was the only reason she had anything to
do with Ivalo—or Bill Cary. I headed on home to the remains
of the Stockholm Scotch.

CHAPTER 13

I WAS IN the Mainio *baari* soon after seven the next morning
and waiting to see if Mikko would turn up, when somebody
shouted that I was wanted on the phone. It was Ivalo airport.

"Pilot Adler has just come on the radio to ask if you
would meet him when he lands," they told me. "He will
land on the river in three quarters of an hour. Do you understand?"

I said: "No, but thank you anyway."

"He said it was very important. He wants your help."

"He wants *what*? No—forget that. Where is he now?"

The voice at the other end sounded as if it were shrugging its shoulders. "Oh, south of here. Near Rovaniemi, I think."

I said thank you and went back to my eggs. My first thought was the hell with Oskar and his troubles. But you can't. Lapland's too lonely to go about saying the hell with other people's troubles; you'll have trouble of your own one day. All of that goes quadruple for pilots.

Still, it would be easier if I weren't convinced that Oskar wanted me to dredge him out of some problem of his own making.

Mikko still hadn't turned up and I thought of going down to his hut to see how he was. I would have, except I didn't believe he was ill but just taking paid time looking for a new job; it would embarrass him if I walked in offering to bathe his fevered brow. In the end I had two more cups of coffee and was out on the bridge by a quarter to eight.

The sun was still low, climbing blearily out of a haze on the eastern horizon. Either the first mist of autumn or smoke from a forest fire over in Russia. Oskar usually landed from the east, upstream towards the bridge. It gave him a wide, straight patch of water, the current to slow him down before he hit the bridge—and the landing could be seen from the dining room of the tourist hotel, which made a nice advertisement.

I lit a cigarette and leaned over the parapet and stared down at the water. I could still see big chunks of the old bridge down there, from when the Germans blew it as they pulled out in 1944.

He must have throttled back well out, because I didn't see or hear the Cessna until it was turning finals two hundred feet up and half a mile downstream.

Whatever you didn't like about that lad, and I didn't like much, you had to admit he could fly. The turn was tight and economical and he didn't need to put on any power at all. His flaps were half down. All he had to do was to put down full flap and he could drop her straight on.

Suddenly the plane flicked on its back. Then it was swerving wildly between the river banks, just ten feet above the water, and completely upside down. He caught and held her there, and then it was coming at me and the bridge, an impossible sight with its damn great floats sticking up at the sky.

I froze in one of the long moments you get only once or twice in a flying lifetime when you're watching an aeroplane and you know the pilot inside is going to die, and you know he must know, too. . . .

He almost didn't. He was that good. He couldn't try and roll right-side-up without sticking in a wing, so he did the only thing he could: pushed on full power and tried to fly her out upside down, over the bridge. And he almost did it.

The engine howled and the nose lifted. Then, slowly and firmly, the nose seemed pulled back down again. The propeller touched and the smooth water exploded into spray. The tail whipped over and the whole plane jumped clear of the water, and the propeller must have broken because the engine wound up to a scream and was still on a rising note when the plane twisted and smashed in sideways. Then there was just the patter of falling spray.

I found myself saying calmly: "He would have had the nose trimmed high for landing; he forgot that that would have pushed the nose *down* when he put on power if he was inverted . . ." Then I was running.

The patch of broken water was nearly a quarter of a mile downstream. As I pounded along the shore the police car from the square went past above me, bouncing like a runaway pram along the slope of the bank. Men were running down to the shore ahead of me. One was pushing out a small boat.

By the time I got there they had one boat almost in midstream and another starting from the opposite bank. Apart from the condition I was in after running a quarter of a mile, there wasn't much I could do but swim out and give them somebody else to save, so I just stood there breathing through my mouth. One of the Cessna's floats had broken loose and was drifting unconcernedly downstream. The tip of the other was showing above the surface, which meant the plane was hanging upside down from it.

One of the coppers had gone out with the boat. The other saw me—he knew who I was—and came over.

He nodded at the river. "Do you know who that was?"

"Oskar Adler. I don't know if he was alone."

"Do you know what happened?"

"I saw *it* happen."

"You don't know what went wrong?"

"I could guess. Maybe Adler can tell you."

The crowd around us gave a mutter and we looked out at the boats. There were two heads on the water and they were lifting somebody into one of the boats. The men bent down over it. Then the cop out there stood up and shook his head at the shore.

His partner on the bank turned back to me and started to say something. I said: "I talk Swedish better."

He looked at me sombrely, then pulled out a notebook with a slow, certain movement. He was a man who would do everything that way: slowly but surely, not wasting any effort. He was a big man, with a lot of beef on his bones and a round, knobbly face with permanently weary blue eyes. In a few years' time he'd have a belly like a barrel; now, he was a man who could reach out with one hand and throw me clear across the river, but would take a long time deciding to do so.

He had a dusty white peaked cap pushed well back on his head and patches of sweat were showing under the arms of his faded blue uniform shirt.

He said, in Swedish: "If that's Adler they pulled out, he won't be telling us anything. You're a pilot, and you may be the only one who saw it happen. You don't have to tell it all to me now, because you'll have to tell it to the chief or the Civil Aviation people later. But I don't want you to forget anything or start inventing anything. Is that clear?"

The crowd muttered again: they were pulling a second body into the boat. The cop out there went through the same performance and shook his head again. The crowd gave a happy, horrified little murmur.

The swimmers were climbing back into the second boat. The cop with me tucked away his notebook and said: "You'd better help identify them." He started walking through the crowd. He could do that: walk through crowds.

The boat ran ashore and an aged character in timber boots and a tan as dark as mahogany climbed nimbly out and held one side. My cop brushed off several eager offers and took hold of the other and just pulled the whole boatload three feet up the beach.

His partner in the boat stood up and bounced out. He was smaller, thinner, with a sharp bird-like face half blotted out by sunglasses.

"Who's he?" he asked busily.

The big one said: "He can identify them."

The other took off his sunglasses and gave me a fast, suspicious once-over, mainly because he was the sort who would do that. "One's Adler," he said. "I've seen the other, but I don't know who he is. Do you?"

I stepped forward and looked into the boat. Oskar had a broken neck; you didn't have to have seen a broken neck before to know that. The other had been thrown around and had broken a lot of his face, but he was still recognisable.

"I know him," I said. "His name's Mikko Eskola. He worked for me."

"For you?" He had his sunglasses back on again. That made him the cold, penetrating investigator. "Did you know he was in that aeroplane?"

The big cop said: "We don't need to go into that now." Then, to me: "Where can we find you?"

"I'm flying today."

The short one gave a snort. The big one said: "If you can be back for lunch, you can fly."

I nodded and turned away and worked my way through the crowd, which was busy telling itself just how it had happened, how many were killed, and just what state they were in. In at least four languages; most were from the hotel.

Somebody touched my arm. I shook it off, then looked to see who: Alexander Judd, the portly one.

"Hullo again." He smiled. "Are you all well, and so on?"

He certainly didn't look as if he'd been in a plane crash the day before. He was wearing another crisp light-grey suit, a cream shirt and another club tie. He looked sober, well-scrubbed and ready to buy Lapland for a well-bargained price. But that wasn't what he was there for.

"When did you get in?" I asked.

"Oh—they got my chap fixed up at the hospital, under drugs and so forth. Wasn't anything else I could do, so I caught the late plane up last night. What was the crash?"

"Finnish pilot and another chap."

"Who?"

Did he sound worried?

I said: "Young Finn. Done some work for me, before this."

"Ah." He nodded. "Afraid for a moment it might have been you."

"I bet you were," I said grimly.

He looked up at me, with a nice startled expression on his fat face. "I don't quite—?"

"Shift up a bit, away from this crowd." We walked a few paces up the bank. "This is the last time I want to see you, Judd. Particularly, it's the last time I want to be *seen* seeing you."

He was looking humorously perplexed, but not yet offended. "I don't understand what you're—"

"All right. I'll give it you without soda. You're SIS—one of the Foreign Office boys. What the mob would call the Secret Service. I don't know what you're doing up here and I don't want to know—but I *do* know you've been spotted by whoever the other side is in this. In case you aren't sure, your engine fire yesterday wasn't an accident. I stopped back and had a look afterwards. Definitely no accident."

He was smiling a nice open smile. "I'm terribly sorry, Mr Cary, and I'd certainly love to be a secret agent, but I'm only a timber merchant. I can prove that, if you like." And he chuckled, a rich, happy sound.

"I'll bet you can prove it. The Foreign Office would be slipping if you couldn't. What you *can't* prove is that there's a timber firm alive that would go to the expense of converting an Auster to floats—and I know roughly what that would cost—just for a trip to Finland. And it had to be a special job: you couldn't use a floatplane around Britain these days."

He pulled a couple of cigars in alloy containers out of his breast pocket and offered one to me.

I shook my head. "Thanks, no. Ruined my taste with cigarettes." I watched while he poured his cigar out of the tube, cross-examined it, and stuck it in his mouth. I waited until he had his lighter going, then said: "And I found your radar detector where you'd hidden it. Had a ten-centimetre horn on it, too; that's the wavelength the Russians use on their frontier radar coverage, so I suppose you were planning to jump the frontier one night?"

The flame of his lighter didn't even flicker. He just lifted his eyes in a sorrowful, mystified look, then took the cigar out of his mouth and said: "Sorry, Mr Cary, but this is all a bit beyond me."

"Look, Judd: I'm not trying to expose you—I think you've done that for yourself already, somehow. When you took off yesterday, your oil tank was full of petrol. Everything your pilot said about the way the oil pressure behaved fitted in with it: generally low, but jumpy as it blocked itself with the sludge it dislodged. But anyway, I opened it up and it all stank of petrol.

"It's an old trick, but not a very good one. It either produces an engine seizure or a fire—but there's no guarantee either will kill you. Still, they may try something more certain next time. Which brings us to the commercial: I don't want to be killed because of you. All offers of my plane withdrawn, and I don't want anything more to do with you. Nothing personal—I've just got enough troubles of my own."

"I'm sure you have, Mr Cary." The cigar was going well and that seemed to be all he cared about. "But I think we'll find we just had an overheating engine."

"Yes, of course." I nodded and lit a cigarette. "Skipping the radar equipment for the moment, Judd, just remember I'm a pilot. Austers have aircooled engines and it's practically impossible to overheat an aircooled engine in the Lapland autumn. But we'll skip that, too, if you like. I've just been giving you evidence that somebody was trying to kill you. I've met timber trade people before. If I'd proved to one of *them* that somebody was trying to kill them, they'd be at the top of the nearest tall tree shouting for mummy. Next time they try to kill you, don't smile so damn much."

I walked away up the bank, leaving him to improve the autumn air with cigar smoke, and went into town.

CHAPTER 14

I SPENT the next twenty minutes buying several yards of wire and a 24-volt electric doorbell, then wangled a ride out to the airport. There I borrowed a few tools and rigged the wires and bell so that when the magnetometer pen arm went above a certain value the bell would ring up near my ear.

It's an old dodge for surveying solo. I just wanted to hear the moment when I got rich.

Then I did a careful check of the Beaver itself. I took a lot longer than my usual morning pre-flight inspection, and by the end of it I was sure that there was only oil in my oil tank, and nothing had been fixed to make me turn upside down ten feet from the ground. I couldn't think of any reason why anybody should want to fix me, but I couldn't forget that Lapland had lost two floatplanes in the last twenty-four hours. Now I had the only one. It was a lonely feeling.

By the end of the morning the bell hadn't rung. All I'd achieved was a sweat that pasted my shirt to my back, a collection of cigarette ends around my boots that looked like the first snow, and the end of the Kaaja contract. I was either a free man, or out of work. You can look at it both ways.

I landed back at Ivalo just before one o'clock and rode in with an airport employee going back to town for lunch. He talked about how sorry he was Oskar had got killed and how he wished he'd actually seen it for himself. I kept quiet and dropped off at the Mainio *baari*.

I was halfway through my boiled beef and potatoes when Veikko came in. He stared around, then fixed on me. The word was getting around that Cary was open for interviews every mealtime.

"Oskar's dead—" he started.

"Speak English," I said, speaking English strained through boiled beef.

He sat down and snapped his fingers for service. He would.

"Oskar crashed and got killed," he said, in English.

"I know. I saw it."

"You saw it? How did it happen?" He was wearing a dark blue suit, a white shirt, a silver tie and an agitated expression.

I shrugged. "He rolled over on the approach."

The old girl wandered out from behind the counter, looked Veikko over as if he were something the cat had coughed up, and said: "Yes?"

Veikko ordered coffee. She wandered away again, hoping they were out of coffee.

"Where was he coming from?" Veikko asked.

"I don't know. Was he working for you?"

Veikko snapped upright as if I'd spilled my lunch in his lap. "No. Who said he was working for me?"

I pushed away the rest of my boiled beef and lit a cigarette. I wanted to watch this; you didn't often catch Veikko looking worried. Life isn't that fair.

Just to keep him simmering, I said: "I don't know. I heard it around somewhere."

"He wasn't working for me. He was *going* to do some work for me, yes." He suddenly got a cunning look in his eyes. "Who are you working for?"

"Kaaja company. That and odd jobs. Flying hunters around."

He studied me carefully. The old girl brought his coffee, and asked me if I wanted one. I said no, thanks.

When she'd gone I said: "Come on, Veikko. You didn't come here just to wish me a happy name-day. It's the wrong day, anyway. Is it still about that Swedish job you wanted me to take?"

"The—?" Then he remembered. "No, no, not that. Some-

body else got that, I heard. No. I want you to fly me somewhere, later this afternoon."

I wasn't over-anxious to be employed by Veikko, but business is business, particularly now the Kaaja job really was
finished.

I nodded. "Where?"

"I'll tell you then."

That sounded like a Veikko idea, all right. I said: "All
right—as long as you remember I may veto the whole idea if
I don't like where you're going or whatever you're carrying."

He sat up straight again. "What would I carry? Why should
I carry anything?"

I stubbed out my cigarette. "I don't know. I just said 'if'
—and it still stands. What time?"

"Five o'clock here. I'll pick you up in the car."

"All right." I watched him for a moment. He was stirring
his coffee. He'd stirred it twice already.

I said quietly: "Strictly between us two suspicious characters, that Swedish job you offered was all hot air, wasn't it?"

He nodded slowly and not at all happily. "Yes. That's
right."

"So you just wanted to know if I was free to leave the
country for a while?"

He nodded again.

I said: "And when you found I wasn't, you set those young
thugs on me in Rovaniemi? Were they supposed to kill me?"

"No!" He said it fast, too fast.

"Which question are you answering, Veikko?"

He shook his head.

"Don't mess about with me, Veikko. You sent three of
them with knives and they weren't good enough to mess about
with me. Why did you send them?"

"I thought—" his hands made a big, hopeless gesture, "—I
thought you must be working for somebody. But I was wrong.
They weren't to kill you, just stop you working for a week or
two. I made a mistake."

"You did that," I said. "Now let's try one of my mistakes.
The *baari*'ll lend you a knife; I've got one of my own." I
slapped the Fairbairn on my boot.

He shook his head quickly and his fat cheeks glinted with
sweat. "Please, Mr Cary, please— Just will you fly me?"

I leant back in my chair. He was badly frightened, but not
by my knife. His eyes were pleading.

"Cash?" I asked.

He nodded.

"In advance?"

"It will be."

I'd got a lot more questions to ask, such as who he thought I was working for when he'd hired the thugs, and who'd got him so frightened now. But the cops might be looking for me, and I didn't much want to be found talking to Veikko.

I nodded and got up. "Okay—*if* I still like the idea at five o'clock."

I walked across to the hotel for a schnapps before I met my police friends again. Mrs Beekman was finishing her lunch. She saw me and jerked her head to indicate I should come and have a word. I thought about ignoring her, then thought that she'd probably send out and hire a couple of roadmenders to come and carry me over. I went across under my own steam.

She looked good. She had on a pair of ivory-coloured trousers so smooth and unwrinkled that they could only have been ski pants, a brown silk blouse, and a black leather waist-coat.

"Sit down," she said. "How's business today?"

"So-so." The waitress came and served me a schnapps and sneered at my flying jacket.

"Somebody crashed this morning, didn't they?" she asked. "I was afraid it was you for a moment."

"Not me. I don't crash."

"I understand somebody got killed?"

"Couple of people."

She lit a cigarette and frowned slightly. "When that other airplane crashed yesterday, you said it hardly ever happened up here. This makes two in two days."

"Maybe there's something going around."

"I wasn't being funny, Mr Cary," she said coldly.

"Oddly enough, neither was I."

She looked at me for a time. Then she said quietly: "Maybe they were friends of yours."

"You might say that."

"And it isn't really any of my business?"

"You might say that, too."

She just nodded. "I'm sorry. You pilots are a damn tight bunch. Still—if I can help . . . ?"

"If you meet a big French-Swiss character called Claude in here, I'd be interested to know something about him, and he'd talk to you. I think Oskar—the man who crashed—was doing some work for him."

"He lives here?"

"He's got a trailer parked somewhere north of here. Still, I think I'll try and drop in on him tonight sometime."

She nodded and there was a long silence while she played with trimming the ash off her cigarette. Then she said: "I made a mistake with you, yesterday. I'm going to make the same mistake again, now—only bigger. That's the only way I can show you how important seeing my brother is to me." She glanced up at me and said quietly: "I think you need a new airplane. I'll buy you one."

I saw it: I couldn't help seeing it: a brand-new silver Beaver with "Cary Surveys" painted in discreet letters on the tail. 108 knots at 300 b.h.p., and at only 23 gallons an hour. Just like it says in the brochures. And maybe a new magnetometer recorder as well? She wouldn't dig in her toes at paying for just that much extra.

I said: "Sorry, Mrs Beekman. I seem to cost more than new aeroplanes. I hadn't known that, before." I hadn't, either.

There was a burble of conversation at the door. My two police friends were standing just inside the dining room, staring around. The big one saw me, stretched out a vast hand, and turned it into a come-hither sign.

I finished off my schnapps and stood up.

She said: "You damned, damned fool. You don't understand."

I nodded. "I said so last night."

Her face crumpled up and she grabbed her hands to it.

I waited a moment, but she wasn't telling me what I didn't understand, so I went across to the door, and the police.

CHAPTER 15

THE BIG COP nodded back over my shoulder: "Good friend of yours?"

"Just another millionairess client. She wants to buy me a new aeroplane."

The smaller one gave me his quick bird-like glance, and wrinkled his nose. "You're one of those, hey?"

I turned towards him. I could get to enjoy disliking him very much.

The big cop said calmly: "We're not going to have any trouble." He patted me on the shoulder and nearly fractured it. "If it makes you feel any better—I don't believe you."

I thought about it, then nodded. "I don't think I believe it myself." We started out of the room. "Where are we going?"

"Somewhere quiet. There's somebody who wants to see you."

We went to the lobby desk. He leant against it and asked the girl there: "Could we borrow a room for a couple of hours? Just for a quiet talk?"

She didn't much want the place infested with either me or policemen, but finally she sorted through the register and gave him a key.

I said: "Two hours? I'll go and get myself another drink."

The big cop said: "You want a drink?—all right." He turned back to the girl. "And send along a bottle of schnapps."

She stiffened. "We can't serve drinks in rooms. The law—"

He smiled gently; it looked like a crack opening across a rock. "It's just for our friend here. He's had a bad shock. You know us—" he spread two hands like tree roots "—we can't drink on duty, can we?" He nodded to me to lead on up the corridor, then turned back to the girl. "And three glasses."

We went into a ground-floor room: small, clean, white-painted, with simple new furniture and heavy curtains to keep out the midnight sun. There were two chairs and a small table. I sat in one, the big man wedged himself into the other, his hips spreading out under the arms of it. The birdey one leant himself against the door and looked official.

"Well," I asked, "where's the somebody who wants to see me?"

The big one said: "He'll be here soon." He took off his cap and ran his hand through thin gingery hair. "Bad business, all this. Lot of fuss."

"Why? It's just an air crash, isn't it?"

Somebody knocked. The small cop sprang aside and yanked the door open in one movement. A waitress marched in and slammed a bottle of schnapps and three glasses on the table.

She looked round at us. "Who is paying?"

There was a silence. Then I said: "I might have known." I paid up and she went out.

The big one smiled and let me pour three shots.

"*Kippis.*" We all swigged.

He said: "Suppose we stamped out every liquor infringement up here. What would happen then?"

"I don't know. Maybe the police would have to buy their own drinks."

"Never. What would happen is that everybody would go blind drinking the home-made stuff. At least the government gets the tax on this. *Kippis.*" We swigged. "You said it was just an air crash. Maybe. But *Suopo* would like to see you."

The other cop turned a scorching glare on him.

I asked: "Nikkanen?"

The small one demanded: "D'you know Nikkanen?"

"Slightly. Probably not as well as he knows me."

I stood up and walked to the window. The river was flowing fat and placid in the pale afternoon sun. The small white, red-roofed houses on the opposite bank looked like children's toys. But downstream to the right I could see a small crowd at the bank and a boat in midstream.

I said: "Roll up, roll up. Great new tourist attraction. Only twenty Finnmarks to see the grave in the middle of the river."

The small cop let out a blast of Finnish, gulped his drink and whizzed out of the room.

The big one smiled gravely and leant to pour himself more schnapps. "Enthusiastic," he said. "But you need someone like him if you've got someone like me. Me, I never even suspected you were a Russian spy."

I turned back to my chair.

I said: *"Kippis,* Comrade."

Nikkanen arrived before the other cop got back. He just stood in the doorway looking at me.

"Hello, Mr Cary," he said in English. "Somehow, you are where things happen. At least, we must hope it is that way round." He gave me the dentist's smile, the one which hopes this won't hurt, but just too bad if it does. "Is that your schnapps?"

"It is."

"Since it is not my work to enforce the drink laws—yes, I will have one."

The cop climbed ponderously out of his chair, collected his colleague's glass and rinsed it at the washbasin. Nikkanen sat in the chair and put down his briefcase, bulge upwards, on the floor beside him. He was wearing a lightweight cream raincoat over a dark blue city suit.

He drank without saying *Kippis,* lit one of his blowpipe

cigarettes, then laid a notebook and ballpoint pen on the table.

"Now, Mr Cary, please tell me what happened. We have a number of statements from people who saw the crash and also some even more exciting statements from people who did not. But none of them are pilots. Why were you waiting for Mr Adler?"

"I got a message phoned from the airport. Oskar had radioed them to ask me to meet him when he landed." Nikkanen must know that already; he would have checked the airport for Oskar's last messages. He was just trying to get me into the habit of telling the truth.

I told him about waiting at the bridge. About Oskar's approach, the sudden half-roll, the long, long seconds while he tried to fly out inverted—the extra seconds of life that are all that being a superlative pilot gives you. And then finding Mikko had been with him.

"I was going to pay Mikko off at the end of the week," I said. "I think he must have talked Oskar into giving him a job; he hadn't told me anything—he was pretending to be ill. I think that's about all I know."

But it wasn't all I wanted to know. I still couldn't see why Oskar should take Mikko on. He wasn't flying any surveys I knew of, and anyway, if he had wanted an assistant he'd have hired one at the beginning of the summer, not the end.

If the same thoughts had struck Nikkanen, he wasn't bothering with them. He just asked: "Do you have any idea why Adler crashed? Could you tell anything from just watching?"

"The Civil Aviation enquiry will tell you that."

"Mr Cary: the enquiry will look at all the pieces—when they are brought up from the river—and they will measure things, and examine documents and draw little maps and then, perhaps in six months' time, they will scratch their chins and say: 'Mind, we cannot be absolutely sure, but we think . . .' And they will probably be right. But I want you to scratch your chin now."

The big cop was sitting on the end of the bed, not apparently listening and not understanding anything he heard, but knowing something was going on, the way a good cop always does.

I said: "I'd say one of his flaps didn't come down to 'full' when the other did. The starboard—right—one didn't. He'd got half flap down already—I saw that—and was just in a position to put down 'full' when he rolled. Anyway, that would have produced the result. I heard that something like that happened to a Viscount near Manchester a few years ago. It went in upside down and killed everybody."

Nikkanen nodded. "The flaps—you will excuse my ignorance?—are used to slow you up to land?"

"Not primarily, no. They *do* slow you up, but basically they let you fly safely at a lower speed. They reduce your stalling speed."

"At what speed did Mr Adler's aircraft land?"

"At something over 50 knots—90-something kilometres. But he was doing more than that when he crashed. Over 70 knots."

"Yes." He made a note in his book. "Would he have noticed earlier if his flaps were not working properly?" He smiled. "Or is that a stupid question?"

"He damned certainly didn't know one flap wouldn't come down full. He probably used half flap to take off, and he might have tested them down to 'full.'" According to the book, he should have done. But what I'd seen of Oskar's flying hadn't always been according to the book.

Nikkanen crunched out his cigarette. He said quietly: "It might be a very important question, Mr Cary."

It might. If Oskar had tested his flaps before take-off, then he'd had a mechanical failure. If not, then perhaps somebody had fixed him. And fixed him in one of of the most certain ways going.

I said: "Your enquiry will tell you that."

He nodded and made another note and lit another cigarette. Then, without any change in the run-up, he said: "And the other aeroplane, the English one, why did that crash?"

"It caught fire in the air."

"The Lapland air is so hot in the autumn, I agree. Was there any connection between the two crashes?"

"I'd say not."

He looked at me thoughtfully. Then he said: "At first, it surprised me to find you, an Englishman, permitted to work up here as a pilot. We have many good pilots of our own, and not work for all of them. So I looked up your work permit. It was many years old, but all the documents are still there."

I said: "What's this got to do with anything?"

"I am just telling you something about yourself—something you might have forgotten. So—I found you were permitted to work here because you had the friendship of a certain man. A very important man in his time, and a very great

Finn. I don't know how you achieved that, Mr Cary. My first thought was that you must, at some time, have done a service for Finland. But of course, the documents do not show this."

"Yes," I said. "Yes, I'm beginning to get the message. That man's dead now. There's nothing and nobody to stop anybody taking away my work permit. All it needs is a bad word from you."

He nodded again. "I think a word would be enough. But it would be a slow business, and not of any immediate help to me. It might help more if I had you put in jail."

"On what grounds?"

"Whatever grounds you choose, Mr Cary. Let us say: 'In the interests of national security.' You might be surprised what I can do in the interests of national security."

"What the hell's national security got to do with me?"

He gave a bleak, small smile. "Anything can be national security until proved otherwise, Mr Cary. Then it becomes just a regrettable mistake." His eyes got cold. "You have no idea how many mistakes I might be ready to make."

We stared at each other for a long time. Somebody knocked on the door. The big cop glanced at Nikkanen, then levered himself up to go and answer it.

Nikkanen said, more gently: "Your trouble is not uncommon, Mr Cary. You just hate policemen."

"No. Only those I've met so far."

At the door, Mrs Beekman said: "Is Bill Cary here?"

The cop turned round and looked at Nikkanen, holding the door almost closed.

The door whanged open and cracked him on the back of the head.

Mrs Beekman stood there smouldering and shaking a sore toe. "I hope I'm not interrupting," she said icily. "I just wondered if you'd be free for dinner tonight, Mr Cary?"

I stood up. "I'd be delighted, Mrs Beekman. But I ought to warn you that I may be in jail tonight."

I glanced down at Nikkanen. He raised his head slowly, looked sadly at me, then twisted round to her. "Mr Cary is exaggerating, Mrs Beekman. I know of no reason why he should not dine with you."

She gave him an ironic little bow. "Thank you, sir." Then, to me: "About eight, then?"

"I'll be there." I might not be, not if the Veikko job took more than three hours, but I wasn't going to admit I was doing anything for Veikko in front of Nikkanen. If he was

looking for an excuse to drop the curtain on me, he'd have to
find it for himself.

Mrs Beekman said: "Fine. Anything I can do for you before then?" It was asked casually, but it had a meaning behind it. Nikkanen knew it, too. And for a moment it was an
attractive idea: I could have used the support of Wall Street
if Nikkanen was really set on making a mistake. But I'd been
following a policy of non-involvement in the Homer family
affairs. I couldn't expect it both ways.

And, of course, there would always be a price.

I shook my head. "Thanks, but there's really no problem.
If I'm not at dinner, it'll be because I remembered another
date."

She smiled, a little pained, but got the message. She went
away and the cop shut the door.

Nikkanen asked: "Did you mean that, Mr Cary?"

"I did. She's nothing to do with any trouble I'm in. So I'm
still vulnerable."

He may have winced a little. He rubbed the end of his long
nose and said: "I think you've been misunderstanding me—"
I hadn't, but if he wanted to make a fresh start, that suited
me: "—what I would most like is just a little discussion." He
smiled sadly. "Just a little more honest than we have had so
far."

"That's fine with me." I sat down again.

He lit another cigarette and said: "There is something happening up here in Lapland, Mr Cary. I think you believe that
yourself.

"Let us go back to the two aeroplane crashes. I asked you if
they were connected. You said you did not think so. Now I
will ask: why?"

I took a deep breath, then topped it off with a snifter of
schnapps. This was where my honesty started getting ap-
proximate. But I had one fair point left to make.

I said: "In one of them two people got killed. In the other,
nobody got killed. There's that much lack of connection."

He thought about this. Then: "You would say it is so certain—if somebody had sabotaged the flaps? And so uncertain if they had caused a fire in the air?"

"Give me a choice, and I'll take a fire any time. Especially
if somebody's forgotten to puncture the extinguisher system.
Flap trouble happens near the ground: you don't have the
height or speed to get yourself out of trouble."

"So the fire was an amateur work? And the flaps professional?"

I shrugged; I didn't see why I should be doing *Suopo's* ground-work for them. "Anyway, why should anyone want to kill the Englishman, Judd?"

"Why should anyone want to kill Mr Adler?"

Good question. "Where was he coming from?"

"Ah, yes." He flicked back the pages in his notebook. "So far, we know only that he took off from the river in Rovaniemi yesterday afternoon. He did not come back for the night. He did not spend the night at Kemijärvi, Kilpisjärvi, Sodankylä or up at Inari or Kirkenes. We are asking other places, but—" he shrugged. "In an aeroplane with floats you do not need to spend the night in any town; just a lake or river will do." He flipped his notebook back to a blank page. "For whom was Mr Adler working?"

"I've seen him with a few hunters and tourists—nothing more. I don't think he had any mineral survey contracts this summer." I didn't think I need mention that he'd been going to do some work for Veikko or my own deduction, from Veikko's denial of the thought, that he'd done some already. Whoever had fixed Oskar, it hadn't been Veikko.

"He was not, perhaps, entirely an honest man?"

I shrugged. "The question doesn't really mean anything. He was a bush pilot; he had his own rules. You don't come down through cloud without being certain of your position; you land as quickly as you can when they report mist at sundown; you refuel as soon as you land to stop condensation in the tanks. He'd have kept to those rules. Flying in a crate of schnapps or going over a prohibited area—those are paper rules."

Nikkanen said softly: "Are you telling me about Mr Adler or yourself?"

I shrugged again.

Nikkanen rubbed his nose thoughtfully. Then he said: "One more thing. Mr Cary. Two floatplanes have crashed—for whatever reason—and you have now the only one left in Lapland. So I would like you to be very careful. And I would like you to tell me if anybody asks you to do any unusual work. You understand?"

I understood, all right. I was the bait. And bait doesn't catch anything if it's kept in the tin.

I nodded, and went out.

CHAPTER 16

I DRANK three cups of coffee in the Mainio and it got to be half past five and no Veikko. I thought of ringing him, but then didn't. Ivalo is a small exchange and they knew my voice. I hadn't got much of a reputation, but I must still have more than Veikko.

For the same reason, I didn't take a taxi. Veikko lived about a mile out, on the road east to Akujärvi. It was a lonely spot, but anywhere out of sight of Ivalo was a lonely spot. Step twenty yards off the road and you were in forest that had grown untouched since the last Ice Age pulled back.

Nobody followed me out of town; I hoped nobody even noticed me go.

I was about halfway there when a big car came pouring down the road towards me, going a lot too fast for the narrow sandy road and trailing a dustcloud like a fog bank. I hopped into the woods while it went past. It was the scarlet Facel Vega, with Claude at the wheel. I didn't think there was anybody else on board, but I couldn't be sure. If Veikko was in it, I was going to look fairly silly tromping on out to look for him.

By then I really wanted to find him. I didn't much care if I flew him anywhere or not, although business was still business, but I wanted to know why he wanted to be flown. I kept on walking.

It was a large house, at least large for Lapland, built in Backwoods Modern style, rather like a Swiss chalet. The wide, heavy roof came down to just above the ground-floor windows, so the first floor only had windows at the front and back. It was made of big horizontal timbers interlocking at the corners just like any forest cabin, but with the projecting ends trimmed to give a reverse upwards slope. It wasn't painted, just soaked in varnish to a bright whisky colour.

The window frames were metal, divided into small panes to give a cross-barred look. The front door was some antique from—probably—Central Europe: a heavy affair of oak timbers and a lot of curly cast iron and big studs. It would have been easier to knock a hole in the wall than punch that in.

It all looked fancy unless you knew Veikko and knew

he must have chosen it for that reason. Anybody who thumped on the door and said Open Up Or We'll Kick It Down would have simply stood there getting broken toes while Veikko shoved his second set of accounts in the stove. To get in through the windows you'd have to rip the whole frame out.

It was almost evening; only the roof was still in sunlight, but there were no lights on that I could see. I took a short cut across what would have been the front lawn if anybody had mown it that year, and pressed the bell. Then I stood back to where he could see me from a window. He'd want that.

After a while, I pressed it again.

After another while I stood back and howled: "Ahoy! Anybody call for a good bush pilot?"

The trees all round the house gulped in the sound and filtered it away with that special muffled echo a forest has, then left me standing there feeling a little lonelier still. I walked around the house. The windows were all shut and covered with net curtains; the back door was almost as heavy as the front and locked solid. Veikko's blue Saab was standing on the drive.

I went back to the front door and pressed the bell for the last time before tromping back to town and finding he'd been in the Mainio for over half an hour. Just to make sure, I pulled the front door. It swung open.

I went in on tiptoe with that creepy, naked feeling of holding my breath and listening for others not holding theirs. Pointless, of course, after ringing bells and shouting my head off for five minutes.

Inside, it was deep twilight between the panelled walls of the corridor. I went down to the end and eased open his study door. There was a little more light in there. Enough to see that the room had been hit by a whirlwind.

Every book had been swept off the shelves; the drawers of the two big plan-chests Veikko used as filing cabinets were lying in heaps; the pictures were off the walls; papers covered the floor like snow. The big teak Danish desk in the middle stood up like a dark island, the tall wing-backed black leather chair behind it was swung away from me.

I stepped aside from the doorway and leant against the tall ceramic stove in the corner; it was warm. I put a cigarette in my mouth and didn't light it, and stared at the mess. After a time it began to have a pattern. Somebody had worked the room over, fast but professionally.

The desk chair was bothering me. I put the cigarette back in my shirt pocket and picked my way across and swung the chair round. He spilled gently out of it and his face hit my feet.

I couldn't have jumped more than two feet up and twelve feet back because the room wouldn't have allowed it. But I jumped. I found myself back near the stove and the cigarette back in my mouth and drawing hard on it.

It still wasn't lit, so I put it in my pocket again and walked slowly back and turned him over. His face had a relaxed, almost friendly look on it. That alone would have convinced me he was dead.

He was wearing the same dark suit and white shirt and silver tie, but now with three bullet holes across the tie. He had bled only a little, and it was nearly dry now. He had left brownish smears on the papers he had flopped onto coming out of the chair. I ran my hands through his pockets without finding anything interesting, and stepped back.

Then I noticed something that had come out of the chair with him: a revolver. For a moment I thought I'd found the murder weapon; then I realised that nobody had been shot with that thing in a long, long time. It was almost as big and almost as old as a Waterloo cannon: the metal was dark brown and pitted with rust. I thought I knew something about small arms, but it took a lot of peering in the twilight to sort that one out: an 1874 model French military pistol. If you fired it now, you'd probably blow your hand off. But it looked as if Veikko had tried.

He must have grabbed it out of the desk drawer—you wouldn't carry a field gun like that on you—and was hauling it up by easy stages into the aiming position when whoever-it-was pulled out something a lot more modern and put three rounds through his silver tie.

There were two things I could do now: get out, or call the police. My vote said get out. But there was a third thing I had to do whatever else I did: sort through his desk papers to see if he had my name in a diary or anything. If I didn't find it now, the cops would later.

Ten minutes of searching brought me nothing but a feeling that I was pushing my luck. He had nothing in his desk diary beyond a few notes about buying groceries, which were probably code for something else. I hoped it was an unbreakable one.

Now all I had to do was get him back into his chair. From

the position of the bullet holes and the small amount of
blood, he must have died almost instantly. Leaving him spread
out on top of his papers implied either that somebody had
searched the room *before* shooting him, or somebody else
had come along and toppled him out of his chair later. Any
cop would pick the second explanation.

It was a long job. He was as heavy as old iron and as limp
as a drunken octopus. Rigor mortis hadn't started, so he probably hadn't been dead two hours.

I collected the papers with bloodstains on them and took
them over to the stove. The small log basket had been over-
turned. I picked up a log, knocked open the stove door catch,
and shoved the papers into the blaze. The log in my hand was
dry, grey and cracked. It had been kept indoors a long time;
so had the others scattered around.

I sat back on my heels and looked at the flames, and the
log in my hand, then at the stove itself. It was another antique: the size of a wardrobe, of blue-and-white ceramic such
as you find in old houses all over Finland. They're cheerful
things to have around, but this one would have burned that
basketful of logs inside a day. I couldn't quite see how these
logs had been kept waiting around long enough to get so dry.

I peered in at the flames and the glowing embers and the
black shapes of half-burned logs underneath them. Then something else struck me. There was no smell of wood smoke.
There was no smell at all.

I found it in the cupboard under the stairs, exactly behind
the stove: a long row of Calor gas cylinders. Logical enough,
for a house in the backwoods—but when you shifted a few
rags the last cylinder was connected through the wall by a
brass pipe. I twisted the cylinder knob shut and went back to
the study. The fire in the stove was out.

I grinned across at the dead man in the chair. "It was
good," I told him. "But you got a little careless with the details. You should have renewed the logs." But he hadn't really
anything to reproach himself for, even if he'd been in the
mood. His secret had outlasted himself.

Behind the dummy metal logs in the stove there was a
blackened metal hatch that was still too hot to touch. It probably had a trick catch to it, but I didn't really look for it. I got
the old sparkplug from my pocket and reached in and jammed
the long spark arm under one edge of the hatch and jerked.
It flopped down forward across the logs.

Among the mess on the floor, there was a decorative green
candle. I dug it up, lit it, and stuck it inside the stove.

At first it looked like an old screw-thread printing press. It
went on looking like that, too, except for a long horizontal
handle atop the broad screw, bent down at each end by heavy
weights. I made a long arm and pushed at one weight. It took
a good shove to get it started, then the orbiting weights kept
it running. The heavy top plate of the press climbed slowly.

The bottom slab had a small round depression in the
centre; exactly above it in the top plate there was another
inset that felt rough when I touched it. I eased a bit more of
my shoulder into the stove and shifted the candle to look
around.

On one side of the press there was a big scorched bowl of
some ceramic material, some ceramic stirring rods, and a few
metal tools I couldn't identify. On the other side was a wooden
box about the size of a shoebox. I tried to drag it out, but it
wouldn't drag worth a damn. I got a hand inside and brought
out a couple of small blank golden discs.

I knew where I was then. All I had to do was prove it. I
planted one of the discs in the inset in the bottom slab of the
press, and gave the handle a hefty pull in the reverse direction. The top plate wound down and slammed shut. I wound
it up again, and the disc went up a few inches with it, then
clattered free.

When I held it near the candle, I had a new-minted 1928
sovereign with the tiny letter I, the made-in-Bombay mark.

I spent a time just thinking about the other discs in the box
—enough to make it too heavy to shift. It was pleasant thinking. But it went on too long. Far, far too long.

Headlights raked across the window and a car squeaked
and grated on the gravel beside the front door. For a moment
I froze solid. Then I heaved the two discs back into the box,
threw the candle in behind the press, yanked up the metal
hatch and shut the stove door.

A car door slammed, then another. Feet marched across
the gravel.

I went on cat's feet across to the desk and collected the
French artillery piece. It just might be that whoever had
killed him had remembered about not having looked in the
stove. Then the doorbell went off, sounding like a 21-gun
salute in the twilight.

I knew who it was, then: the killer would have known the

front door was left open. I grabbed hold of the telephone cord, yanked, and it came loose.

A voice said: "Open up or we'll kick it open." I recognised the outlook, if not the voice. But I couldn't see what brought them out here. Then I remembered the Facel Vega on the road. All Claude had needed was a telephone; now all I needed was a very good lawyer. I put a foot to the door and it swung open. Two torches blazed in my face.

The voice of the big cop said in calm Swedish: "You do seem to get around in your job."

The other one suddenly yelled something about me having a gun and his torch took two steps backwards. I took the pistol in my left hand and held it out butt forwards. A huge hairy hand came out and grabbed it.

I said: "It belongs to Veikko. He's in the back room. The study."

The small cop rushed past me into the house.

I said: "Tell him not to put fingerprints on everything. This is a police job."

The big voice said amiably: "And what did you think we are—game wardens?"

"I mean not your sort of police."

Inside the house, the other cop called: "Here. Come here." His voice was slightly shrill.

The big one asked me: "Dead?"

"Yes."

"You?"

"You wouldn't have caught me here if I'd killed him. I'd been going to report it to you, but the phone was out of order."

"You did your best, in fact?"

"Naturally. Also, there's no gun."

"No gun?" The big French revolver waved in the torch-light, looking like a toy in his hand.

"That didn't kill him. That would have blown down the house, as well. And you need to find the real gun before you can get a conviction."

The torch looked me slowly up and down, like a big single eye. "We've been hoping for somebody to come and push Veikko out of the daylight—" he used the quaint old Finnish slang phrase "—but it's going to be a long night for all of us, all the same."

CHAPTER 17

WE ENDED UP in the same room of the same hotel doing the same thing: waiting for Nikkanen. At first this surprised me: I'd expected to be bounced straight into jail. Then it occurred to me that probably the 4:10 Dakota up from Rovaniemi had brought a few newspapermen who'd be besieging the police station trying to get an angle on the two-air-crashes-in-two-days story. Being a *Suopo* man, Nikkanen wouldn't want to be seen going anywhere near the cop-shop.

He'd gone down to Rovaniemi on the 4:10 turnaround; he couldn't get back before the 11:20. We waited.

Nobody had told me whether or not I was under arrest, and somehow I hadn't got around to asking. We just waited. No schnapps this time. All I had was a weekly newspaper I'd picked out of the police car and which I was pretending to read.

The big cop was sitting directly opposite me, across the table, with Veikko's revolver lying on the table pointing my way like the sword at a Navy court martial. The small one was sitting on the bed.

"Three shots," he said. "Just three shots—bing, bing, bing. As close as three fingers. He must be good." He said it in Swedish, so it was obviously meant for me.

I went on pretending to read the paper.

The big cop said: "Your friend Oskar wasn't so innocent, either. *He* was carrying a gun. Did you know that?"

"I don't remember."

The short one snorted. "He doesn't remember. Ha!"

I said: "Maybe it was the one that killed Veikko."

The short one got half off the bed and said: "We never thought of—" before he remembered that Oskar had been dead and his pistol in police hands seven or eight hours before Veikko got shot.

He scowled nastily at me. If it had been light enough, he'd probably have put on his sunglasses and given me an inscrutable stare.

The big one leaned back, but not so far that he couldn't grab the revolver if I started a civil uprising.

"Personally, I don't think you killed Veikko,'" he said. "But probably nobody will ask me what I think."

The small one said: "Why waste effort? We caught him in the house with a fresh body, trying to intimidate the police with the victim's gun. Get an easy conviction."

The big cop seemed to think this over. "We could do that, yes—but I'd still rather get at the real truth."

"Why bother? He isn't going to help us. Why help him?"

They both looked at me. The game wasn't helped by them having to speak Swedish, to make sure I understood, and yet still seem to be just chatting among themselves. I went on reading.

The small cop said: "He thinks he can talk his way out when Nikkanen gets here. Ha! What Nikkanen will do to *him*." He almost shuddered.

"Go on like that," I said, "and you'll scare yourself to death."

"You think we can't involve you with Adler, don't you? Well, we can. And once we've done *that* . . . You don't know about that pistol he was carrying, do you?"

They were both watching me again, with small expectant smiles. They had something good and juicy to reveal at just the psychological moment.

I said: "I'll bet it was loaded, too."

"Yes, it was loaded," the big one said.

"And I'll bet there was something else."

"Yes, there was something else." He gave it a dramatic pause. "The number was filed off."

Silence. Time for me to go pale and cry: 'He was *that* sort of monster? If only I'd known.' Cary cracks and confesses all. Local police solve case. *Suopo* goes home and sends them a medal.

I said: "And what does that mean?"

The short one snorted. "What does it mean? Only that he was a professional—a real professional. Now, what was his game?"

I said: "You can get the number back. Just polish it and etch it out with hydrochloric acid and ethyl alcohol."

The big cop lowered an eyebrow at me. "Now, how would you know that?"

"You ever heard of stolen cars or aircraft engines? That's how you can check their numbers."

He turned ponderously to his partner. "He's educated, this one. We ought to have him on the force."

The short one said: "We ought to have him in some quiet

place where nobody could hear him scream. I'd solve *him*."
He sounded sincere for the first time since we'd met.

"You boys are straining yourselves over nothing," I told
them. "No professional gunman would carry a filed gun,
simply because it *looks* professional. You might talk yourself
out of being caught with a gun; you couldn't talk your way
out of being caught with a filed gun. All it proves is that
Oskar wanted a pistol so badly that he didn't care what sort
—or he just didn't know what it meant. The interesting question is why he thought he needed a gun at all."

They were staring at me again. "Except," I added, "that
your real problem is catching that Swiss Facel Vega."

I got that sort of hush you get when policemen are thinking. They knew the car, all right.

Then the big one said calmly—too calmly: "Who's in it?"

I shrugged and picked up the newspaper again and rolled
it up nervously. "If you've let it get away, I'm not saying
anything."

The short one leaned forward eagerly. "It's still north of
the river. Who's in it?"

The big one frowned at him warningly.

I unrolled the paper, then rolled it up again. "I don't
know who Oskar's been working for this summer. He hasn't
been doing mineral surveys . . ." I shrugged.

The big one looked me over thoughtfully. He didn't trust
me worth a bent Finnmark. But he didn't have anything else
to trust. Nikkanen clearly hadn't mentioned the Facel Vega—
but what would Nikkanen say when it came out that I'd
mentioned it and they'd let it get clean away?

He said something fast in Finnish that I wasn't supposed
to catch and didn't, but was probably a proposal that somebody go and put a watch on the bridge. There was no telephone in the room.

The small one didn't want to move. If anybody got me
alone, he wanted it to be him.

I went on rolling and unrolling the paper.

Finally they decided it: the big one stood up and said, in
Swedish: "I'll only be just down the corridor, so I'll be able
to hear anything that goes on." He seemed to be saying it
to his partner as much as to me.

The partner gave a sour grin and picked the big revolver
off the table. "You won't hear a thing."

The big cop hesitated, then went on out and closed the
door.

When we were alone the short one jerked his head at the door and said: "He's getting old, that one. He doesn't realise a case like yours is urgent: all *Suopo* cases are urgent. You don't think Nikkanen's coming back here to drink another schnapps with you?"

I watched his feet. "You don't know what Nikkanen wants, so don't try and solve his cases for him. He wouldn't thank you even if you did solve them. He's got expenses to justify."

He said: "You think we're just village hicks, don't you?"

I looked up at him: "Yes."

The revolver slammed onto my left cheek. I lifted a hand and touched it with my fingertips. The gun stared straight into my face.

"Resisting arrest," he said thoughtfully. "If they can't prove anything else, Nikkanen would like some charge to hold you on. We need a little evidence for that. Just a few bruises. Or, of course, you could make a statement."

I went on watching his feet.

He said: "You needn't tell us everything—just the stuff we'll find out anyway. Just enough to get us some of the credit. We don't always like the big *Suopo* men from Helsinki coming in and telling us what to do. We might even put in a good word for you."

One wisecrack and he would hit me again; I knew that. Which was a silly situation for him to get himself into, because it meant I knew what he was going to do before he did himself.

I said: "I'd feel degraded."

He swung the gun away. I stabbed him in the belly with the rolled newspaper, an upward thrust. Rolled tight, it can be like wood. He folded up like a mousetrap, the gun somewhere down around his ankles. I stood up and aside and chopped him under the ear with the side of my hand.

He bounced off the bed and onto the floor with a thump that shook the room. But we were on the ground floor; nobody's ceiling fell in.

I picked up the revolver and went to the door and eased it very slightly open, and waited. I didn't want to wait. But I hadn't given myself any choice.

It seemed to take a long time. The hotel creaked and muttered around me, and the night outside made distant humming noises and the man on the floor made loud breathing noises. I was wound up like an alarm clock when I heard the ting of the lobby phone and feet along the corridor.

I had the door shut behind him and the revolver rammed up under his chin before he realised the script had been changed at all. Strictly, it was a silly way to point a gun at a man. No professional would have done it. But professionals never kill cops; I wanted this one to think I might be going to.

He didn't say anything or try anything. I stepped aside. "Sit down."

He moved to the chair, then looked around at me and saw the bruise on my face. "He came close to you. He made it easy for you."

"In more than one way. Sit down."

He sat, with his back to me. "I shouldn't have left you alone with him. I think you have experience with guns—and things."

"Some. More than you two, anyway."

"That Facel Vega—was that just a bluff?"

"You went out to Veikko's because somebody rang you, didn't you?"

"Perhaps."

"I wasn't bluffing about the Facel Vega. Anyway, it'll be nice to have somebody in the cage when Nikkanen comes, won't it?"

I chopped him under the ear in the place I'd been sizing up.

Which left me with two laid-out cops on my hands, which isn't the sort of problem the etiquette books are much help on. And no idea when they'd wake up. You can never tell. When you slug a man you can only compromise between dazing him and killing him—you hope.

So now I should have tied them hand and foot and gagged them, all with just two sheets off the bed. But I wasn't going to play Sister Susie sewing shirts all night, so I just had to leave things as they lay.

When the corridor was clear I locked the door behind me and headed away from the lobby, hoping for a back way out. I found one; nobody saw me go.

The night smelt sweet and fresh and oddly satisfying, as if that were all I had been trying to achieve. The pain in my cheek snapped me out of that; it was swelling and starting to throb, and every single damn one of my teeth ached.

I went around the back of the hotel and up the dark river bank to the square by the bridge. There was just one taxi left, an old Mercedes 220 with rags stuffed in its side air intakes to keep the engine running warm.

Keeping my left cheek out of the lamplight, I asked the driver: "Do you have a tow-rope?"

He had.

"I've got a car that won't start, down there—" I pointed south. "Can you take me out and give me a tow?"

He could. As I got in, the town's police car drove up to the bridge and parked so that it blocked most of the roadway, its headlights shining north across the bridge.

We went about half a mile out of town towards, among other places, the airport. I told him to stop. Then I showed him the pistol and told him to walk home.

He wanted to argue the point, but I persuaded him that the gun and I represented a majority opinion, and he started walking. I drove the car another two hundred yards, stopped, slung the tow-rope over the telephone wires and pulled. It took a lot more pull than I'd expected, but finally I got them all down. Now, unless word had been passed already, the airport wouldn't know I was coming. I drove on.

I could have spent a lot more time being a lot more subtle in my getaway, but nobody would have believed it anyway. They knew I'd head for the Beaver; without it, I was stuck up in Lapland like a butterfly on a pin.

I stuffed a wad of Finnmarks in the glove compartment, then left the Mercedes parked just outside the airport. Nobody tried to stop me reaching the Beaver.

CHAPTER 18

I FLEW SOUTH-WEST, in the general direction of Sweden, with my lights on so that the tower could get the wrong idea good and clearly. After a quarter of an hour I went down to 500 feet, switched off the lights and turned north with the engine throttled back.

It was a still, almost windless, night with some broken stratus cloud and a young moon dwindling in the west. There were shreds of mist on the lakes and river bends, but nothing too serious yet. I cut the Arctic Highway just south of Inari and went on out over Lake Inari to gain height where nobody would hear. Then I turned back, cut the engine, and started to glide south down the road towards the lights of Ivalo, flickering through the mist fifteen miles ahead. I was looking for a sixty-foot trailer.

It wasn't so difficult as it might sound. You could never get that thing far off the main road, and there were no worthwhile side roads between Ivalo and Inari. And you couldn't hide it under trees, any more than you could a house. In the faint moonlight, it was going to show up like a cathedral.

I found it. It was parked about a hundred yards off the road, up what must have been an old logging track and behind a belt of trees that probably hid it from the road itself. I tried to memorise the layout of the place, then turned away over the lake.

The nearest possible landing place was over a mile away, and not an easy landing even then: it was a narrow inlet studded with small islands. The islands actually helped, giving me a reference point for my height which I couldn't judge from the still water in bad light. I got two islands in line out to port, waited until they merged into one, then hauled back on the stick and stalled in with a splash.

She ran out of effort before we reached the shore, and I didn't want to rev up the engine, so I had to blow up the dinghy and tow her the last thirty yards.

I ended up cold and wet from the lake and hot and wet from the paddling, and wondering why I wasn't really heading for Sweden. But I was sober and I had Veikko's cannon shoved in my belt. I was ready to talk to a man in a custom-built trailer.

I tied up the Beaver as near under some trees as I could, then walked up through the trees and boulders to the road. Then along it. It was quite empty—the time was after eleven o'clock—and no cars passed either way.

When I reached the logging track I went up alongisde it in the trees with the pistol in my hand. I wasn't sure what I expected to meet, or whether I was prepared to shoot it when I met it, but at least the gun gave me a choice. Always assuming it would actually shoot, of course.

In the dark, across a small clearing, the trailer looked just like a long, low bungalow. Its windows were all dark. The Facel Vega was parked just off the top of the track.

I stood leaning against a tree for a while studying the thing. At the end of that time it was still just a damn big trailer parked in a Finnish wood. I moved off carefully, circling round the clearing in among the trees to come up behind it.

When I'd done that all I had was a closeup of one corner

of the trailer and a nasty feeling that I was about to barge
in on some honest citizen in the middle of a perfectly legal
night's sleep. The whole thing looked too solid and suburban
and respectable. Now I should go and press the doorbell and
say: "Look, I'm most frightfully sorry, but . . ."

I didn't. Either there was somebody in there whom I
wanted to talk to, in which case a gun was what I needed, or
there wasn't—in which case I should quietly fade away to
Sweden without pressing any bells at all.

Something nudged my leg. I did a vertical takeoff and
came down with the revolver cocked ready for Cary's Last
Stand. But after a few agitated moments, all I could find
within range was a grey cat giving me an affronted look.

A bear or wolverine would have surprised me less: the
Lapland woods don't support much to interest a home-loving
cat. Then it occurred to me that if you can afford to haul a
sixty-foot trailer of comforts into the Arctic Circle, you could
afford to bring the cat, too.

I put on a forced grin and stretched out a friendly left
hand. The cat went on looking suspicious. Then a car door
slammed. The cat and I jerked, and froze. Feet moved at
the far end of the trailer. I lowered myself down among the
roots of a tree, in the pious hope that I looked more like a
grey cat that way. A figure came around the end of the
trailer and moved cautiously up towards me through the trees.
Something glinted dully in its right hand—and I had come
to the right place.

He was about three yards away and I was going to have
to speak or shoot, when the cat's nerve broke. It whizzed for
the deep woods. The figure spun around.

I said: "I've got a gun on you, Claude."

He stayed dead still.

I said conversationally: "Drop the gun, Claude."

He took a long time. For him, it would have to be a long
time; he had his pride to think of. But the decision had
been taken when he didn't shoot at my first word.

"Move around into the open." He moved—after a time, of
course. I came in behind him and scooped up his gun. It was
a Browning Hi-Power 9 mm.—I could tell that from the
thickness of the butt, which holds 13 rounds. It was a relief
to have a pistol which wouldn't blow up in my hand if I
tried to fire it; I switched guns behind Claude's back.

He said over his shoulder: "This will get you into a lot
of trouble, Mr Cary."

"Friend, tonight I'm already in trouble right over my head. After that, depth doesn't much matter."

"Mr Cary, I am *not* your friend."

"You're the nearest thing to a friend I've got tonight. Now, whichever's the front door, open it. And do it sensibly."

He got what I meant. He went up a small set of steps to the nearest door, opened it—it opened inwards—leant in and switched on a light. Nothing sudden or startling. Nothing that might get him shot in the back.

I said: "Absolutely splendid. Now lead the way in."

I followed him. Just as I was kicking the door shut behind me, the grey cat rushed in past us.

We went down a short hallway and past a zipped-back curtain and Claude put on the lights in the living room. For a trailer, it was a vast room, and furnished to look even bigger. The walls were panelled in squares of light grained wood, set so that the grain ran in alternate directions. There was a fawn wall-to-wall carpet, and a load of slim, light birchwood chairs with coloured leather seats, a few small coffee tables and even a couple of sizable rubber plants climbing out of black glass pots by the curtained window. The lighting was all concealed, giving the walls a warm glow and leaving the centre of the room the darkest place.

There was a rug of blending blue and green rectangles hanging on the opposite wall.

"Well, well, well. That'll be a ryiji, won't it?" I asked. "That's the way to treat 'em; you don't go paying all that money to go treading all over them, do you?"

A small sneer flickered across Claude's face. "You are standing on one, Mr Cary."

And damn me, I was: a lump of the same pattern in reds and browns.

"Of course," I said, "an original Rembrandt would look better up there, but I suppose you were too mean. And aren't rubber plants just a little *passé* this year? Why not a simple old bank of orchids?" I sat down. "Forgive me, I've had an over-stimulating evening. I just slugged my first policeman. Better go and wake the boss; I've got a complaint to lodge."

"Mr Cary, I am the only one here. I am 'the boss,' as you call it." He was wearing a waisted olive-green leather jacket, yellow silk scarf, rather crumpled dark trousers and a pair of brown moccasins.

I shook my head. "All that fancy business down at the

bridge the other day: you were trying to make us think you might be weird enough to haul this thing up here just for yourself alone. You overplayed the part. Now wake him."

"Mr Cary, I assure you I am the only one here."

"Bosses don't sleep in the car and they don't sleep in their clothes. Get him out here, *chauffeur*."

His face got even more expressionless, then he turned and went to the door just to the right of the ryiji.

I added: "And stay in plain sight all the time. These must be thin walls."

He got that point, too: a 9 mm. slug will go through eight inches of solid pine, so it would probably shoot clear through from one end of the trailer to the other. He went down the passage and knocked at the next door along, opened it, and there was a mumble in what sounded like German. I got out of my chair and moved over to keep him in sight.

A light went on in the room and after a little time a thin, slight man with rumpled grey hair, wearing a striped red-yellow-and-black dressing gown came out. His hands were empty and nothing was dragging down the dressing gown pockets. That made him a neutral.

I looked past him at Claude. He stared into the room for a moment longer, then closed the door gently.

I said: "Hold it. She comes too."

For a long moment the atmosphere said that these two were going to jump me. I took a backward step to get my back against the wall and crunched my thumb knuckle hard down on the safety catch.

"You boys are determined to act tricky, aren't you?" I said. "I've got thirteen rounds in the magazine, so I don't have to skimp the shooting if it comes to it."

The man in the dressing gown half turned his head and called sharply: *"Komm her, Ilse."*

The room seemed to start breathing again. He got a small carved wooden box out of his pocket, took out a cigarette, and lit it. We stared at each other through the smoke.

He had long thin mandarin hands coming out of his wide sleeves. His face came down to a sharp small chin, with the skin stretched very tight over the bones. Big blue pop eyes and a mouth that couldn't stay still around the cigarette. It was a face that was both ascetic and voluptuous; an expressive face, one that could express anything except happiness. It was a face that remembered death, and it belonged back in the age when men painted skulls at the bottom of their drinking mugs. The man behind that face would need a lot of something—faith, drugs, drink or women—to stay sane in this world.

I said: "You'd better do the introductions, Claude."

Claude said: *"Das ist der Pilot."*

"Would *he* have a name?" I asked.

The man jerked his thin shoulders to show the name didn't matter. "Koenig, if you wish." He had a faint German —or Swiss-German—accent.

Then she came in. She was wearing a long quilted dressing gown with a pink rose pattern, and the middle of the night wasn't her best time. She was tall and well built in the conventional places, with a face that was on the edge of getting heavy, a tangle of blonde hair, and grey eyes that would have been wide if she'd been awake. She looked as happy as a wet cat.

She said to Koenig: "Cigarette."

He got out his box and gave her one. Then, to me, he said: "And what do you want here?"

I crabbed back to my chair and sat down. "I might just be looking for a job, mightn't I?"

Koenig bared his teeth in a fast, skull-like grin. "What sort of job?"

"Claude was telling me something about a job, a few days ago."

Ilse padded across to a chair and went down into it with a thump that shook the caravan.

Koenig grinned again, meaninglessly. "I'm afraid that job has been filled, Mr Cary."

"By Oskar Adler?"

He frowned, just as meaninglessly, and sat down himself. Claude stayed standing, and I stayed with the Browning pointing in roughly his direction. He was the expendable one.

Koenig said: "Adler did a few errands for me, yes. You think that now he's dead you might take his place? You didn't need a gun to ask that, Mr Cary."

"Did you send him on the flight when he got killed?"

"Why are you asking?"

"Dammit, answer the question," I said; he just grinned. "I've got the gun. According to the rules, that means you've got to answer."

He went on grinning.

"Whisky," I said. "Is there any whisky in this place?"

"I think we might manage a whisky. Claude—"

"No," I said. "She gets it. I trust her."

Koenig said: "Ilse—would you give Mr Cary a glass of whisky?"

She gave me a look that should have split me down the middle, then hauled herself to her feet and went across to a small cupboard built into the wall beside the ryiji. The door hinged down to make a table, and I caught a glimpse of half a dozen or so bottles over her shoulder.

"Oskar's flight," I said. "I was asking you about Oskar's flight."

"And if I don't answer, will you shoot us all?"

"No. I'll just leave you stuck up here north of the river for the police to pick up. I thought we might be able to do a deal."

The room went quiet. Ilse broke it by coming across with a big tumbler half filled with what looked like whisky. She shoved it into my hand without getting in front of the gun.

"It's neat," she said. "If you want anything else, get it." She padded back to the cupboard.

I sniffed the tumbler and sipped. It was rough, but Scotch, and you get used to some odd whiskies up in Lapland.

Koenig said suddenly: "You're in trouble with the police."

"True."

"So you've come running to me for help?"

"We're both in trouble," I said cunningly. "I thought we might be able to reach a mutual aid pact."

Ilse said: "So we're in trouble, are we? Nobody tells me anything." Koenig glanced around at her. She was wearing a bottle of Bols in one hand and a glass of it in the other.

Koenig said: "And why should we want anything to do with you, Mr Cary?"

"Because the police are watching the bridge at Ivalo, and I expect the Norwegian frontier up north, too. You won't get five miles with that car, let alone the trailer. From here, you're walking home—unless you're flying. And I have the aeroplane."

Claude said quietly: "In summer he flies mineral surveys. In the winter he can't find work. He usually has to store his aeroplane."

Koenig ignored him, and said in a voice as hard and concise as a slide rule: "And why should the police be watching for us, Mr Cary?"

"Because somebody fixed Oskar's flaps so he'd roll in and kill himself on landing."

I got a silence. Not a shocked silence—I was in the wrong company for that—but at least a fast-thinking silence. Claude stiffened up off the wall he'd been leaning against. Ilse froze the glass of Bols halfway to her mouth.

Koenig said: "How do you claim to know that, Mr Cary?"

"I saw him crash. They're hauling up the wreckage now. When they get a Cessna expert up from Helsinki, they'll have proof. And *they'll* want to know who Oskar was working for." I leaned forward eagerly. "Now let's get things settled, before the night wears out. For 10,000 Swiss francs I'll drop you in Southern Finland. For 20,000 I'll make it Sweden or Norway —you name it."

Koenig smiled gently. "I think I could persuade the police that Mr Adler was not working for me on that flight."

I nodded. "And then, of course, there's the Veikko killing. Your car was seen on the road just before it was discovered."

This time I got a real hush, even from Koenig. His face ran through a pointless series of scowls and grins, but behind them all his eyes were like shotgun barrels.

"Who told you that?"

"I saw that, too. I told the police; but by now they'll have other witnesses who saw it come through town. Sorry and all that, but it was only fair. It was your boy Claude who rang them and tried to get me framed for it." I finished the whisky and leaned back in the chair.

"You're imagining things, Mr Cary." But perhaps there was just too much pause while he thought the possibility over.

"Go ahead and ask him. He was the only one who could have done it. Nobody else saw me on the road, and nobody could have seen me go into the house and got to a phone in time to get the police out there. There isn't a phone nearer than town. Anyway, Claude doesn't like me. But go on— ask him."

Koenig turned his head slowly towards Claude. Claude moved his shoulders in the slow French shrug of what's-it-matter-anyway. Compared with his face, his shoulders were star-part actors.

Koenig said something fast and nasty in German.

Claude said: *"Il n'importe—"*

Koenig just fizzed. Claude shut up.

I tossed my empty glass at Ilse. "More, please." She surprised herself by catching it, then surprised me by not throwing it at my head. But by now she knew I was carrying something more than a pistol.

Koenig said slowly: "So you have—with the help of Claude—implicated us in two crimes. Now you want us to pay our way out. Am I right, Mr Cary?"

"Quite right."

He smiled. "Claude underestimated you in what he told me about you. You are not merely a survey pilot, are you?"

I leered at him. "I've got hidden depths."

Ilse brought me the tumbler half full of whisky again. She looked down at me with the lazy, contemptuous smile of a big cat. Just to keep in practise, I leered at her, too.

Koenig said: "Of course, we might be able to explain away Claude's little drive this afternoon, too. With all this—" he flickered a long hand around the room's furnishings "—I feel the police would not bruise our faces as badly as they seem to have done yours."

I moved my hand over my cheek. It was swollen to quite a lump by now, although it had almost stopped throbbing. Then I looked at my watch: it was half past midnight.

"All right," I said. "Let's talk about the Veikko killing a bit. I've got the time and the whisky."

I settled back in the chair and waggled my gun hand to stop it getting stiff. A fully loaded Browning Hi-Power weighed—what was the figure?—yes, 41 ounces. I swigged my whisky.

I said: "Let's assume you're some sort of currency dealer in Switzerland. All Swiss are either that or watchmakers, so let's assume you deal in currency. And that you've been selling sovereigns, British gold sovereigns, to the Russians. Through a whole lot of channels, probably, in Germany and Austria. And one through Finland; through Veikko.

"It wouldn't be a bad idea. The frontier isn't much guarded up here, except by Russian radar stations. You could fly the stuff across—bulk loads—in the spring and autumn. Four or five hundred pounds weight at a time—that's what? nearly thirty thousand sovereigns. Nearly £100,000-worth. Perfect air freight: small bulk, high value. The principles of air freighting don't change just because it's all crooked."

Koenig was running a series of smiles around the cigarette in his mouth. "And who was doing the flying?"

"Oskar Adler, of course. It had to be him or me, and I

know it wasn't me. But of course he'd be working for Veikko, not you. And you must have known Veikko as well as I did: you knew the first idea he'd have would be how to hang onto some of the sovereigns. Whatever you paid him wouldn't be enough. Nothing ever was; that's why he stayed a Lapland crook rather than a big-time Helsinki one. Hell, it's why he got killed, in the end.

"So to stop him latching onto any of the load, you'd tell him the Russians were warned of how many sovereigns to expect in any consignment. The only way round that would be for him to start melting down all the coins he got, diluting them with copper, and re-stamping them on his own press."

I looked up at Claude. "You missed it. It was in the back of the stove in his study, along with a whole lot of prepared blanks."

Claude went on looking at me as if I were a stain on the chair-back.

I felt like yawning. That surprised me; apart from seeing one crash, finding one body, slugging two policemen, holding several people up with a gun and a bit of flying, I hadn't done much work that day. I took a gulp of whisky and ploughed on.

"A sovereign's got eight or nine per cent copper in it any-way," I said. "Let's say he shoved in another fifteen per cent, and maybe a bit of silver to stop it going too reddish. That'd save him fifteen sovereigns in a hundred. In a full load he'd save over 3,000. At £3.10 each, that's not bad.

"Still not enough, though." I shook my head; it felt heavy. "Nothing would be. So he'd boil down the 3,000 and dilute them into 3,450 and sell them westwards; maybe even in Switzerland. That would bitch him. Or maybe the Russians started complaining. Maybe they tested one or two. I'm guessing on this part."

The corners of Koenig's mouth were twitching. "I'm glad you admit to some guesswork, Mr Cary. But let me assure you—if there were forged sovereigns on the market, it would have become well known."

"Like hell it would." I finished the whisky and dumped the tumbler on the coffee table beside me. I was beginning to feel the 41 ounces of the gun in my hand; I laid the hand along my knee. "Like hell it would. The big thing about sovereigns is that they're worth about fifteen per cent more than their gold value, aren't they? Well, that's only because they've got a reputation for never being forged: you don't have to waste time and trouble testing them. If you found some forgeries on the market, you'd keep damn quiet about it—*and* take off running to get the forgeries stopped. That's why you came up here to kill Veikko, isn't it?"

Another hush. I beamed peacefully at him. I'd got my bedtime story told. I could rest in peace.

Koenig said: "But we didn't kill Veikko, Mr Cary."

His voice was oddly distant. When I looked at him, so was his face. Like a skull at the bottom of a drinking mug, perhaps.

"It's what you came here for." My voice sounded distant, too, like an old gramophone running down. Maybe, after all, it *had* been a hard day.

Koenig said gently: "But why should you care who killed Veikko?"

I grinned sleepily at him. "Maybe I don't. Veikko's old enough and bad enough to look after himself. Or was. It's Oskar Adler I care about. Pilots have enough problems without people trying to kill them, too. Who was he flying for?" Cunning, cunning Cary, twisting the conversation round to just where he wants it to be.

Koenig said: "You aren't really selling a flight out of Finland."

I said: "And you're not getting one." My voice sounded faint and faraway.

Koenig said soothingly: "Nobody's going anywhere tonight."

I could have done it, then. I could have shot the lot of them, just by lifting the Browning on my knee. But I had to stand up, instead. And that took everything I had left to give.

"You bastards," I said slowly and heavily. "You bastards."

I lifted the gun. And a small voice from long, long ago was telling me never to fall backwards when you're using a pistol. Always fall towards the enemy, so that you can keep on firing. So I tried to fall forwards, and it was easy. The only shot I fired hit the ryiji on the floor about a second before I did.

CHAPTER 19

MY FIRST THOUGHT was that I'd been drugged. The second thought was pure reflex: I had an intercontinental-size hangover. I must have gone to bed loaded like a musket. The third thought grew on me slowly, starting with the feeling that somebody had been burning old tires on my tongue. I *had* been drugged.

I lay there with my eyes shut, listening to my breathing; it was slow and deep. My hands and feet were cold, almost numb. Surely they hadn't left me lying out in the wild woods for the bears to nibble my toes? All you have to do, Cary, is open your eyes and look. A man in my condition?—you can't be serious. Let's just go on lying here.

Heavy breathing and cold hands and feet: that sounded somehow familiar. The old knock-out drop. You can smell it and taste it a mile off, unless it's wrapped up in something strong like whisky, and better still if you're up in Lapland where it's no surprise when the whisky tastes a bit lefthanded. The oldest trick in the game. And I'd even asked for the whisky. But all you have to do is dig a pit and Bill Cary will come and fall into it—if he can find it.

It was time to open my eyes and damn the consequences. It turned out to be heavy work, all right, and all I had then was a view of a stainless steel light-fitting in a dove-grey ceiling. So at least I hadn't been dumped in the woods. Against that, if I was still in the trailer, I was still in captivity.

That woke me. I rolled on my side and lifted myself on an elbow. I was lying wrong-ways in a big double bed, halfcovered by a red-and-white Regency-striped silk counterpane.

Behind me a voice said: "There's no hurry, *Liebchen.*"

I said. "Who's hurrying, for Chrissake?" then looked to see who it was. Ilse was leaning in the doorway with a small automatic in one hand and a cigarette in the other.

I added: "And who the hell are you calling *Liebchen,* come to that?" and swung my feet onto the floor. Mistake. It started a fit of coughing that nearly squeezed my stomach out through my ears.

"Cigarette," I croaked.

"If you brought any, you still have them."

I found a packet of cigarettes I'd slept on and got one lit by holding both hands on the match. Daylight was filtering in through the venetian blinds over the window. When I looked at my watch, it was nearly ten o'clock. But I'd expected that; if they'd fed me a dose to put me out as fast as I remembered going, it would have taken time to wear off.

Ilse said conversationally: "Please don't try to be clever. I will shoot, and Herr Koenig is in the next room also."

"Yes, I love you, too. How about something to drink—and with a little less chloral hydrate in it this time?"

She studied me. She was wearing a loose orange jersey that came most of the way to her knees, with a series of coloured bands round the left cuff like a military rank badge. And grey slacks. Her hair was pulled back off her face, leaving it thinner and somehow both more tired and younger looking.

She shook her head. "I don't think they'd give you the job." She said it as if it were something that had taken some thinking out.

I nodded. "Nobody in their right mind would give me a job. How about a drink?"

"I don't think you'd be good enough."

"Uh?" It was all I could think of to say.

"Why would you come here? Of course, they may be being very subtle."

I wiped a hand slowly over my face. Maybe the part of my brain that lets me know what women are talking about was still drugged.

"Look," I said. "I'm talking about whisky. Now you tell me what you're talking about."

"No whisky. And if you do not know what I am talking about it does not matter. Because then I am right."

I followed that thought halfway, then it jumped on a bus and lost me. I wiped my face again and tried to think of other things. By now it had been light nearly four hours. The police would have checked up the road as far as Inari at least. They'd be checking the side roads now. They might have spotted the Beaver by now, too.

I asked: "Have you worked out how you're going to cross the river?"

She smiled gently.

I said: "You won't enjoy the walk, you know. I don't know if you've ever looked out of the window, but it's rough country for high heels out there. And with the police looking for you. Bears, too," I added, probably overplaying it.

She said: "Don't be silly, *Liebchen*. They've never heard of Herr Koenig or me; they don't even know we're in Finland. Claude brought the trailer up here all on his own."

I should have thought of that. You can come into one Scandinavian country—Sweden or Norway or Denmark or Finland—and when you move into another, nobody even asks for your passport. A form of mutual trust and tourism, and damn useful for crooks.

I kept on my grim expression. "You're still walking. They'll be pretty jumped up in Ivalo today, after letting me get away. Any foreigners will get a good going-over. And then you're going to have to prove how you got there: they won't believe you walked from Norway or Sweden."

"They're looking for you, *Liebchen*, not us." She smiled and reached behind her and brought out a glass of what looked like Bols. She sipped.

I stared down at my boots. They were old and dry and cracked and dusty; I knew just how they felt. I dragged on the cigarette and heaved myself back into the firing line.

"There's still two killings to solve, and they know I couldn't have done one of them. They're still looking for the Facel Vega and the trailer—and the longer they don't find them, the more they'll think they need them."

I stood slowly up off the bed and stretched carefully. The automatic in her hand twitched and followed me.

"You'll crack," I said. "You personally. You'll be the one they work on, and you'll tell them everything. It's a *Suopo* case now, and they'll have their best counterespionage men from Helsinki up to work on you. And when they've done it, they'll shut you away for ten or fifteen years in one of their fresh-air prisons and when you come out there won't be anyone wanting any shopsoiled blondes today, thank you."

If she was cracking at all with my working on her, I couldn't see any sign of it. She took a last draw at her cigarette, looked around for somewhere to put it out, then just dropped it into the fitted carpet and screwed it out with her toe. That shook me.

She looked up and smiled. "Don't worry about the carpet, *Liebchen*. We're going to burn the whole trailer before we leave. And you inside it." She really enjoyed saying that.

A car horn pooped outside.

I stepped round the bed to the window and opened two slats of the blind with two fingers. There was no sign of the

Facel Vega, but a dark blue Volkswagen was just pulling up in front of the trailer.

"You expecting any dark blue Volkswagens?" I asked.

"Get from the window!"

She sounded emphatic enough for the Volkswagen to be a real surprise. I turned and grinned at her, then looked back at the car.

"I said, get away!"

Mrs Alice Beekman got out of the Volkswagen.

The blind jerked and the window exploded. The little automatic sounded very loud in the room. I got away from the window.

Ilse was looking at me through the whisp of smoke from the gun. "You will learn, *Liebchen*, that we are serious."

Mrs Beekman's voice filtered in through the broken window. "Hey—who's playing stupid with a gun in there?"

I grinned at Ilse, a little shakily, perhaps, because being shot at or near takes it out of you. But a sincere grin.

"Go on," I said. "Be serious with her, too. All it'll get is the F.B.I. and Strategic Air Command down on your neck, as well."

The doorbell buzzed.

Ilse glared at me. For a moment I thought she was going to shoot me simply as a way of getting rid of one problem before starting on the next. I think she thought so, too.

Then Koenig called. *"Ilse, komm schnell."*

"Get out there and pretend you are just visiting," she hissed. She stepped back from the door.

I went slowly out and down the passage. Ilse and the little gun stayed well out of grabbing range.

Mrs Beekman was just coming in through the curtain at the other end of the living room. Koenig was just behind her.

"Hi, there." She smiled at me. She was wearing a white suit with a long jacket that looked as if it were made of old sacking but was probably champagne-fed lambs'-wool. A brown silk scarf tucked neatly in the neck.

"Morning, Mrs Beekman," I said. "Sorry about last night—"

"That's okay. I got it from the cops. Who was doing the shooting?"

Koenig said smoothly: "I was demonstrating to Mr Cary one of my hunting guns. Unfortunately, there was a cartridge left in it. I hope you weren't alarmed."

Mrs Beekman cocked an eye at me.

I nodded. "They've been showing me guns, all right."

Behind me Ilse made a movement. My spine felt suddenly vulnerable.

Mrs Beekman nodded. "I know it's early, but isn't anybody going to offer me a drink?"

Koenig waved a hand at the cupboard. His left hand. His right was resting sort of casually in the pocket of his dark blue anarak jacket. "Please to help yourself," he suggested.

I waited for the explosion: nothing she'd done before suggested she liked being told to pour her own drinks. But she just went over to the cupboard and got a glass and a bottle of whisky and started pouring.

Koenig watched her, the usual meaningless grins and scowls running over his face. Finally he asked: "And what can we do for you, miss—?"

"Mrs Beekman. Alice Beekman."

He nodded; he knew the name all right. He knew the size of his problem.

She said: "I came to see Cary. I just want some information from him." She sipped her drink, then topped it up again from the bottle. She puzzled me; when you start carrying the bottle around with you at ten in the morning, you're usually working up for a scholarship to the alcoholic ward. But I'd seen her drinking before. I knew she could leave it alone.

Koenig asked: "What made you think he was here?"

"He was talking about you yesterday. So I thought he'd come here. So I came here."

It was so simple and logical and it must have been peeling Koenig's confidence away like a skinning knife. Instead of being hidden away cosily, he was sitting right out in the open where anybody could see him.

"And who told you where the trailer was?"

"I had a word with that cop—Nik-something." She looked at me.

"Nikkanen. The *Suopo* man."

"That's the boy. He said it was up somewhere between Ivalo and Inari, so we just came looking. Didn't take us long."

It took a little time to sink into him, what with not being his own language and after the shocks she'd given him already, but when it sank, it went deep.

"*We?*" He darted his head forward. "You are not alone?"

She had the bottle raised to top up her glass again. Her

eyes flared at him. "Alone? Of course I'm not alone, you—you peasant. D'you think I drive myself?"

It was superb. And he ate it, bait, hook and halfway up the line to the rod. He jumped for the window, tugging at his pocket.

She whipped the bottle up and over and smashed it on the back of his head. His face slammmed into the window, then he started to slide to the floor, dripping blood and whisky.

I got my attention away long enough to grab Ilse's hand as it came out from behind her back with the automatic. I got one hand on her wrist, then two, and twisted in opposite directions. The gun fell onto the rug. Ilse kicked me.

I pushed her against the wall and looked back at Mrs Beekman in time to see her put a high heel into the back of Koenig's right hand, which had a gun in it. I winced; I don't know what Koenig did. She kicked the gun to me.

I picked up the two guns. Mrs Beekman said: "I think that makes you the new Master of Ceremonies." She propped her hips against the back of a chair and sipped her whisky.

I said to Ilse: "Sit down and keep quiet."

She sneered at me. "And if I do not? You will shoot me?"

"No, but she might belt you on the head with another bottle."

Ilse sat. Mrs Beekman grinned at me across her glass.

I said: "If it needs saying: thank you. But couldn't you have used anything but the whisky?"

"They should have some more." She went to the cupboard and started routing around in it.

I turned Koenig over to give him more breathing space. He wasn't quite unconscious, but he didn't much care what was going on.

"It's not serious," I told Ilse. "And he's damn well disinfected, anyway." He smelt like a Saturday night in a lumber camp *baari*. "Wrap up the back of his head to stop the bleeding."

She got up and went out of the room. I shifted across to watch her go down the corridor.

Mrs Beekman turned around from the cupboard with a full green bottle labelled 'The Antiquary.' Koenig knew his whisky, all right, even if it always seemed to get used for the wrong things.

"Fill up your own," I suggested. "The lot you're drinking may be doped."

"I don't really like the stuff this early." She put down her glass, opened the bottle, and poured me one. She brought it across.

"Thanks. What's happening in Ivalo this morning? And how come yóu found us before the cops did?"

"They found the Facel Vega abandoned on the north bank about a couple of hours ago. They reckoned that meant they'd crossed the river on foot, so they started looking south of it."

I nodded. "That would be why they dumped it. Were the cops watching the lake?"

"I don't know. They seemed short of men; that's why they haven't searched the road up here. I told Nikkanen I'd tell him if I spotted anything."

Ilse came back down the corridor carrying a tin of first-aid bits and pieces.

"I'll bet," I said, "Claude was sent off to dump the car and then pinch a boat. They could row across the lake and land on the south bank of the river." I was watching Ilse as I said it. But she wasn't reacting. "They'd still have to walk or pinch a car from there, though," I added. "And if they've got any sense they won't pinch a car; they've got to go eighty miles south before there's a choice of turnoffs. They'd get picked up long before that."

Still no reaction from Ilse.

I shrugged and finished my whisky. It didn't exactly put me in Olympic form—after no supper, no breakfast and a dose of chloral hydrate it would take more than a stiff whisky to do that—but at least I felt ready to look fresh air in the face.

I looked round the room. I'd have liked to search the trailer; if I'd been by myself, I probably would have, and risked Claude coming back. But if I were still by myself I'd still be sitting on the bed with Ilse holding a gun on me. And no whisky.

"I'm ready," I said. I picked up the whisky bottle and nodded to Ilse, who was winding a bandage around Koenig's head. "Give my regards to Claude."

She looked up at me and her eyes were vicious. "I think you *are* one of them, after all."

That didn't mean anything to me—at the time, anyway. Mrs Beekman led the way out.

Outside, she asked: "D'you want to drive?"

"No. Get in and start moving. They may have other guns

in that place and there may be somebody else dropping in at any moment."

I stayed outside the car with a gun in each hand until she started it and did a U-turn back to the head of the track. Then I hopped in.

She grated the gears and said: "Where now?"

"I'll get out at the road."

"Like hell you will, friend. I came to find you, remember? Before the cops catch up with you, I want to know where my brother is."

I nodded slowly. I'd sort of forgotten the Homer family problems in the last twenty hours. Silly of me, of course.

I asked: "Where did Nikkanen think I'd gone?"

"He figured you'd flown out to Sweden or somewhere. Anyhow, that's what he said he figured. Is your airplane near here?"

I looked at the two guns I was carrying. One—Ilse's—was a small Sauer and Sohn handbag gun, the sort you sneer about as having no punch—unless somebody happens to be pointing one at you. The other was a Browning, but I couldn't tell whether it was the one I'd taken off Claude the night before or another. Pistols were definitely the autumn fashion in Lapland.

"Turn left at the bottom," I said. That took us towards the Beaver, but more important, it should stop us bumping into Claude if he was heading back from Ivalo.

She dragged the Volkswagen round in a spray of dust and stones and clashed the gears again.

"Is your airplane up here?"

"Yes."

"How far?"

"Keep going." I had a moral problem to think out, and I'm not good on moral problems. Did anything she'd done to rescue me from fiery death—and not just for my beautiful brown eyes, either—over-ride Homer's unwillingness to meet anybody from his own family? Strictly, it didn't, of course.

But he'd also left it to my judgment, and said he'd see her in a few days. Well, my judgment was that I wasn't going to be anywhere near here in a few days, and that if I didn't tell her where he was now, I wouldn't be able to ever. Probably that was the way she was thinking, too, if she'd been talking to Nikkanen about my future.

And I was going to have to fly into my private lake now anyway, partly because it was a damn sight less conspicuous

than leaving the Beaver on Lake Inari all day—since I daren't
fly out before dark—and partly because I needed some refuelling, and my island was the only place I could get it now.

She said: "Where do I stop?"

"In about a quarter of a mile. Look, Mrs Beekman—I *could*
fly you in to see him, but you'd do better if I gave you a
marked map and you hired some pilot up from Rovaniemi or
Helsinki to fly you in."

"What's wrong with you?"

"I'm a wanted man. If you fly with me, there's a presump-
tion that you helped me escape from the country."

"Is that all? Nothing about slugging people with bottles?"

"They don't count; they're wanted, as well. They won't
complain."

"Okay. Where's your airplane?"

I took a deep breath. "This is a serious business, Mrs Beekman. Three men have got murdered in the last two days.
Two planes have crashed. The Finns think it's an espionage
affair, and I dare say they're right. But I don't know how it
all ties up. I do know I haven't killed anybody myself yet,
although that's partly luck since I've been waving pistols
around fairly freely, and that's always a likely start."

"In fact it's serious?"

"Yes."

"Fine. Now you've convinced yourself your problems are
serious, will you start convincing yourself mine are, too?"

I said: "The whole damn thing started when they gave
women the vote."

"If I hurt your Goddamn pride by rescuing you from that
trailer, you can always go back and surrender and start over.
The blonde grandmother in the admiral's sweater seemed
sorry to see you go."

"They were going to fire the trailer—with me inside."

She thought about that. Then she said: "That would be
pretty stupid. They'd set the whole woods on fire, at this time
of year."

I said wearily: "I know stones that bleed, too. Stop here."

We pulled up with a lot of gearbox noise and her stirring
the gear lever like somebody mixing a pudding. She said:
"Damn European cars." And we got out.

Then she said: "I can't see any airplane."

"Just keep quiet a minute, will you?" I yelled. "Of course
you can't see it. If you could see it, the cops could see it, and

they'd have hauled it away by now." I got my voice back under control. "Now—how long did you hire this car for?"

"I didn't. I bought it."

I might have known. I leaned my head against a tree and tried to think. Then I said: "Now, look: if the cops find this car abandoned, they may worry what's happened to you. They may even think you're with me, if they start thinking I haven't left the country yet. On the other hand, nobody's likely to start worrying until after midnight, when your hotel may get het up. And you should be back before then."

She said impatiently: "I'll bet you can go on like this for hours. Where's your airplane?"

I got back into the car and found the whisky bottle and took a quick one. It didn't help much, but at least it was a decision I'd taken for myself. Then I drove the car off the road on the inland side, to distract attention from the lake, locked it, and led the way down towards the water.

The wind was light, easterly; the sky was broken stratus again, and the horizon, when you could see past the islands, was hazy with late mist or—more likely—forest fire smoke.

The engine took some starting, and when it started one cylinder wasn't pulling its weight. While the rest of the cylinders warmed up, I picked a course out across the lake, then south into the forbidden zone. I gave Mrs. Beekman the map and sent the Beaver scuttling out of the inlet with sharp bursts of throttle.

When she unstuck from the water I held her down close to it and we went away low, weaving slightly between the islands.

CHAPTER 20

IT WAS ninety miles down to my lake and we landed not long before noon. I'd circled over Homer's cabin to let him know we were there—if he was there himself. Then I dropped Mrs. Beekman at the beach to wait for him while I taxied across to the island to refuel.

I remembered having about 120 gallons left there, and wasn't planning to leave any behind. What I couldn't get into the tanks, I would carry in the back.

I didn't have 120 gallons: I had 85. Somebody had knocked off 35 gallons. At first I thought of Homer, but nobody would need 35 gallons, no matter how bad he was at lighting fires. Then I found a stack of empty tins down by the bank.

The only thing in these parts that could carry away 35 gallons of 80 octane petrol without using the tins it came in was Oskar's Cessna—or had been, until the day before. And Mikko could have told Oskar about the fuel dump. I hadn't touched the fuel for several days.

I poured in as much as the tanks would take—all but twenty gallons—and stacked the others near the rear bulkhead. Then I punched a hole in the bottom of each can and threw them into the lake to sink. No need to leave more clues than I had to.

I taxied back to the shore with enough fuel to go 400 nautical miles in my tanks, but still a nasty taste about somebody pinching my petrol.

Mrs Beekman was waiting alone at the beach.

"No sign of him," she reported.

"We'll go up to the cabin."

"If he'd been up there, he'd have come down here."

"That's right. But at least we can steal some of his food. I missed dinner and breakfast."

She just stood there on the sand with her feet planted apart and her hands on her hips. "You're sure you didn't bring me to the wrong place?"

"Why the hell should I?"

"I'd hate to guess." She went on glaring at me.

I was beginning to know this mood. "You've guessed it: after lunch I'm planning a little rape. It's the only crime I haven't been suspected of these past few days, so I may as well give them that as well."

I headed towards the path. When I looked back, she was still standing there.

I said: "If all this fuss is just because you can't cook, don't worry: I can."

"That sounds fair: I've done all the fighting today," she said bitterly. I winced and led the way.

Halfway there, I remembered that this was supposed to be bear country and that I'd forgotten to bring the shotgun from the Beaver. But I had Koenig's pistol—and his whisky. If thirteen rounds from a Browning Hi-Power didn't stop a bear, I could always offer him a drink.

The cabin was empty—at least of Homer. But his cases were still piled up under the window, and three guns on pegs along the wall.

"You recognise the luggage?" I asked, and went to look at the guns. One was a rifle, the 7 mm. one for deer. The other two were a pair of matched Purdey shotguns: clean-lined hammerless jobs with no fancy engraving on them. A fourth set of pegs was empty.

Mrs. Beekman said quietly: "This is his stuff. I'm sorry."

"He's taken his bear rifle," I said. "Well, he said he might be going on a hunting trip." His sleeping bag was still rolled up under the guns, but the groundsheet with it had gone.

"How long would he be?"

"He said two or three days. That was two days ago. He may not have started until yesterday, so he could still be two days."

She was routing in the cardboard boxes I'd brought his supplies in. "Where would he have gone?"

"You can't tell. He could be just ten miles away and it would still be worth making a three-day trip of it: this is pretty rough country."

She straightened up from the box with three tins in her hands. "Well, he's left enough stuff, so I can wait."

I said: "Like hell you can. You're out in the wilds, here. The nearest road's more than a day's walk away—with your shoes, anyway. And it's bear country. No—if he isn't back this evening, I'll put you down near Inari on my way out. Then you can get some Helsinki pilot and bribe him into bringing you back in a couple of days. I'm sorry I can't stay on myself."

"You think I'd be safer if you did?" She glanced at me with a small twist of a smile.

"From bears, anyhow."

She nodded and looked at the tins in her hands. "Salt herrings followed by beef stew and peas for your lordship?"

I waved a hand. "Make it so."

She found a tin-opener and started work. "And I'll be staying," she added.

"Like hell."

"You'll drag me screaming down to the airplane and out to Ivalo?" she asked calmly. "Lay a finger on me and I'll sue for a million dollars."

I said: "I still say they shouldn't have got the vote," and went looking for tin mugs to make a whisky issue.

We ate and I put the blackened old coffee-pot full of water on the stove, then shoved in some coffee when it got hot. I never understood how, but the Finns make the best coffee in the world just like that. I wasn't quite up to their normal standard, but I managed something drinkable.

We pulled Homer's sleeping bag out onto the door-sill and sat on it sipping coffee. The wind had died, and there was the lonely stillness of a held breath in the stiff, straggly trees around us.

"D'you like this country?" she asked.

"In a way. It's sort of quiet and tough without being interfering or grandiose."

"I guess those forests could be pretty spooky." She was staring down through the trees, and I knew she was seeing her brother somewhere: a small, tubby, balanced figure with an alert rifle, trying to beat the forest at its own game.

I poured whisky into my coffee. "Pretty spooky. The Lapps have got as much of a tradition of *shamans*—witch-doctors —up here as they have in the Congo."

I looked down into the forest, and sipped at my mug. I had mixed feelings about Lapland myself. I liked the quiet trees and I hadn't got any ambition to prove I was as good a woodsman as them. But flying over it, I saw it as one big lousy emergency-landing ground and was looking for a reason to see it torn up into pit-heads and slag-heaps.

Mrs Beekman said: "And now you're getting run out. What are the cops after you for?"

"Bashing two cops, holding up a taxi-driver, stealing a taxi . . . You saw Nikkanen—what did *he* say he wanted me for?"

She lifted her shoulders. "Oh, you'd been found holding hands with a corpse and had escaped before they finished questioning you."

"I did that." I rubbed my fingertips up the side of my face that had got questioned.

"Do they think you did it?" she asked.

"I don't think so. I didn't have the gun that killed him, and I gave them a good story about trying to ring them to report it but the phone was busted."

"Was it?"

"Of course. I busted it myself when I thought they were going to grab me." I sipped at my coffee. "No—they just want me in a general way. Finding me with a corpse gave them a good reason for putting on the thumbscrews. They think I know something about what's going on up here."

She lifted an eyebrow at me. "Well, what *is* going on up here?"

I lit a cigarette and took a deep drag on it. Here we went. "Basically, the characters in that trailer have been smuggling gold sovereigns into Russia. The man who got killed was the one who was handling them on this side of the frontier."

"Why's Russia interested in sovereigns?"

"Same reason that Britain keeps making them: for espionage payments in the Middle and Far East. They're internationally recognised coins, got a gold value of their own, and no embarrassing numbers that you can trace like you can banknotes. Smugglers use them for the same reason."

I seemed to have finished my coffee and poured another cup. "Most international crookery and espionage is backed with gold—and most of that with sovereigns, when they can get them."

"How did the man who got killed fit in?"

"Veikko? He'd started forging sovereigns—diluting them with copper and re-stamping them. He never saw that that would make him International Enemy Number One: the Russians didn't like him, the Swiss didn't like him. No crook or spy in the world can have liked him; he was undermining the whole sovereign market." I sook my head. "But he wouldn't have thought of that. He believed being a crook meant you had to cheat everybody on everything. He was too dishonest to be a good crook."

"I beg your pardon?"

"Crooks are honest men—they have to be, when you think of the deals they do with each other and that they daren't put anything in writing. You couldn't run an underworld for five minutes with the cheating that goes on in big business: breaking contracts, sub-standard goods, fighting law-suits."

She nodded slowly. "I guess there's something in that. So what happened to the pilot who got killed?"

"I don't know how he fits in."

"The cops think he does. They're making a hell of a fuss about getting up the wreckage."

"He was flying the sovereigns for Veikko, all right. But he probably got fixed by the last passenger he picked up—and nobody knows who that was. Or where they went."

She nodded again. "Have you got a cigarette?" I gave her

a cigarette, and lit it for her. Then she asked: "And how do *you* fit in?"

"Me?" I spread my hands. "Honest, Judge, I was just standing there."

"Horse crap," she said, in the fashion of fine old Virginia families. "You know just a bit too much about gold and sovereigns and crookery. And busting out of arrest. I'm seeing the police point of view, now. I'd have you under the bright lights every time somebody stole the cat's milk."

"Can I help it if I'm brighter than a Lapland cop?"

"And modest, too."

I stubbed my cigarette out carefully. "Let's just say that Lapland's a small parish. This business involved flying, so sooner or later it involved me. And I rather want to know who fixed Oskar Adler. I was worried the cops were distracting themselves from that by concentrating on me. So I removed me."

She studied me carefully. "I'm sure you got your motives from the same shop as King Arthur. But how come you're so *good* at escaping from cops?"

I stood up. "I think I'd better do some maintenance work on the plane. Be seeing you later. Don't speak to any strange bears."

She watched me go with a still, set expression.

Down at the lake I took the cowlings off the Beaver, then started the engine. It was still missing badly on one cylinder. After a few minutes I stopped the engine, then climbed up on one float and laid a wary hand on each of the nine cylinders in turn. Only one didn't burn me: the Number 5 cylinder, down at the bottom left. I smoked a cigarette while the whole thing cooled off.

When I got them out, Number 5's sparkplugs were as dirty as a Brighton weekend. I scrubbed them with my toothbrush, washed them in some of the spare petrol, and screwed them back. Then I washed the oil filter in petrol, too. After that, there wasn't much more I could do. One of these days I would give Pratt and Whitney back this engine and they could send it round airports as an advertisement, wearing a little brass plate reading *This engine actually worked in this condition thus enabling Bill Cary to work in his condition. If you, too, are an idiot, P & W engines may save you from yourself.* Grateful, they should be.

It was getting on for five o'clock and the occasional gleams of sunlight were dying behind the trees at the far end of the lake. Two shots sounded faintly up towards the cabin. I frowned at them, then decided it might be a recall signal of some sort, and started shoving the cowlings back on.

When I got there she was waiting at the door with two black grouse lying beside her and one of Homer's shotguns propped up against the wall.

"You wouldn't have a sharp knife, would you?" she asked.

I unclipped the Fairbairn off my boot and handed it over. "Did you shoot those?" I asked. Not the brightest question, of course.

"No, they walked up and borrowed the gun for a suicide pact. *All* Homers get taught to shoot—*and* to cook." She looked at the Fairbairn dubiously. It looked as much like a kitchen knife as a samurai sword does. "I'd hate to think what the Carys get taught. Do you feel it's the cocktail hour?"

I routed out the bottle and the mugs and brought her a whisky. She had her jacket off and the sleeves of a raw silk blouse rolled up and was getting in among the grouse with the knife in a crisp, economical way. She was kneeling on the sleeping bag plucking and gutting the grouse just off it. Every now and then she stretched to straighten her back and her breasts thrust sharply against the blouse.

I leant against the doorpost and sipped my whisky and watched. After a while she looked up.

"You happy?" she asked.

I nodded. "Fascinated."

"You like housewifely women?"

"It wasn't that I was watching."

She lifted an eyebrow at me, then went back to work, completely unembarrassed. Nothing would ever bother this woman, not if she was doing a job she thought had to be done. Like gutting a grouse—or raking the Finnish backwoods for her brother. And nothing would shift her off doing it, either. She was the sort who met trouble with her jaw and then hired the best men to fix her jaw so that she could meet more trouble the same way.

I smoked and watched while she finished the grouse, shoved them in a mess tin with tinned onion soup as a gravy, and put them on the stove. I searched around and turned up a paraffin pressure lamp, lit it, and hung it from a strap Homer had rigged from the ceiling.

Outside, the sunset was just a slow bleeding away of all the colour. The trees turned black, the sky grey, the ground a darker grey. I brought in Homer's shotgun, cleaned it, and stuck it back along the pegs. Then I poured out more whisky all round. Then I lit another cigarette.

By now I knew Homer wouldn't be back that night, but I was too much of a coward to tell her. Leave it a bit longer. After all, I could be wrong. He might be the sort that likes walking the Lapland woods at night, making about a third of a mile an hour and busting an ankle at every fifth step.

We ate the grouse and it was the best meal I'd had since my lonely banquet to celebrate not finding nickel. I said something like that.

She just nodded and asked: "When were you planning on going?"

I looked at my watch. "About nine o'clock, maybe."

"Where'll you go?"

"Sweden or Norway." I hadn't yet decided which. Everybody knew I had contacts in Sweden, so Norway might be the best place. On the other hand, the nearest Norwegian town was Kirkenes, up on the north coast, and they'd certainly have been warned to watch out for me. On yet another hand, I wanted to stay in close contact with Lapland to know when it was safe to go back. Nikkanen would be forced to frame some real charges if he wanted me extradited. I didn't think he'd make much of 'escaping from arrest' unless he could produce a good reason for the arrest. And the Norwegians wouldn't touch a general 'suspicion-of-espionage' charge—too political. Anyway, I could always pretend to be working for NATO. It would probably take them an age and five-eights to find somebody to swear that I wasn't.

"Will you find out who killed that other pilot from there?" she asked.

I shrugged. "As much of a chance as I'd have from a jail here. I can always come back."

"Will you?" She was getting her chin up.

"If I feel like it."

"You wouldn't just be—"

"Yes, I am running away. Just remember—you're the one who's travelling light. You aren't carting your Virginia estate on your back. All I've got is that aeroplane. Well, it's damn useful for running away in, but it's also very difficult to hide. If Nikkanen wanted to confiscate it and made me fight a law-suit to get it back, it'd break me. I'd have to sell the plane to fight the suit."

Except even selling the Beaver wouldn't bring me much more than enough to defend myself on a spitting-on-the-pavement charge.

"I'm sorry." She held out her mug. "Could I have some more whisky?"

I poured it.

Then I said: "He won't be back tonight, you know." I'd knocked her down: now was the time to kick her. The King Arthur touch.

She just nodded and said: "I know that. I was doing a bit of walking in these woods myself. I knew that as soon as it got dark."

I waggled my head and poured myself more whisky. She got up and walked across and sat on the sleeping bag under the guns, legs stretched out straight in front of her, ankles crossed. The lamp hissed faintly and threw a raw yellow light.

"Why d'you want him back?" I asked quietly.

She leant her head back against the wall with her eyes closed. "The estate."

I opened my mouth to say there must be more to it than that, then didn't. If she didn't want to tell me, I wouldn't get told. I knew that much about her by now.

"You've been running the place by yourself?" I asked.

"For the last few months."

"Why the divorce?"

She opened her eyes. "Why should I tell you that?"

"No reason, Mrs Beekman. What else shall we talk about until nine o'clock?"

She leant back again. "I didn't like his hobby: other women."

"Sounds a pretty reasonable objection."

"It's been said that he couldn't stand being married to a rich woman. That he had to assert some sort of independence." Her voice was suddenly weary.

"Man must be crazy," I said. "All you and money too."

She opened her eyes again and smiled lazily. "And how would you have made out?"

"I've always held to the belief that I could handle big money without spoiling the essential lovable me. Trouble is, nobody ever tried me on it."

"You don't know the first thing about money."

"You tell me the first thing."

"Grab it when it's offered. I offered you a new airplane the day before yesterday; you turned me down. Today I get the same service for—what? Fifty dollars?"

"*And* you did the cooking. But maybe you're right." I shrugged. "I must have been keeping a stiff upper lip at the time. But you could still give me a new plane, of course."

"I've already got what I wanted: I'm here. The plane was just a bribe."

"Oh, I knew that. Maybe Mr Beekman's trouble was that he took the bribe."

She took a deep breath and said quietly: "Give me a cigarette."

I walked across to her. I saw her hang swing just too late to duck it. My head creaked on its hinges.

"And that," she said calmly, "ends that particular conversation." She took the cigarette.

"You still owe me fifty dollars," I said, rubbing my cheek. It had had to be the sore one.

"The game's over."

I held out a match. "I'm just learning the first thing about money."

She breathed smoke and relaxed and smiled. "You're a weird one, Cary. What are you really wanting out of life?"

I sat down beside her. She turned quite naturally so that her head was on my shoulder. I ran my hand gently through her hair. The cabin was quiet and close around us.

"I want to find nickel," I said.

She looked up at me with a wry smile. "Not gold or diamonds?"

"Just nickel, I heard that some people make money just by finding oil."

"It's happened." She moved her cheek gently against my hand. "And what'll you do when you find it?"

"Get myself a new plane, or two. Maybe start a real company."

She turned further and her breasts crushed against me and her hair was in my eyes, and I wanted her. Not hungrily or frantically, but very strongly and certainly. From loneliness, perhaps, but not the loneliness of the forest or of Lapland itself. And maybe because she carried her own loneliness with her, too.

"Maybe I'll buy you a new plane after all," she said sleepily. I could make money at it. I think you'd be a good risk."

I lifted her head and kissed her and her body reached

against me, strong and soft at the same time. And there was no world outside the cabin.

Then she pulled firmly away and sat back on her heels; looking at me with her grey eyes wide and not at all sleepy now.

"Just because I'm getting divorced," she said gravely, "doesn't mean I can be got just by grabbing."

"I know: I'd get sued for a million dollars."

"And don't get tough with me, Cary. I can't take much more."

"Yes, you can." I reached and ran a knuckle down the sharp line of her jaw. She shivered suddenly and then caught herself. I said: "You've got enough guts and singlemindedness for the whole United States Marines. If you hadn't, money would have loused you up a lot more than any one man could."

"You pay the prettiest compliments." But her eyes relaxed. "You're a bit of a hard bastard yourself; that's why I think you'd be a good investment. But of course, you're only here to nine o'clock." She smiled lazily at me.

"I thought that big business knows no hours."

"You're learning, Cary. You're learning."

She leant slowly forward and I reached for her. And there was no hunger; just a gentle strength moving from loneliness to a great calm.

Later she said sleepily: "We go well together, Cary."

I was reaching around in the darkness for my cigarettes. In the match flare I looked across at her. She shut her eyes and smiled lazily, then let her head fall into a tangle of silvery fair hair across her bare arms.

I said: "It wouldn't work," and blew out the match.

"It'd be a fight. But I wouldn't win."

"It wouldn't even be that: we wouldn't meet often enough. I'd be up in Rovaniemi or Kirkenes or Dawson, Canada— and you'd be somewhere else."

"You wouldn't be there the whole time."

"My job would be. I'm a mineral survey pilot."

"You'd have your own fleet of planes. You'd just run them."

I said gently: "You're still trying to buy me."

She sobbed suddenly and angrily. "*Damn* you, Cary." Then: "Would it have to be like that?"

I drew on the cigarettte. The red glow lit the angle of her

bare shoulder, and the tangle of hair. I said carefully: "I didn't hear you say you were ready to give up Virginia."

She cried softly in the darkness, a lonely distant sound as much beyond my or anybody's help as the far cries in the forest.

After a while she said: "I guess I was trying to win the fight." Her hand reached out and found mine and took the cigarette. "At least will you let me buy you a fleet?"

I reached and stroked her hair. "Quiet, darling. I don't need anything else to remember you by."

She said: "I've got nothing else to give you but money."

"Fifty dollars'll cover it."

After a moment, she started laughing quietly. "You're still a hard bastard, Cary. But you could use a fleet."

"Not necessarily. People don't come to a man because he owns aeroplanes—and they'd get to know how I got to own them. They might come if they knew I'd earned a fleet by finding nickel."

"Already he's thinking how to make his second million."

"Something like that."

"So I've taught you something, anyway." She stretched past me and crunched out the cigarette on the cabin floor and then put her arms around me.

CHAPTER 21

SHE WAS MIXING coffee on the stove when somebody fell over his own feet outside. She jerked up her head and her eyes were wide with hope—and perhaps apprehension.

I shook my head. Homer wasn't the sort to go falling over his feet on his own doorstep. I took a step towards the pistols in my jacket on the back of the door.

Then the door opened and Judd said cheerfully: "Ah, I was hoping to catch you," just as if he was merely popping into the club bar. "Longish walk here," he added, and came in and shut the door.

He was right about the longish walk. It must have been over twenty miles on a direct line, and the last four hours of it in darkness. He was wearing a bronze-coloured mackintosh jacket over a dark grey suit and thick-soled suede boots that were covered in mud.

He ducked his head at Mrs Beekman. "How d'you do. Hope I'm not intruding."

She looked at him, then me. "Were you expecting visitors?"

"I was not," I said firmly. Then, to Judd: "How did you know I'd be here?"

"Oh, I didn't. The police think you've gone to Sweden, but I couldn't very well look for you there, so I took a chance on you coming to your fuel dump. Nowhere else to look, really."

"How did you know about it?"

"Somebody mentioned it. Can't remember who." He chuckled at me. The secret service doesn't tell secrets to strangers.

Mrs Beekman said to me: "Is *he* part of all this business?"

"I rather think he must be." I looked at Judd thoughtfully. "He represents the British secret service. I hadn't realised they cared."

Judd gave me a sad, reproving smile. Bad form to reveal the profession, and all that.

Mrs Beekman said: "Well, if you want this one slugged with a bottle, do it yourself. I'm not coming between two Englishmen. Like some coffee?" she asked Judd.

He unzipped his jacket. "That would be very kind. I have a cup." He pulled out a pigskin-covered hip flask with an oversize cap, unscrewed it, and held it out to be filled. "Thank you very much." He sat down on an upended suitcase.

"Well," I said grimly. "What d'you want?"

"Just a couple of questions." He sipped his coffee and chuckled at me. Finding Cary had certainly made his day. I didn't yet know what it might do to mine.

Mrs Beekman asked: "Want me to take a walk?"

"No," I said quickly. "I've got no private business to do with this character."

Judd shrugged and smiled helplessly. "If you insist. Well —the fact that you got arrested suggests you must know something about this business up here." He put a question mark on it with his eyebrows.

"I know about the sovereign run that Koenig and Veikko and Adler were doing. I suppose you're up here to stop it."

"Something along those lines. Well, you obviously know as much as we do," he lied cheerfully. "May I ask you—were you helping on this at all?"

"Not at all."

He nodded thoughtfully. "I'll have to take your word for that."

That got me. "You can take it and stuff it. I don't give a damn whether you take it or not."

"Ah, well," and he peered down into his coffee. "You see, the second question is—I wonder if you could help us?"

I got a sudden small cold feeling that seemed familiar from a long time ago.

"To do what?" I said.

He glanced at Mrs Beekman. He hated talking in front of her, but I wasn't giving him a choice. And it would have taken a bulldozer to shift her now. She was watching us with a fascinated look of disbelief.

"Well?" I said.

Judd said: "We've got somebody on the other side of the frontier whom we're supposed to pick up tonight. I was going to do it in the Auster. Now, I wonder if you'd do it for us?"

The cabin was as quiet as an unexploded bomb.

Then Mrs Beekman said: "Are you asking him to fly across the Russian frontier?"

"Er—yes, that's right," and he smiled at her. "It shouldn't be too difficult," he added.

I shook my head. "I just don't see the point of it. Why put a man across the frontier on a job like this? You can't close down the Russian end, whatever you do."

"Well, it's a bit of a long story." He waved a hand to show that he truly wanted to tell it, except for the time factor. "But—you do see my problem?"

"I see it," I said. "And I see another one: I ain't going."

He nodded. "It is rather vital, you know."

"Not to me it isn't."

"You're resolved?"

"I am. And something else: you should have got your London end to check up on me before you asked."

"Oh, I did that. We found you used to be one of us yourself. Coincidence, isn't it?"

For a while nobody said anything. Judd was looking into his coffee; Mrs Beekman was examining me curiously, as if I were a new spring fashion that she wasn't sure would catch on.

"And I thought you were just a reformed smuggler or something," she said. "You're a close-mouthed bastard, too, Cary."

Judd chuckled. "We're delighted to hear it." He got up and poured himself more coffee.

"Remind me of the good old days," I said grimly. "Does the sun still glint on the massed monocles staring out over Green Park? Do they still call it The Firm, and you a Salesman, and the people at home Spare Parts?"

Judd smiled. "One keeps up the old traditions."

Mrs Beekman: "You used to be a spy?"

Judd winced and I remembered the old hatred of the word. "Not exactly. I was one of their wartime pilots—delivering agents around Europe and picking them up again."

Mrs Beekman asked: "So what happened?"

"I got fired."

"Why?"

"Ask him," I said. "He's just got the word from London."

Judd smiled a small sad smile at me, then said fast and tonelessly: "He brought an agent out to Finland at one time, then refused to go and pick him up again. Said the agent was a 'double'—had gone over to the Germans. So they sent somebody else and the somebody never came back. Finally they decided Cary had been caught by the Germans and bought his way out by betraying the agent he'd just delivered.

"Such things *have* been known to happen," he added.

I nodded.

Mrs Beekman looked at me: "Well? What really happened?"

"It doesn't matter, now. It was all a long time ago."

"It matters to *me*." Her chin was up and her eyes giving off sparks.

I looked at Judd. He lifted his shoulders slowly. "Go on if you like," he said. "I'd quite like to hear it myself." He looked at his watch. "We've got time."

"We've got all the time in the world," I said. "Let's be clear about *that*."

He smiled.

I said: "It happened in a thing called Operation Counterweight. Bit before your time, Judd, but you've probably heard of it." He nodded gently. I went on: "It was the British Foreign Office's idea of restricting the Russian sphere of influence after the war. They guessed what would happen: any country that got liberated by Russia would end up in the Communist bloc. So, in late 1943, they started Counterweight. Putting agents into countries the Russians were likely to invade, to make contact with the more conservative underground and stir them into being the first to form a government. Assuring them of British recognition, and so on."

Mrs Beekman said: "Didn't work too well, did it?"

I shrugged. "Austria might have gone, too. Maybe Finland. That's where I came in."

I came in from Spitzbergen, in an old Noorduyn Norseman ski-plane borrowed from a Canadian bush airline. No radio, no radar, just a magnetic compass that, up in those latitudes, wasn't pointing to much except Tuesday week—and a ten-centimetre radar receiver. The landing point was an inlet on frozen Lake Inari. The man to be landed was a man I'd known as Hartmann.

Because we were going into rough country, the SIS relaxed a rule and sent us on a number of Special Operations Executive courses on rough living, fast shooting, sabotage and related arts. Generally, the SIS regarded the Special Ops—our contribution to the French and other resistances—as a little crude and uncouth. The SIS didn't blow up bridges—it just looked at them and estimated how long it would take an armoured column to pass over them, and from that it deduced that . . . almost anything you cared to name. It never got around to deducing that Hartmann was as bent as a paperclip.

The Special Ops boys didn't quite trust him, but nobody asked them for their opinions. I didn't trust him myself, but nobody asked me, either. As it turned out, I was right. It also turned out that being right wasn't enough.

The flight into Finland was a long, cold, dark business in February 1944. You never saw the sun the whole day and the only time you had to avoid was a couple of hours twilight around noon. Nobody did much flying up there at that time—but we were shadowed by a Luftwaffe night fighter on the way in. What worried me more was that he didn't try to jump us; as I'd heard, this was supposed to be a shooting war.

I was still worried when I reached Lake Inari, so I didn't close up to the shore. I stopped a hundred yards out and Hartmann was just climbing out when they rushed us. They should have fired: at a hundred yards a burst from a machine gun could have carved the Norseman like a Christmas turkey. And Hartmann should have jumped back in; he was walking straight into Gestapo hands. But they didn't shoot and he didn't jump back—he ran towards them.

I shot. I loosed off a burst from a Sten that blew out the cabin window, chipped the port strut, and knocked down half a dozen of them. But I missed Hartmann. Then I got the hell out. On that leg, the night fighter really did try to get me—but he wasn't as desperate as I was. He wasn't prepared to come down twenty feet above the sea on a dark night and sort it out at that height.

I lit a cigarette. "So when I got back—they just politely refused to believe me. And when I wouldn't go back for him, a month later—that did it. It also killed the boy they sent in my place."

I stood up to go and get more whisky, then didn't. I'd been pouring whisky on the memory of that boy in the Norseman for eighteen years and it hadn't helped yet.

Judd was nodding gently and rhythmically. "I imagine they argued that your story meant Hartmann had turned pro-Nazi in 1944," he said thoughtfully. "And, of course, people just weren't doing that, so late in the war. I see their point."

I shook my head. "I never knew why he did it. It sounds crazy to me—and it gets crazier. When I came back to Finland after the war, I tried to trace him. There weren't many German records left, but I established that he stayed in Ivalo about a month. Then they tried to fly him south—at least I found a record of an unnamed passenger sponsored by the *Abwehr*, German Intelligence. And the *Abwehr* can't have had much to do in a small place like Ivalo.

"The flight went missing and I assumed Hartmann was dead. Just a few days ago, I found out what had happened. He must have forced the pilot to land on this lake here—" I nodded at the door. "Then he killed him. The pilot and plane are still down in the lake. So he sold out the Germans, too. But why? Just to get stuck *here*, in the middle of winter? That's crazier still."

Judd nodded.

There was a long silence. Then Mrs Beekman said to Judd: "Well—do you believe him?"

Judd said: "He may well be right. It doesn't matter now."

"Doesn't *matter*?" she flared at him. "How d'you make *that* out?"

"He's right, you know," I said. "It isn't important any more."

She stared wonderingly from one to the other of us. Finally she said: "I just don't get it. Is this the jolly old British idea of fair play?"

I said: "Who told you secret service work was supposed to be fair?"

Judd nodded again. "Just secret," he said. "And, of course, serviceable."

After a long while of staring at us, she shook her head. "No—I still don't get it."

I said: "I never expected it to be fair. However you dress it up, secret service is nationalised gangsterism. Wherever it operates, it's against the law. What's fair about that? Where are the rules? It just has to be secret, that's all. It keeps its successes secret—and its mistakes. The SIS files must be full of mistakes; I happen to be one of them. I never expected them to come round Finland after the war asking 'Did this happen?—or that happen?' They couldn't admit that *anything* happened. I always knew it might be like that. I never expected it to be fair."

Judd said: "Only way to run a secret service, when you think about it."

Mrs Beekman said: "You must have been a pretty dedicated character."

"Just a hired hand," I said. "You don't start questioning what you're doing. You're not hired for that."

"And *all* wars are just wars," Judd said. "Provided, of course, that you win them and get to write the history books."

He took a cigar in an alloy container out of his breast pocket, decanted it, and started looking it over for subversive slogans. "Of course," he said, "it must be a bit difficult when you've been kicked out."

I said: "It is, I can assure you. You become a man without a past. I've got no war record, no flying logbook; in 1945 I didn't even have a flying license. I had to start all over again. That's half the reason I came out here. I've built it up from scratch in Finland. Although I dare say the SIS would have been happy to hear I'd flown into a mountainside in bad weather. Up to tonight, anyway."

Judd nodded. "They would, I understand. You were an awkward loose end. And now, you see," he explained to Mrs Beekman, "after kicking him out, here we are asking him back—not because we think we made a mistake, mind you—but just because we happen to need him. So we're suggesting he risks getting shot or jailed or—if this ever leaks out—at least ruining his career in Finland. Just to help us." He stuck the cigar in his mouth and started making passes at its nose with his lighter. "Now, you couldn't call that fair, could you?"

She shook her head slowly. "No, I wouldn't call that fair. I thought I'd met some hard cases along Wall Street, but . . . Anyway—you've given some damn good reasons why he isn't taking it on."

I said: "He's harder than you think. He was just challenging me to admit I'm an incompetent who's likely to get caught or a coward who's scared to get caught." I grinned at Judd. "All right—take it that both are true. It still isn't the important reason why I won't go."

He took the cigar out of his mouth. "And that is?"

"Finland."

He put the cigar back. "Oh yes?"

"I owe them something, Judd. I don't think I owe them this."

He said: "Oh yes?" again, and his voice was the polite faraway one they specify for use on the man who's gone native and started wearing shark's-tooth necklaces.

I said: "When I came back here, after the war, I got in touch with the man Hartmann was supposed to have contacted. A politician, and rather a big man in his way. He's dead, now. He knew about Counterweight and knew it had gone sour somehow. When he found out who I was—who I'd been—he backed up my work permit. I still hold it mainly because of him."

Judd studied the end of his cigar. "You talked about the operation?"

I grinned. "You still think I should be holding to the faith? Well, as a matter of fact, I am. I don't go around telling people I've been in the British Secret Service. Probably I'd just get thrown in the asylum, but I'd be a lot worse off if I was believed. Foreigners are funny people, Judd. They don't like having British agents crawling all over—particularly they wouldn't like them flying their own planes up near the Russian border."

Judd said: "I know. Go on."

"I owe that man—and his ideas about Finnish independence—something, Judd. Had you thought what you might do to Finland?"

"I'm not concerned with Finnish—er, sales."

"Maybe not. But supposing we got caught over there, Judd? You'd be bad enough—they'd know you could only have come in through Finland. But me—I'd be a real birth-day surprise. I've been here a long time. Finland harbours British spy. How many times has he flown our frontier be-fore? The Russians could use that, if they wanted to. It wouldn't do Finland any good at all."

Mrs Beekman walked over to the whisky, picked it up, and came and splashed some into my mug. Then she reached out a forefinger and dragged it along the line of my jaw. Her grey eyes were very steady on me.

She said softly: "You've kind of got something, haven't you, friend?"

Then she walked back past Judd and filled his flask cap. "Offer him money," she suggested. "That brings out the best in him."

He smiled briefly at her and went back to studying me. Then he said: "Supposing I talked about Britain—told you this was an important mission for Britain?"

"You could try it, but it wouldn't get you anywhere be-cause you just wouldn't know, yourself. You think it's impor-tant because the SIS has told you to do it. That's what *im-portant* means to you, Judd. I'm not sneering: as you said, it's the only way to run a secret service. But I'm not in the secret service any more. You just tell me what the operation is and what it's supposed to achieve and *I'll* tell *you* whether it's important or not."

He took the cigar out of his mouth. "Well, well, well," he said quietly. Then he broke the long ash off it on the edge of the stove. "Do you know what you've gone and done? You've gone and developed a sense of personal justice. You think what you think is right, *is* right."

I smiled at him. "I have to, Judd. I've got nobody else to tell me: I'm not married and I don't have an organisation behind me. That's also something that happens to you when you're booted out of the SIS."

He shook his head gently. "It makes you a terribly danger-ous man, Mr Cary. A man who thinks he's being just. Ooh." He shuddered at the thought.

I said softly: "Some day, it could even happen to you."

"I hope not. Being fair would be far too much of a strain." He sucked his cigar thoughtfully. "But it leaves me wonder-ing if, since you aren't *for* us—are you against us?"

"You haven't told me what this operation's about—why you've got somebody over the other side. In connection

with the sovereigns, I can't think of any good reason. Yes—
you could say I'm against you."

"There's a man over there whom we promised to pick up.
We have to try and stick to our promises."

"Right. So you should have been better at the job. You've
already been spotted and had your plane knocked out from
under you."

He winced slightly, then nodded. "Perhaps. But, with the
position as it is—" he spread his hands and smiled wanly.
"Is it any good my saying that I can make this a pure business proposition?"

Mrs Beekman said: "Ah—money. I knew we'd come down
to that. Try offering to buy him a new airplane and see where
that gets you."

Judd turned to her. "Madam, I don't think you're really
helping—"

"Sure I am. I'm telling you something about this boy. You
stick to the loyalty angle. He's crazy on loyalty."

I grinned at her. But the money offer was an important
step: it meant he'd stopped thinking of me as 'one of us.'
The SIS is crazy on loyalty, too. They believe that a man
who can be bought, can be bought by somebody else for a
little bit more.

Judd asked me: "No good?"

"No good."

He took a long pull at his cigar and his face was weary.
He looked older, and his features were sagging.

He was a good man. Some of them are. Some are just
faraway characters with their brains soaked in invisible ink,
and some are ex-military types who look as secret as the
Eiffel Tower, and some are just that special Foreign Office
type the Foreign Office recruits. But some are good. Under
his fat face, this was a sharp tough boy who'd just walked
over twenty miles through some of the roughest country in
Europe and was planning a night out in old Russia to follow.

Which still left him with the problem of how to get me
into the driving seat of the Beaver and across the frontier.
The only thing left that I could suggest was for him to stick
a pistol in my face and tell me to get weaving. But, as I remembered, the SIS didn't do things that way. They'd been
very fond of telling me that they were intellignece, not executive. Pistols came under 'executive.'

At that point, he had another problem: his cigar had gone
out. He investigated the end of it, sighed, and leant sideways

to dig in his pocket. And the SIS had changed while I'd been away.

He pointed a short-barrelled revolver at my middle.

He said: "Welcome back to the secret service."

CHAPTER 22

FOR A LONG TIME nobody said anything. Then Judd chuckled in an apologetic way and hauled himself up and walked over to my jacket on the back of the door and tipped it off. It clanked like a load of scrap iron. He chuckled again, bent over, and picked out the two pistols.

He waddled back to his seat looking like a pistol bargain week. "I'll trust you not to be carrying more than two guns," he said cheerfully. Waving a pistol about seemed to have done wonders for his sense of humour.

I got up slowly and walked over to pour myself more whisky. The pistol followed me.

Mrs Beekman came out of shock and asked in her diamond-cutter voice: "Are you pointing that thing at *me*, too?"

Judd said: "I'm afraid so, yes."

I watched her anxiously. I recognised the symptoms: in a moment she was going to walk up and clout him with her handbag just as a gesture of individual liberty.

I said quickly: "He means it. They don't usually use guns, so when they do they're really serious." Then, to Judd: "Let's get one thing clear: are you honestly proposing to fly the frontier with that gun on me?"

He sighed. "It's really the only thing left to do. In the face of a sense of personal justice, one does rather need a gun. Unless, of course, you're prepared to come to some agreement."

I shook my head. "No agreement, Judd. If I go, it'll *have* to be under a gun."

"If you insist. But I do want you to appreciate that I will shoot you if—well, if the question arises." He sounded honestly concerned that I might get myself shot needlessly, as if he were telling me to be sure and wrap up warm. I believed him anyway: compared with the idea of flying the Russian frontier, the idea of shooting Bill Cary was everyday common sense.

I sat down again. "All right. Tell me the plan."

He asked: "Did you hang on to my radar receiver when you found it?"

"Yes. I don't know if it works still, though."

"I think it does. That makes the whole thing a lot easier." He groped around inside his jacket and pulled out a folded map and a newish-looking novel, and tossed them at my feet.

The map was an RAF one-millionth-scale sheet with the contours coloured in shades of mauve for reading under red cockpit lighting. This one was number 91, Mount Khibiny, which covered southern Lapland and about 120 miles into Russia, up to the shores of the White Sea.

There was nothing suspicious about it: you can walk in and buy them at any serious map shop. I already had one in the Beaver's map pocket.

The novel had a bright yellow cover loaded with enthusiastic comments from book critics. When you read them the second time, you realised they were talking about some other book by the same author. The first inside page had a big sprawling dedication scribbled on it: ALEX JUDD WITH BEST WISHES and signed by the author.

It had to mean something. I looked up at Judd.

"You put the right-hand side of the page up longitude 32 with the bottom corner on latitude 66-30," he said. I bent the book wide open and tried it.

He said: "The tail of the 's' at the end of 'wishes' is on the pick-up point. Should be the north shore of a lake. The dots on the 'i's' are where we think the radar stations are."

There was a clean simplicity about the idea that reminded me how good the SIS could be on details. The only mistakes they made were big ones.

I lifted the page to see where it reckoned the radar stations were. The page covered about 100 miles from the top to bottom and it had three 'i's' on it—the author had one in his signature. That located three stations, each about thirty miles apart, each fifteen or twenty miles back from the frontier. I took away the book and studied them. Each was on the highest available ground, within easy reach of the few roads, railways and 'winter trails' the map marked. The map would be years out of date and by now there might be more roads than it marked, but the layout of the stations still seemed logical for an early-warning 10-centimetre band line.

Just to be on the safe side, I asked: "What grade information is this?"

Judd said: "Oh, it's very reliable."

"I didn't ask that, for Christ's sake," I snarled. "You're not talking to some boy seconded from the RAF now. *What grade?*"

"Two."

Grade Two meant something they were pretty sure about, but nobody had actually seen it with their own eyes. In this context it probably meant some aircraft wandering about up across the Barents Sea, outside territorial waters, and using a radar receiver to plot what stations latched onto it. You can do it fairly accurately, but never better than Grade Two—and even that at 200 miles range.

I looked up the pick-up point. It was just beyond where a long thin lake joined a fat square one: the point was on the north side of the square one.

It was only about 45 miles inside Russia on the shortest route, and I wouldn't have to pass over any villages, roads or railways—or at least none the map admitted to. But the lake was only twenty miles short of Kanalaksha, the only sizable town in the area, on the shore of the White Sea.

I looked up from the map. "I suppose you haven't any information about a second line of radar—on the three-centimetre band, perhaps?"

Judd took the stub of his cigar out of his mouth and said: "It's there, but not far forward enough to worry us. It's pretty complicated trying to set up anything but the simple ten-centimetre stuff out in the wilds."

"I know that. But what about Kanalaksha? They must have an airstrip there: they might have a three-centimetre station, too."

He nodded: "Probably have. But I think we can keep high ground between us and it."

I looked back at the map, and he was probably right. And I could dodge the ten-centimetre stations for a lot of the time, staying down in valleys or with a background of high ground, against which they shouldn't be able to spot me. That still left one or two bits of high ground I had to cross—and where they'd probably see me.

Still, the receiver would tell us when they did. If the three-centimetre station caught us, we'd never know.

"Incidentally," I said, "why didn't you get issued with a broad-band set? We could have picked up anything on that."

"I agree. But the old style equipment was too big to go in the Auster without the Finnish customs spotting it, and the new miniature equipment is too secret for them to risk it if we get caught." And he smiled politely.

I nodded slowly. The bastards had thought of everything —including how to cut their losses. The trouble was, one of the losses was likely to be me.

"All right," I said. "How about fighter stations in the area?"

"I understand you needn't worry about missiles, at the altitudes we're likely to be flying."

"I wasn't. I was worrying about fighters."

"Yes." He took out his cigar and frowned at it, then crunched it out under his foot. "We tend to think there may be a few at Kanalaksha."

Just twenty miles from where I was supposed to land.

I took a deep breath, couldn't think of anything to say, and went back to studying the map.

Mrs Beekman said quietly: "Are you really going to do this, Bill?"

I stood up and walked round my suitcase. "I don't have a choice."

"Will you get back all right?"

I stopped. It was about time I faced up to that question. I thought about it, then said: "I'll be doing the job *I* was doing seventeen years ago, the same kind of aeroplane, the same radar receiver. The trouble is, I think the rest of the world's got a bit more complex since then; I've just got older. No." I shook my head. "I think we're going to get caught."

Judd may have got a bit paler; he certainly hadn't changed his mind.

I said: "When d'you want to start?"

He looked at his watch. "The pick-up's timed for one in the morning. How long will the flight take?"

"Nearly an hour. I won't be going in direct. I'm taking the scenic route."

He nodded. "We'd better start down to the aircraft in . . . say half an hour?"

"All right."

He looked at Mrs Beekman. "I wonder if you'd be terribly kind and find me something to eat?—I haven't had anything since I finished some smoked-reindeer sandwiches on the march up here."

Mrs Beekman looked at me. I said: "Feed the brute. He won't be any slower on the trigger without it."

She got up slowly, gave Judd a look that should have stuck out of his back, and went across to the boxes by the stove.

I lit another cigarette, and went back to the map. The room was small, warm and close, and thick with tobacco smoke in the swaying lamplight. Soon there was a smell of cooking drifting through it. It all seemed reluctantly familiar, like a pain you've forgotten about.

A small crew-room on the edge of an airstrip in the Shetlands or Spitzbergen; thick with tobacco smoke like this; red lamplight to keep my night vision intact; somebody cooking me a last hot meal on a stove in the corner; everybody carefully avoiding me, talking in brief whispers, so as not to distract me. It was familiar, all right. And me in a corner hunched over a map trying to plot a course between mountain peaks, Grade Two information on what radar stations there were, Grade Three information on the latest flak posts and Luftwaffe fighters, and a Grade Fifteen guess that I was going to the right place anyway. Then climbing into the Sidcot suit and slinging a Sten gun round my neck to lie in my lap in the cockpit, so that it would be the first thing I could grab, and sticking the rubber-coated cyanide pill to my left wrist with sticking plaster so that it would be the second thing. . . .

And outside, waiting, the vast empty cathedral of the night. And my job to sneak up through the pews and pinch the altar cloth. The trouble with jobs like this was that you always had a vague feeling at the back of your mind that you *ought* to be caught.

I jerked my head up from the map. Judd was just putting down an empty plate and smiling encouragingly in my direction. Mrs Beekman was back in her corner, breathing on a cigarette and watching me very calmly.

Judd asked: "How are you getting on?"

"Badly. I'm beginning to think like a spy again. I don't like it."

He chuckled and decanted another cigar.

I kicked the map over to him. "There's your route. It's the best you'll get."

It was in four legs. The first three, heading roughly southeast, east and north-east, made a wide swing through the valleys and across the frontier to take us between the middle and southernmost of the three radar stations. Each leg was around 25 nautical miles long. The fourth was a sharp turn back to south-east and a run of fifteen miles down a river valley to our destination lake.

Judd examined it dubiously. "Looks a little complicated. Complicated plans have a way of going wrong."

"So have simple plans—like the simple idea of popping across to Russia to pick up a pal. If we're going to get caught, we may as well go down calculating."

He still looked dubious. "If you took a simpler, shorter route, they'd have less time to react if they did spot us."

"Judd, in this business you've got to forget anything about a quick dash and a bit of faith in having led a good life. Even if you've led a good life."

"Well—" and he shrugged. "You're the boss." Which should have got him the Nobel Prize for hypocrisy.

Then he stood up and zipped up his jacket. "We'd better be going."

Mrs Beekman came over to me. "D'you think you can get away with it, Bill?"

I rubbed the stubble on my face. "If anybody can, I can. But pilots always have to think that."

"If you'd left at nine o'clock, you'd have missed him."

"Among other things."

She smiled gravely. "I'll see you back here." She turned to Judd. "If you *don't* get back, I'm going to blow this whole thing in the newspapers."

Judd nodded. "If we don't get back, the important people will know about us already." He was stripping the magazines out of my two pistols. Then he looked at the shotguns and rifle on the wall, and I knew he was thinking of what might happen when she was left alone with them behind his back.

I said: "She won't try and use them."

He cocked an eyebrow at her. "Promise?"

"I don't want you starting any gunfights," I told her. "I know more about them than you do, and if there's any reasonable chance, I'll start one for myself."

She nodded reluctantly. "And don't *you* start anything, unless you're sure . . ."

Then I was holding her against me, small but strong and warm. I lifted her face and kissed her.

She stepped back and said with very careful calmness: "Whatever happens, I won't ever hate myself."

I nodded, and turned away, then back. "Lend me a lipstick, would you? Useful navigation pencil."

She dug one out, and smiled, and said: "Remember to bring it back."

I smiled back, and led the way out.

CHAPTER 23

THE NIGHT was thick rather than dark. There were no stars; the layer of stratus had solidified and the sky was a dirty cobwebby ceiling that began at the treetops. The points of the trees didn't have the crisp sharp shape they should have. The shadows on the ground were pale and blurred.

In the hard, deep shadows of moonlight I'd have tried running for it. Or maybe in moonlight I'd have wanted clouded dimness. Maybe I just didn't like the idea of getting shot in the back.

Judd's pistol, as far as I had been able to see in the lamplight, was one of the Smith and Wesson .38's with a shrouded hammer. A handy, easily hidden gun, but the short barrel meant it wasn't accurate enough for much more than suicide. That didn't encourage me: Judd probably wasn't much of a shot himself, and an inaccurate shot and an accurate gun can cancel each other out.

We reached the lake at about twenty to eleven. I climbed into the Beaver, and Judd got up on the float behind me to watch what I was doing. I just let off the brakes, climbed down, and pushed her back into the water.

I got back in, put across the master switch, and turned on the cockpit lighting. I dug in the door pocket and found a scratched old protractor. The Beaver swayed as Judd hauled himself in through the port passenger door, behind me.

"I'll stay back here," he decided. "Where's the radar receiver?"

"I never mounted it up. It's in the baggage hatch in the rear bulkhead."

The aeroplane swayed again as he worked his way aft. A Beaver cabin isn't much more than four feet square, so he had quite a job hauling himself back over the seats. But for the same reason, it wasn't going to be easy for me to start a fight, not with him in the seat behind me. And impossible, once we were in the air and flying only a few feet up.

After a while Judd called: "Where can I mount the aerial?"

"You're probably standing on a drop hatch in the floor. Pierce the lid of that and shove it through." I went back to measuring angles.

The gun went off with a muffled crack. As soon as I realised he hadn't shot me, I jerked around to see what he *had* shot.

Judd said: "Sorry. I was just piercing the hatch. Should have warned you." He went on calmly unscrewing the long shaft on the horn aerial.

I dimmed the lights and looked out over the lake. The water was as flat as plate glass and the far trees were faint and blurred. Mist doesn't begin to build in more than a five-knot wind, so it didn't look as if I would have to worry about wind at all at the heights I'd be flying. But I'd rather have worried about wind than mist.

Judd fought his way forward and shoved a wire over my right shoulder. "Can you plug this in?"

My R/T set was British-built, so the radar receiver plug fitted the same outlet. And I wasn't going to be sending or accepting any messages on this trip.

Judd said: "Thank you," and scuffled his way back.

"Don't switch that thing on until the engine's running," I warned him.

"Won't do." He grunted around at the aerial handle. "If anything picks us up, I'll try and give you a rough strength, and the direction in relation to us. All right?"

"All right."

He hauled himself back into his seat. Behind the two front seats, there were another pair, then a space which had the drop hatch in the floor before you reached the aft bulkhead. He was sitting in the seat diagonally behind me with the receiver parked on the seat beside him. Sticking up behind him was the handle of the aerial, so that he could reach back and turn it.

He smiled happily at me. "Ready when you are."

It was five to midnight. I passed him a piece of paper. "From here on, you're the navigator. Read this back to me when I ask you."

He took a little pencil torch out of his jacket and scanned the paper. "Looks more complicated than ever."

"Don't let that worry you: it's all wrong anyway, since I don't know what wind there'll be."

His smile was just a slight unstiffening of his features. "Whatever you say."

"*I* say let's forget the whole idea and run down to Helsinki for a quick beer."

"Except that, of course."

I nodded and started the engine. He hadn't once come within safe grabbing range. Now I was really going to have to go to Russia.

We took off at seven minutes past midnight. There were a lot of things I could have done: flooded the engine or left the emergency fuel cut-off down and tried starting a dry one, and he probably wouldn't have known what. But he'd have known I'd done something, and that could be enough. He was a dedicated man, and he might have shot me in just a general way, to prove he was serious.

I circled over the lake and straightened out at 200 feet on a course of 156 magnetic. I punched the timer clock on the dashboard and asked: "What time on this leg?"

The pencil torch flickered behind me. "Er—25 nautical miles; 14 minutes, 20 seconds."

I scrawled 14-20 with the lipstick on the panel beside the clock and settled down to hold 105 knots. There may have been a glimmer of light among the trees far back over my left shoulder, but that didn't concern me any more. There was nothing but the night ahead.

Most night flying is very different from day flying. Mostly, you just sit there in a small dim office watching the dials, jotting down things on maps, making minute corrections to the controls to bring up better readings on the dials. Slowly you get detached: it all turns into one big, sprawling sum of speed, direction, wind, height, temperature. Solve it —get it near enough right—and you're safe. You never know about the deaths you didn't die: the mountain peaks you missed, the collisions that didn't happen. It's a warm cosy feeling. It's the way the airlines fly.

This wasn't like that.

I wasn't doing sums in a cosy cabin. I was scuttling across the floor of the sky, watching anxiously all round—but mostly ahead; lifting over small ridges that rushed at me out of the dimness, searching for the stainless-steel glint of a river to fix my position. I had the cabin lighting turned right down and I was pretending to be hidden—but I was hiding in something that gave off a racket that could be heard at five miles and a radar trace that could be seen at fifty.

The book says *higher, slower,* but this sort of flying isn't

in the book. My hope was in keeping low and fast. I was
a small insect running around in a land of big boots.

The timer said 5 minutes 40 seconds. The fourth of a
series of small rivers, crossing at right angles to our track,
ran away behind me. The ground began to rise ahead; just
the usual ridges that rut the whole of Lapland, but each
one higher than the last, rolling like waves towards me. I
edged the throttle forward a fraction and the nose lifted and
we crawled up the slope.

"What time to the top of this crest?" I asked.

Behind me, Judd was peering down at his receiver. The
dial on the face of it was giving off a faint yellow glow that
lit the fat curves of his face. He glanced up at me, then
routed out my piece of paper.

"Er—seven minutes thirty seconds."

"Thanks. How're you doing?"

"No trace yet."

The timer said 7.20. The next wave of trees didn't happen.
I hesitated a moment, then pushed down the nose, eased
back the throttle, and tried to skim the crest as close as
possible. These, the crests, were the dangerous places. Up
on a hilltop, with no high ground behind us, we were spitted
like a butterfly on a pin for the radar to catch us.

We zipped across the spruce tops at a thirty foot clearance;
it looked less. Jud said: "Ah—hah . . ." but it faded off,
as if disappointed.

"Thought I had something there," he said.

"Just remember you're looking for them looking for us. If
you don't see a thing, I won't complain."

We slid down the slope into a valley, crossed just left of
a lake parallel to our track, and started climbing up the far
side. This time I pushed the throttle a little further forward.
The timer read 11 minutes 10 seconds.

The timing seemed almost dead on. The track-keeping
wasn't perfect: I should have passed straight over that lake.
But I was more interested about keeping a good look-out
than keeping a perfect track. I remembered a voice from
long ago saying: *I could name you a stack of pilots who'd be
wearing their wings on their fronts instead of their backs if
they'd put a bit more faith in a damn good look around and
a bit less in an inch of armour plate.* I grinned. He'd been
right, but he was dead now. Not many had lived through
the whole war. Getting fired before my luck ran out had
saved me.

The crest of the slope, the last line of trees, steadied ahead. I flattened the climb but kept the throttle up, aiming at the treetops.

Judd said: "Ah," then, very fast: "Radar almost ahead—about five degrees off to the left . . . It's gone now."

We were rolling down the slope. I pulled the boost right back and the propeller as coarse as I could get it, to slow its drag. We were doing 125 knots—for the moment.

The cabin went quiet but for the wavering roar of the air on the badly fitting doors.

Judd said: "What are you doing?"

"Crossing the frontier as quietly as possible. Any objections?"

The Beaver swayed as he jerked to the window and peered ahead. The valley floor was smoky with mist. Then there was the dull glint of a river—and then another. Just ahead of my right float, they blended into one. And just beyond them, a wide, unnatural gap in the thin trees. Then it wasn't just a gap but a lane hacked out of the forest and fading away into the dimness on either side. The frontier.

"New course?" I demanded.

Judd fumbled and flickered his pencil torch. I bent the Beaver gently to the left, keeping it easy so as not to lose more speed than I had to; so as not to put on more power until we were as far past the frontier as possible.

Up here the frontier was just a few strands of barbed wire guarded by a man and a dog and a telephone. But it wasn't the man or the dog that worried me.

Judd said: "106 magnetic. Fourteen minutes."

I punched the timer to stop, reset and start again. I left the 14-20 scrawled on the panel in lipstick. It would do.

I said: "From here on, we're really illegal. You sure you don't want to scrub it all and run down to Helsinki for a quick beer?"

Judd said: "Afterwards. I'll buy the beer."

"On SIS expenses?"

"We'll put it down as medical necessities. Would it be an idea to put on a bit of power before we run into this hill?"

"Thanks for reminding me." I left the throttle and pitch where they were. The speed was down to 90 now and fading. The first ridge, with its ragged line of trees, hovered ahead of me, misty but hardening like a photograph in the developer tank, and gradually reaching up to overtop me. Speed down to 80. The timer said 40 seconds from scratch. Say just about a mile past the frontier. I pushed the pitch and throttle gently forward, trying to catch and hold the speed at 70 in a climb. The engine wound up to a howl. The speed shivered at the 70 mark. The first line of trees slid past thirty feet below.

Judd said: "You left that a little late."

"If you've got any complaints, put them in writing to the Head of Records. He'll tell you I practically invented this business."

"He told me already."

"All right. Wrap up and give me the details of this leg."

The torch glowed. "After this crest you get a river at 10 nautical miles, five-and-a-half minutes. Then a hump at over a thousand feet, then a bend of a river at fifteen-and-a-half nautical miles . . ."

"That'll keep us going."

We crawled up the hillside holding about 75 knots. I'd have liked it higher, but that would have meant full power. Full power on a Wasp Junior would wake the Siberian garrison.

We crawled on up the slope. We were going across a shoulder, with the ground sloping both up in front of us and up right to left.

Judd said suddenly: "Radar. Strong—out to the right, about forty degrees. Very strong. He's—he's about twenty miles away, that's all."

"That's your southern station. He'd be about twenty miles away from here."

"He's got us. He's getting us every time round. The needle's going off the dial."

"Get a new needle, then."

"Can't you *do* something?" He sounded angry more than worried.

"Certainly. I'll just run back to the stores and get a submarine instead; you wait here." I paused. I was down to thirty feet and the waves of trees were coming at me suddenly, like flat cut-out silhouettes, darkening from a misty grey to a sharp black, then sliding away behind.

"He can't see us," I said.

"What?"

"High ground behind us—on our left. We're lost against that. Switch your aerial round 180 degrees and you'll get nearly as strong a signal: his ground return. He can't see us in that."

He tried it; he wasn't taking anything I said on trust. Or perhaps he was just learning that sometimes you have to sit in the sky and hold your breath and wait. No dodging and swerving, because that would probably make you show up more, and get you lost into the bargain.

After a while Judd said: "He's still on the same sweep interval. He'd be doing a localised sweep if he'd seen us." After another while he said: "Sorry. I forgot you must have been through this before."

"I once tried to forget it myself." I pushed the Beaver over the crest and started picking up speed down into the valley.

Judd said: "It's fading out." Then he said: "It's gone, now."

I flattened out in the valley. The bad moment for radar was yet to come, and I knew where: at the turning point onto the third leg. Up there, for a time—and for as short a time as I could manage—we'd be in line-of-sight for two stations. But that was ten minutes ahead.

The valley was flat-floored; a rubble of spindly spruce, small ridges, and bare patches that were baby lakes or patches of swamp or just plain naked rock where not even spruce could grow. I wavered over it, keeping as low as I could, but not liking what I saw on the small lakes: mist.

It wasn't definite, yet. Just a blurriness that made you think you'd got your eyes focussed wrong. But it was only just after midnight. The air was still cooling, the difference between air and water temperature getting greater. Unless there was a wind, this mist would go on building until first light.

I eased nervously up to about sixty feet and looked at the timer. It said five minutes. About a minute to the river and for the ground to start to rise beyond it.

Judd said: "Nothing showing."

"We're down a hole. They couldn't catch us here." I scrabbled in my pocket for a cigarette and passed it back to Judd. "Light this, would you? I don't want to ruin my night vision."

He knew what I was talking about. It takes half an hour for your eyes to adapt fully to darkness, and several minutes to re-adapt after you've lit a match in front of them.

A faint light flared behind me. He passed the cigarette back.

"Thanks. Incidentally, what *are* we picking up over here?"

"Just a man."

"And what else? How much does it weigh?"

The river passed underneath, a glint of water blurred at the edges. Judd made non-committal noises.

I said: "It can only be weight, Judd. If it was just a man, he could walk out 45 miles a damn sight safer than we can fly in and pick him up—if he's got the sort of training your firm gives. Well, I hope you know how much weight the Beaver carries."

"I know. I checked with London."

He would have. I said: "I still don't see what he's doing over there, on a job like this."

He didn't say anything.

The ground began to climb again, and I climbed with it. This was just a spur of high ground dividing the river we'd passed from one of its tributaries. Over the spur, we'd meet the tributary and fly up its valley towards the main crest of the hills: the most exposed point.

We got a flicker of radar interest at the top of the spur, but nothing the operators would have noticed. Then we were sliding down into the tributary valley.

There was a small glow from Judd's torch. "You should meet the river at 10 minutes, 20 seconds from the start of this leg."

"Thanks." The timer said 7.40. The real time was 28 minutes past midnight.

He said: "The next hill's going to be a dangerous place, isn't it?"

"Yes."

"What d'you think'll happen if they spot us?"

"Don't *you* know? What did your briefing say?"

"Just that they'd send up aircraft, probably. I don't know what sort, of course."

"They won't put up jets in this weather. You can't fly those things visually low-level on a misty night. No, they'll use some communications plane, something like this one, to start a search. What I'm hoping is that even if they spot us up here, they won't spot us landing. So they may not guess where to start looking."

"I see." He thought it over. "I'm beginning to see your point about a zigzag course."

There was a broken line growing in the trees over to my right. The timer said nearly ten minutes. I edged over towards the line and it edged towards me, and it was the river. I turned in above it and started flying its line rather than a compass course. One thing you knew while flying a river was that sudden hills weren't going to jump up and hit you in the teeth.

I found myself trimming the nose higher and adding a touch more throttle. The ground was beginning to rise again. About four minutes to the top.

Judd asked: "When we get radar, where d'you expect to get it from?"

"Both sides."

"All right. I'll let you know as soon as I've got anything."

"You do that." It wouldn't be much use, except as a rough check on whether we were in the right place or not.

"Tell me one thing," I said. "How come you managed to mess up this mission and get yourself sabotaged? What leaked?"

"Oh, we did. We had to let it be known we were coming to investigate the sovereign line."

"*Had* to? Why?"

"It was the only way to get the Swiss end out into the open. Useless trying to sort it out in Switzerland. Everything's done at fifteen removes and through numbered bank accounts. We knew if we threatened the Finnish end, somebody would come rushing up to close it down. Then we'd have a personal lead. It worked, too. We know who they are. I'm getting some radar about 90 degrees to the left. Weak."

"They're shooting down hill; we're all right. But they know who you are, too. I'll bet it was Koenig who fixed your Auster."

"I rather think so. I found Koenig was in Rovaniemi that day. We thought he'd gone up with the trailer. Still, we had to take that sort of risk."

The ground was climbing more steeply, now. I edged on more power. I didn't like the visibility ahead much. I was up to a hundred feet above the ground, now—not dangerous at this point, still in the tributary valley, but I didn't want to go over the crest that high. I just hoped I'd know the crest when it came.

I said: "That explains some of the troubles I've been having this summer. The rumour that the SIS was coming must have got around pretty well: half Lapland's been offering me phoney jobs to see if I was already booked to work for you. Veikko, then Koenig's boy, Claude." The crazy conversation with Ilse was making sense now: *I think you* are *one of them, after all.* Also why they hadn't killed me when they'd got me drugged; they'd want to ask a few questions about how much the SIS had discovered.

Judd said: "Yes, we had to run that risk, too. We thought it might be useful—distracting attention from us."

"*You* had to run the risk?"

"Well, we thought you'd be able to look after yourself. We didn't think you'd have forgotten all of our training." He paused, then added: "And officially, you aren't one of our nearest and dearest friends, you know."

"So if I'd got killed, it wouldn't have worried you."

"As it turned out, it would have been very awkward. Still, you didn't, did you?" he said cheerfully.

"As it turned out, it wouldn't have made much difference."

The timer said about a minute to go.

Judd said: "Ah—" Then he said: "Thought I got something, then."

"Which side?"

Judd said: "I'm getting something now. Not much, but regularly. About 120 degrees right." He paused. "Nothing to the left, yet."

I looked out to the left. Beside me, the trees curved up into misty darkness. There was probably high ground still between us and the station on that side.

The timer said thirty seconds to the crest, but it didn't have to be accurate to a few seconds. I hadn't kept a steady enough speed for that.

We crawled on up the slope, me trying to stare the crest out of the dimness ahead.

I couldn't do it. With visibility like this, even at my height, and even climbing a hill, the horizon was below me.

Judd called: "Radar strong on the right. Very strong." He paused while he twiddled his aerial handle. "And on the left, coming stronger. About—about 100 degrees. They're both getting us."

Then I knew I must be at the crest. Whatever I could see, the radar couldn't be seeing us if there was ground higher than I was. I pushed forward the nose.

Outside, the big electronic whips waved by radar stations flicked us on each circuit of the scanners, about once every ten seconds, flick and away, flick and away, from each side. Each time, we were coming up as a little luminous green trace on two radar screens; each time, the whip showed we'd moved a little further in a certain direction.

Long ago, I'd tried to think what I could do in that ten seconds while I was out of sight, something to convince them they'd made a mistake, that I wasn't really there, that I was really flying in a different direction. . . . There wasn't anything. And this time there were two stations. One might make a mistake, might decide I was a flock of geese or perhaps miss me altogether as he reached for a cup of coffee. But not both.

My hope was in the turn onto the third leg. If they knew I was there, the turn could throw them off knowing where I was going. That was why I'd picked this as a turning point. I heeled her over through about forty degrees.

Judd said: "He's changed his sweep—the left one. He's looking for us."

Now the scanner wasn't revolving in a big circle, but wig-wagging from side to side, sweeping just a small segment of the sky. The whip was lashing faster, beating at the under-growth of sky and hilltop, trying to pinpoint us. Now he had us every two or three seconds. Now he *knew*.

The crest line curved round behind me and up away to the left.

Down right and ahead, the ground fell away—*had* to fall away, if the map was anything near right. I cut the throttle right back and we tumbled down the slope like a barrel over Niagara.

CHAPTER 24

JUDD SAID: "Radar gone from behind . . . gone from the left." He waited while he made sure. "They've lost us."

I asked: "What course am I supposed to be on now?"

He fumbled around; the torch glowed. "56 magnetic. 15 minutes, 20 seconds." Then he said: "They've got us, now, haven't they!"

"If they're any good, they have."

"What'll they know?"

"They know we've gone down into this valley. They shouldn't know any more than that." From the map, the valley widened out a few miles ahead and then became part of what was more or less a plain stretching to the shores of the White Sea. Our destination lake lay about forty degrees off to starboard from the line I was now flying. I was keeping to the right of the valley, with a ridge of high ground just on my right, planning to turn right round the end of it. We were through the line of radar stations, now. They were behind me or off to my left, and the high ground made a nice confusing background for me. I hoped.

The river swerved across my course, then back again. The high ground on the left began to fall and fade away into dimness.

I called back: "You'll pick up some radar on this leg, but I don't think they can see us." Then: "If they *do* catch us, what about my lethal pill? Or don't they issue them now?"

"Oh, you needn't worry. I'll make sure they don't take you alive."

"You hadn't told me *that* was in the contract."

"I think it would be neater that way, don't you?"

I gave the oil pressure gauge a sickly smile. Well, I'd known he was a hard case. I lit a new cigarette from the old stub.

As the valley got lower, it got mistier. Occasionally, among the trees, I could see small pools of white darkness, the individual trees sharply silhouetted against it. I kept a nervous watch out to the right, for sudden spurs that might jut out from the high ground. But it seemed to be fairly gentle country—except for the inevitable small ridges.

Radar was hitting us regularly now but not seeing us—at least he wasn't going onto a local sweep. Judd caught a weak, distant sweep from the third station, to the north.

When the timer said 13 minutes he leant over my shoulder and said carefully: "Turning point is a lake about a mile and a half long, running north-west, south-east. Turn right onto 148 magnetic."

"Thanks."

"Time on the last leg is 8 minutes, thirty."

I lipsticked 8.30 on the panel. I was holding my course very carefully: this was the only leg on which accurate navigation really mattered. On the other legs I'd been flying to the shape of the land as much as to a compass course. But now I was getting out onto a flat plain, with the lake as the only landmark. If I missed it, a few miles further on was a railway—and perhaps people to notice and report.

A whiteness grew among the trees ahead, then the trees ended and I was flying over nothing. Then I realised it was a vast pool of mist—the lake.

I said: "Blast," and stood the Beaver on her right wingtip, thumped the timer twice, and slammed her upright on a new

course. Behind me, Judd said something that was mostly ex-
pelled breath.

High ground began to climb ahead. I edged right of it,
looking for the line of a river that would carry us on straight
down to the lakes we wanted.

"I don't like that," I said. "That lake was just mist. I didn't
see it until we were on top of it."

"The other lakes are bigger."

"I'm not worried about missing them. All I have to do is
follow the river, if I can find the river—" I saw it then, and
swung back to port. "I'm worried about landing. If it's got ten
feet of mist on top of it, we're going to go in with a hell of a
splash. We could stick in a float and turn over."

"We're going to have to try it, whatever happens."

"If it looks too bad, I might be going to take the chance of
you shooting me. What did you tell your pal about setting out
lights?"

"A green light flashing from the north side of the lake when
he hears the aeroplane. Then two white lights in the water
about 30 yards apart, along the length of the lake."

Just possible. On a good night, no trouble at all. The lights
in the water would be far enough apart at 30 yards to give
me some idea of my approach angle. On a night like this, I
could lose them both in the mist on an approach, where I'd
be seeing them not through ten feet of mist from dead
above, but maybe eighty feet of it from an angle to one side.
And the second light from nearly twice that distance. But I
needed both lights to have any idea of where I was.

I was winding down the river now. Three minutes gone of
this leg. The real time was seven minutes to one.

Judd said: "Well, at least the mist may hide the aeroplane
once we've landed. That would be useful."

"There's a good chance the water'll hide it. And us."

"There's a long lake before we get to the one we're landing
on. We can see how bad the conditions are on that."

"And if they're too bad, what then? We run down to Helsinki for a beer instead?"

He didn't answer. I pushed down a bit lower over the river;
we were in a wide valley with no danger of high ground, and
we were probably getting towards inhabited areas.

The river itself wasn't too bad: wide and shallow and fast,
it hadn't collected much mist; just an occasional blurriness on
the slow inside of a bend, and a few shreds drifting
around the feet of the black trees on the banks.

Without consciously starting it, I was doing a landing check. Brakes—no interest in a water landing. Undercarriage —still retracted. Mixture—into rich. Fuel—about 25 gallons left, and flowing all right.

"Strap yourself in tight," I said. "If it can be done, and if your friend's remembered to put the candle in the window for us, I want to slap her down as quickly as I can."

Five minutes of the leg gone. There was a whiteness among the trees ahead. Then we were past the last tree and running down a long, thin lake—or what must have been a lake. I never saw any water. Just a thick scum of mist and in front of us two clumps of spindly pines sticking up clear and black from islands that were lost in the mist. I swerved around them with the floats just brushing the top of the mist.

On one of the swerves I said: "Take a look down. That's what conditions are like."

I felt him move to look, but he didn't say anything.

The lake was about seven miles, or four minutes, long. That meant I was going to come over the throat where it joined the destination lake at just on one o'clock. I'd got that right, at least. It didn't amount to anything if I couldn't get down. And by now, I wanted to get this right.

I edged over to the shore, to see if I could pull the old trick of landing parallel to it while looking out sideways to make it my horizon. On flat calm water, which gives you no idea of your height, it works fine. It didn't work with mist. I lowered the floats gently into the mist, then gradually lower until it was shredding through the propeller, then finally breaking over the nose at the windscreen. The shore vanished, I was suddenly nowhere.

I reared out of there with the back of my neck as cold and wet as a dog's nose.

The lake bent slightly to the left and I bent with it. Three minutes to go. Time for a little calculation.

My eye level was about eleven feet above the lowest point of the Beaver, where the half-retracted main wheels stuck down out of the floats. So if I sank to eye level in the mist, the floats were eleven feet below it. Give or take a foot or two for the effect of the propeller churning the stuff up.

It didn't mean a thing. I didn't know how deep the mist was. It could have been eleven feet or fifteen or twenty.

Judd said: "How does it look?"

"It looks impossible."

"I thought you were good at this sort of thing."

"It takes a good pilot to recognise the impossible. How d'you think bad pilots kill themselves?"

No comment.

After a while I said: "It all depends on the lights. If they're any help at all, we might make it." I didn't sound convincing, even to me. And it was me I was working on. He probably thought I could have made it if only I were still wearing the Foreign Office tie.

We came over the connecting channel between the lakes—just a gap in the trees thirty yards wide and a bit longer, floored with mist. The second lake opened ahead. There was no horizon. The mist reached as far as I could see. Gaunt thin pines on small islands poked through in clumps, fading away across the lake like the rotting masts and sails of dead, half-sunken ships. It was as quiet and still out there as a cave of ice. The Beaver must have sounded very loud and looked very obvious.

I swung left to keep near the north shore, then pulled the nose up and cut back the engine to get the noise down. I felt Judd stretch across behind me to peer out.

The time was a few seconds after one. I stopped the timer and reset it to zero. The north bank was just a forest of root-less pines standing out of the mist. I pulled the nose up and into a wingover to reverse course along the north shore. The speed was down to 75 knots, but I was putting out a lot less noise.

"All right," I said. "Where's your friend? You're sure you didn't write down the date or time wrong in your diary?"

A green light blinked blearily from the mist among the trees. Judd jerked in his seat.

I said: "All right, I have it." I dipped the nose and snapped the navigation lights quickly on and off, then swung out in a big S-turn over the lake and back again along what would have to be the landing run.

There were no islands closer than a quarter mile from the shore, which at that point was a very slight headland, a gentle bulge into the lake. If somebody was going to heave floating lights into the water from there, they were probably aiming to mark a landing path just skimming the bulge. As good as anywhere.

A spark twinkled through the air and then turned into a steady misty glow on the west side of the bulge.

"What are those things?" I asked.

Judd paused to think if he was revealing any important

State Secrets. "New type of floatation torch. It always stays the right way up."

Another one twinkled sharply and brightly and then became a dull glow on the water below the mist. I turned back, put down half flap, and went down on a reverse landing course, just to try the lights. I aimed for the nearest light, keeping half an eye on the further one. The nearer light got gently bigger, but not sharper. The further one started to fade appreciably while I was still at fifty feet above the mist. At thirty feet it died away entirely. I rounded out, skimmed the top of the mist, and pulled away. The lost light glowed suddenly below me.

"Did you see all that?" I asked.

"I saw it."

"You know enough about flying to know why there were supposed to be two lights? So that you can have something to give you a perspective on the ground—which one light won't do?"

"I know about that," he said, and his voice was heavy and old. "I see what you mean." He didn't sound like a man with a gun.

I turned at sixty feet, turned down the cockpit lighting to just a glint, and dipped towards the nearest light, aiming just short of it. The floats squashed into the mist, sank, then I pulled back sharply. The light flared under the nose and for the first time I saw water: a glimmering flat sheen for a few feet around the torch. I climbed out and away.

Judd asked: "What would happen if—if you got it wrong?"

"We might turn on our backs. We might just dig one float in and tear it loose. One of them's a bit out of line anyway. Either way you'd have three people stuck here instead of just one."

Then I said: "I have an idea. I've a nasty feeling it may be the first time anybody's had it, so it could be a very bad one. But I think I can land on one light if we can get it to show up a bit more water."

"Is there any way to do that?"

"My idea covers it. I want to drop something in the water between the lights; that should start a few ripples that'll catch the light a bit further than it goes now. It's too damn calm."

"Such as what?"

"Unstrap yourself. There's a baggage compartment in the rear bulkhead, and there's a few tins of food—emergency supplies—in there. Then open the drop hatch and wait for my shout. Chuck out three or four in a string." I felt him move back.

I turned in a slow circle to bring us back to a reverse run up the landing line. The mist and the black, tattered trees fading across the lake still looked as dead as the far side of the moon. The time was four minutes after one.

I heard the rush of air as the hatch came open. Judd called: "I'm ready."

"Okay. In about fifteen seconds." I pulled back the pitch and then the throttle, and dipped down on a line with the lights, staying on the line after the far light had vanished. I flattened out gently on top of the mist.

"Ready," I called. The first light flared and disappeared under the nose.

I counted *and one* and shouted: "Now!"

The second light suddenly glowed ahead, swelled, and passed beneath. I rammed up the throttle, not caring about the noise. Now we were committed. If we were going to make it, it had to be before the ripples died. I climbed into a turn.

Could I still use the second light? Round out at—say— three or four feet on the glow from the first light, then coast through the mist at that height and drop her on by the ripples from the second light? Could I still work it?

No. I couldn't try it with a split mind. It had to be just one idea and one only. Forget that second light.

Judd scrambled heavily back into his seat.

"I didn't close the hatch—"

"Skip it."

I came out of the turn at fifty feet above the mist, about two hundred yards back from the first light. I eased back the throttle and put down full flap. The Beaver slowed, swayed, and then shook herself into a new slightly nose-up attitude.

I shuffled her in gentle small turns, lining up with the lights while I could still see two of them. The speed drifted down off the dial. At 50 knots I let the nose droop. The far light faded and vanished.

I kept my eye on the one light. I was aiming short, shorter than on the previous runs.

We were about thirty feet above the mist and a hundred yards from the light. It was beginning to fade—just slightly. Speed down to 47 knots. She was heavy at this speed, and sluggish on the ailerons.

Twenty feet up and the light was fading. I had to hold her down; some part of me wanted to haul up so that I could see the light better. But I had to aim short; I had to round out and then touch on the light itself. Beyond it was nothing. Nothing.

Ten feet above the mist the light was just a faint glow. I was about sixty yards short of it. I was in the right place. I made a hand go out and pull back the throttle and pitch. I raised the nose slightly.

Suddenly the inside of the cabin seemed as quiet and still as the mist and the black trees above the mist. The light was the only live thing in the world, and it was just a dying ember. The speed slid down off the dial. The floats broke the surface of the mist. It foamed and rose and streamed away, suddenly moving, but sluggish, a dead thing in a tide. The mist climbed and shredded through the propeller. The light disappeared.

I was alone. I was falling. There was nothing. And I was inside it, part of it. I wanted to haul back, rear away, slam on the engine to hear something else besides me trying to escape from being nothing. I didn't want to die in the quiet.

Then there was light. A glow that was nowhere, too diffuse to be high or low, but growing fast, spreading outwards and at the same time hardening in the centre, high, too high. I jerked back on the yoke and it shuddered under my hands, on the brink of the stall. The light flared, close and dazzling in the mist, and beyond it little twinkling ripples. Suddenly the flat world snapped into place underneath me. I knew where I was.

Four feet up—too high. I jerked the yoke forward and back and the Beaver dropped a two-foot step in the air and the yoke shuddered again and I pulled back and she suddenly stopped flying and sagged with a splash into the water.

Mist swept over me. Nothingness, but a different nothingness, because I was on the earth again. The second light glowed, brightened, and drifted astern, a couple of yards to port. I let the Beaver wander to a stop.

We rocked gently in our own disturbance of the water. The engine made early morning coughing noises; it couldn't take much slow running. But for the moment, I liked the quiet.

Judd made a long breathing sound behind me. "Yes," he said. "Yes."

I said: "Welcome to Russia."

"Yes," he said again. Then, more cheerfully: "I had a nasty moment back there."

"You got it second hand, friend. I'd already squeezed it dry."

"Did you know you were going to lose the light like that?"

"Yes. I had to—if I was going to find it again in the right place."

"You must be as good as London said."

"They said I was good?"

"The best they'd known."

"Just lacking in moral fibre, though?"

He didn't say anything.

I said: "When you do too many trips like this, you begin to want to be sure the people who send you know what they're doing. You get intolerant of other people's mistakes. You could call that lacking moral fibre—if you're sitting behind a desk in London."

He didn't say anything to that, either. I pushed up the throttle, turned onto a bearing of about 310 degrees and trickled through mist in what I hoped was the direction of the shore.

The small peninsula suddenly loomed out on the starboard wingtip. I swerved away, then turned back to follow its shoreline. A flat grey beach grew out of the mist ahead. I cut the throttle. The port float bonged on a rock, but not hard enough to do more than put another dent in it.

"Now all we have to worry about is if it's a trap or not," I said. Judd was crouched by the open door, with his pistol in his hand.

"If there's more than one person, take off as fast as you can," he said.

"And you start shooting."

The rock had swung the Beaver side-on to the beach. It looked empty. Now I could see the thin dark blurs of the trees behind it. It was a dead, colourless world like the bottom of a lake, and the mist washed aimlessly through it like water.

The engine was turning over with loud smokers' cough. I felt cold and badly wanted the feel of a gun in my hands.

Then somebody walked out onto the beach.

Judd leaned forward, peering hard.

The figure on the beach shouted: "Judd—it's all right!"

Judd said: "Thank God." He scrambled up. "Can you beach her?"

"I don't want to leave marks. Find the rope and moor her." I switched off the engine and the world went very quiet.

Judd stepped down onto the float with the rope, wrapped it round the aft float strut, then stepped off into the water. It went up to his knees. Halfway to the shore, he turned and called at me.

I said: "Coming," then undid my straps and worked my way down to the back of the cabin.

CHAPTER 25

THEY were back at the trees tying up the end of the rope as I started to wade ashore. Then they moved down the beach towards me. I let them get well into the open and within fifteen yards, then brought my hands from behind my back.

"Just stand where you are, you bastards. I've got a 12-bore shotgun pointing at your middles."

They stopped.

I said: "Hands well up and drop any guns."

Judd said: "Now, Mr Cary—this is quite unnecessary."

"Of course it is; I'm doing this for fun. Now drop your gun, Judd."

"It's in my pocket."

"Get it out, then. I'm not worried. You've been waving that gun around all evening. Let's see you try and use it; let's have the bright line about shooting me if the question arises. Well, the question's arose. Come on—it's been a dull night so far."

Judd moved one hand slowly and pulled the gun very carefully from his pocket and dropped it at his feet.

"Absolutely splendid," I said. I waded ashore with the shotgun at the 'point,' looking just like the pictures of D-Day.

They were standing several feet apart. I waved them back without introducing myself to the new friend, then bent over to pick up Judd's gun.

Judd said: "What happens to us now?"

"You start walking. It's only 45 miles to the frontier."

The revolver was a Smith and Wesson, all right, and somebody had cut away the front of the trigger guard, to give a faster grab at the trigger. *That* was the sort of thing professionals did to guns—not fooling about filing off numbers. I broke the cylinder out one-handed, and caught a glint of light on five cartridges. Fully loaded. I snapped it shut again.

Judd said carefully: "I'm sure you don't really mean that."

"Don't I?" I lifted the S & W until both it and the shotgun were lined up on his belly. "You wrote the rules, Judd. You were going to shoot me if I didn't fly you. All I'm asking you to do is take a walk. You'll probably get away with it." I had the shotgun butt propped against my hip. All I had to do was pull on both trigger fingers and he'd get a load of bird-shot, a solid 12-bore slug and a .38 Special through him. After that, he'd be mostly a hole.

I came close to doing it.

Then I said softly: "You shouldn't do this, Judd—come barging in on people's lives, pointing guns at them. It gets them all nervy. They end up wanting to shoot somebody. They may even shoot somebody without really meaning to. There's a lot of killings been done by a gun or a knife without the man himself really wanting to do it."

He kept very still. I watched him carefully, and slowly the feeling wore off. "All right," I said. "All right—I'll fly you back. But never try guns on me again, Judd."

I had watched him too long. The other man suddenly threw himself forward. He wasn't jumping for me, though. He was widening the angle so that to shoot at him, I'd have to turn my back on Judd.

I whipped round, jerked both triggers on the shotgun, then dropped it and took a jump backwards, lifting the pistol. The other man was just a cloud of sand.

Judd was just starting to move.

The man shouted: "Don't shoot—don't shoot!" and the sand drifted away and left him kneeling with his arms spread sideways.

I jerked the pistol at Judd and he stopped. Then I swung it back to the second man. He had his head down and was shaking it angrily. Just in front of him, there was a long narrow trough scooped out of the beach. Then I realised he'd just got two eyefuls of sand from the shotgun blast.

I straightened up, walked across, and pushed him over backwards with my foot. He just lay there, his eyes shut and his face working as he tried to clear them.

He was a short, grey-haired man in a dark woodsman's jacket, rough trousers and woodsman's boots.

He said: "I should have known better than to try that on you, Bill."

He was the man I'd known as Hartmann.

It was very obvious and logical when you thought about it.

If I was the traitor on the Counterweight mission, then he must be the innocent party. So when he turned up again—probably with some brave story about having escaped from the *Abwehr* and walked the whole way home living on turnip tops—they'd welcomed him back. They hadn't told me, of course, but by then they wouldn't have told me the time by my own clock.

The only surprise was that he'd gone back to them. But probably he didn't until he'd heard how they bounced me. He'd have ways of finding that out.

And once you accepted all that, it was common sense to find him doing the same job for the same people in the same part of the world as eighteen years before.

"Do you mind if I rub my eyes?" he asked calmly.

"Go ahead. And you seem to have dropped a gun—" there was an automatic down by his feet "—If you feel like grabbing for that, I'd be happy to see you try. It would take you all the rest of your life."

He lay where he was and rubbed the heels of his hands into his eyes. "Thank you, no," he said. "I've already tested your reactions. The gun's all yours."

"Thank you." I kicked it away, picked it up, and threw it into the lake. Then I walked back to the shotgun, picked that up, and broke out the empty cartridges.

"To whom it may concern," I said, looking at Judd, "this shotgun is unloaded. So don't get killed trying to snatch it." I shut the gun with a snap. "Did you know who we were coming to pick up?"

Judd said: "Yes, but I didn't think it would help to tell you. I thought you might try to kill him."

"I still want to, friend. But first I want to hear what he's been doing these last few days."

"Oh, come now, Mr Cary. He's one of the Firm, you know. He's not going to talk just by your asking him. We'll be here all night."

Hartmann was up on his knees, still wiping his eyes, and staring experimentally at us. He had a tight, square face with a few more and deeper lines in it than I'd remembered eighteen years ago. But the voice was the same: he still dragged out his vowels and moved his lips too much ever to pass as a Briton—but he could pass as somebody from any one of a dozen present or past countries east of the Elbe. I hadn't an idea of what nationality he'd been born.

"All right," I said grimly. "I'll *tell* him what he's been

doing. And if he doesn't like it, he can always swallow his lethal pill."

Hartmann smiled briefly at me, and staggered onto his feet.

I said to Judd: "How did he get in here?"

Judd moved his shoulders slightly. "Walked, of course. Safest way."

"You really think he walked? You don't know this boy. He prefers flying. But he has a neat little way of stopping the pilot telling anybody where they've been: he arranges to kill him. So far he's managed it on at least two; the Luftwaffe man—and Oskar Adler."

Judd said: "That's nonsense, Mr Cary. Whoever killed Adler was obviously the same people that sabotaged my Auster. And that *couldn't* have been Mr—er, Hartmann. He was depending on me to get him out of here."

I said: "You don't know enough about sabotaging aircraft, Judd. *I* do—and so does he. We both learned it at the same Special Ops sabotage school, and at the same time. Knowing how to fix Oskar's flaps was a highly professional business; anybody who could do that wouldn't try anything as childish as filling your oil tank with petrol. Look at it that way round for a change. And remember I know Hartmann knows how to do these things.

"And I know Adler: I know he'd have taken the job on, if he was asked. He hadn't made much money this summer, and he couldn't have done any sovereign runs for Veikko since the spring. I know he was worried, too: he'd taken to wearing a gun that he didn't know much about. He must have heard about your firm and Koenig both coming up here. He was trying to make friends with Koenig's crowd; he'd try to make friends with your boy, too."

My voice was getting hoarse with breathing mist. It still sounded loud and pointless, like somebody preaching a sermon in an empty hall. But I wanted to get it said.

"But he'd still be worried," I said. "So when Mikko asked him for a job, he took him along for protection—or maybe as a witness, in case things went wrong. Mikko told him about my having a petrol store on my lake. Adler used some of it, on their flight into here. And Hartmann must have told you about the lake; must have left some message and a map in Rovaniemi. There's nobody else *could* have told you, Judd. And only Mikko could have told him, through Adler."

Judd said: "Quiet a moment."

I swung the pistol at him—but then I heard it, too. A faint, fast *whut-whut-whutting* out across the lake behind me. At first it sounded like a big, flabby, two-stroke outboard motor. Then I realised what it was, and I should have thought of it before. A helicopter.

The perfect search aircraft for this sort of weather. Maybe as fast as the Beaver was, but with none of the landing problems. If they saw anything, all they had to do was hover, lower a rope ladder into the mist, and send down a search party to sort us out.

It seemed to be moving fast across behind me. I didn't turn round, not with those two characters in front of me. I said: "Can you see it?"

Judd peered over my head. "I think so—yes. I think it's a Hound."

"A what?"

"MI-4. NATO code-name 'Hound.'"

"How many does it hold?" I was a bit out of date on my Russian aircraft.

"Sixteen or twenty, about."

Hartmann said: "It's going past."

Heading for a bunch of lakes to the north-east: we'd last been seen heading in their direction, and here we were on a direct line from Kandalaksha to them. But when they didn't find us there . . .

I said: "He'll be back."

Judd said: "Well, let's get going, then."

"You and me, yes," I said. "He stays."

"We can argue this out later," Judd said impatiently. "Let's just get back to Finland."

"Sorry. The Pilots' Union just voted him untouchable. He's killed too many."

He sighed. "Your sense of personal justice is showing again, Mr Cary."

"You just think about the timing, Judd. You've done a bit of walking in this sort of country yourself; you know how long it takes. We're two clear days' walk inside the frontier and it'd take him another day to walk from the nearest road to the frontier on the Finnish side. So if he's been here only a day—and I think he's been here two days—then he must have started four days ago. *Did he?*"

A red light suddenly flashed in the forest, rushed towards

me, bounced off a rock near the water and howled into the sky. Behind it, a rifle cracked.

By then I was flat on the beach trying to look a lot smaller than I felt and groping in my pockets for shotgun cartridges.

Judd was slower: finally he subsided into a big heap on the sand, breathing hard. Hartmann had dropped into a crouch but hadn't gone any further.

Judd said: "Get down, man."

Hartmann said: "I think it's all right—"

Judd said: "Lie down!"

Hartmann started to get up slowly, watching the trees.

I snapped the shotgun shut, got to my knees and swung it at his head. He flopped sideways and stayed there.

I shuffled the gun back into my shoulder, sighted it on a large piece of forest, and said: "Get behind me into the plane. I'll cover you."

"What about him?"

"The hell with him."

"We came to collect him. We can't—"

"*I* can. Get in the plane."

Instead, he started crawling across my line of fire to collect Hartmann. On that beach, outlined against the mist on the lake, crawling was nonsense. It just made you a slow target instead of a fast one.

I swore at Judd and rolled left, to get a clear line on the forest. The rifle flashed again and sand jumped by my left elbow. This time it wasn't a tracer bullet.

I marked the flash of the rifle but didn't shoot back. I had an odd idea that the man wasn't really trying—yet.

Judd had Hartmann by the back of the neck and was hauling him towards the water. They made a target a blind man couldn't have missed. The rifle flashed.

When I got my head up again, all I had was a load of sand in my hair.

I said: "Hold it, Judd. That character isn't trying. I think he's just pinning us down until somebody else gets here."

Judd grunted: "What makes you think so?"

Three misses made me think so. And a man who could put two shots within a few inches of my left elbow could have knocked me down with his first shot. Instead, he'd fired a tracer round that I couldn't have helped seeing—just like a shot across my bows. But Judd would probably have turned it into an interesting discussion.

I said: "Never mind. I'm going to try and knock him off before the someone else gets here."

"Is that a good idea?"

I nearly shot him.

Instead, I got the pistol out of my pocket, fired two careful shots into the forest at where I thought the rifleman was, and then ran.

I ran diagonally to my left, up and across the beach, to hit the trees out of line with the rifle. I wanted to get away from that background of mist.

I crunched off the sand in between two trees, trampled a lot of grass and moss and small bushes, and arrived at a rock of my own height. I was about ten yards in from the beach. I leant against it and started to collect my breath and my hearing.

The forest began to creep in on me.

CHAPTER 26

IT WASN'T one of those tall, dark cathedral-like forests; no northern forest is. The trees were small and thin and sparse, and didn't stop much of the dim, misty light from the low clouds overhead. The mist itself had pretty well stopped at the edge of the forest; all that was left was a faint blurriness and weird bottom-of-the-sea light that had no source and left no shadows and faded off not into darkness but uncertainty.

What worried me a lot more than the light was the ground itself: nobody had ever touched this forest. The floor was thousands of years of rotted branches, and bracken and bushes and great sponges of moss. And rocks.

Rocks anything up to the size of small cars and bigger, half sunk in the ground and coated with moss or lichens. You would see a man stand up thirty yards away, in this light, but he might not stand up; he might be sitting on the other side of the rock you're leaning against. Or in a deep little gulley cut by thousands of years of melting snow, just where you're going to put your foot.

I slid carefully down the side of my rock until I was flat on the ground. The forest seemed to be breathing on the back of my neck.

This is some of the worst fighting country in the world:

ask any Finn or Russian or German who tried fighting over it. Now it was my turn.

I wouldn't have minded a bit of real mist: it might throw his aim off, and with a rifle he needed to be accurate. The shotgun gave me a bit more scope.

That reminded me. I broke the shotgun gently open, pried out the solid round cartridge, and pushed in another dose of birdshot. Then I eased myself forward out of the protection of the rock and started working deeper into the forest. If anybody got outlined against that lake mist, I wanted it to be him.

I made about five yards in five minutes, and every time I put down an elbow or knee it sounded like a pane of glass shattering. At least to me. You could hear a lot more than you could see in that forest. The rifleman hadn't fired again. As I judged it, he had been about twenty-five yards to my right and, by now, about on my level. Except that he probably wasn't there by now. He would have moved, too. He certainly wouldn't sit there and be outflanked. And he'd know a lot more about moving around in these woods than I did. He'd be moving twice as fast and hardly making a sound. . . .

I lowered myself flat, sweating and trying to look fifteen ways at once. I was up against a seven-fingered troll with feet as soft as snowflakes and three eyes that could see in the dark. All I could do was get up and run and run. . . .

I dragged myself back from the edge of panic, hand over hand, and let my breathing calm down. I was sane again, but I'd lost any belief that I knew where the rifleman was. After I'd got into the forest, he'd certainly have moved—either deeper in, to catch me head-on, or coming across to creep up behind me. Either way, I had to change my line of advance. He'd expect me to keep going or turn to my right. So I had to go back or turn left.

I turned left; going back meant going towards the lake. I made a couple of easy yards across soft moss, then ran up against a waist-high rock. Going round would take me through a bush or the skeleton of a dead tree, and there wasn't any quiet way of doing either. So it had to be over.

I turned my head and watched the forest behind me carefully. From my level I couldn't see much, but nothing I could see was moving. I reached up and laid the shotgun on top of the rock, then slid myself after it.

A bullet screamed off the rock by my knee. I grabbed the gun and went over the far side of the rock like a waterfall, and hit the ground rolling. That time, he'd really been trying.

There was a slight slope to the ground and I didn't try to stop myself rolling down it, taking the undergrowth as I found it. It made a noise like an avalanche, but he wouldn't hear it or anything else for a few seconds after loosing off that rifle within a few inches of his ear.

The flash had come from almost directly into the forest from me, about twenty-five yards away.

I crashed against another dead tree, crawled quickly round it, turned right—towards the deep forest—just because there seemed to be more cover that way, and scuttled up into the shelter of another rock.

I'd made a good fifteen yards and I didn't think he'd seen any of it; I knew he couldn't have heard it. But earlier he'd made at least forty yards with me both watching and listening and I hadn't known a thing about it. I peered out round my rock and started examining where I thought he'd fired from. I took a small piece of ground at a time, and searched it as well as the light allowed. At least I'd done *that* sort of thing before, quartering the sky for enemy aircraft.

Somewhere deeper in the wood, a bird squawked like a creaking hinge and nearly got itself shot at. I calmed down and went back to searching.

Slowly, the forest started to creep up and breathe down my neck again. I could see a dozen things I couldn't explain that could be him—sitting, kneeling, leaning against a tree. But none of them moved.

I was beginning to understand the Scandinavian legends of trolls and *tontut* and *taikuri*. Get into that quiet, worn forest and look around and you start seeing things that couldn't just have happened that way. Somebody must have carved the rocks to that shape, twisted those trees just that way. And you never feel lonely. There are always the eyes that you never quite see.

He must have gone by now. He must be crawling, quiet as a puff of smoke, another forty yards, to come up behind me. I could feel the rifle barrel lining up on the back of my neck. . . .

Then he moved. He was the same distance from me, and only a few yards from the centre-point of my search. With the slope of the ground, he was up-slope from me; all I saw was a blurred small shape slide from one tree-trunk to the next.

But suddenly the eyes weren't watching me any more. I was the watcher; I was behind the eyes.

I lined up on the base of the tree and waited. Firing uphill gave me the worst of it, but with this customer I had to take every chance he gave me. I might never see him again.

He took his time. He must have lost me and was moving only a few feet at a time, then stopping to see if his new position had opened up a view of me.

Then he moved again. I fired both barrels, then jerked back behind the rock to reload while I was too dazzled and deafened to do anything else. When I poked out half my head again, it was on the other side of the rock. Nothing moved.

I was a damn fool. I should have worked out a new firing position and jumped for it while he was still wondering if he was dead. By now he was loking for me again, and I was still where he thought I was.

The watched feeling began to seep back.

Then he called: "I'd hoped you'd have some of your solid rounds with you, sir!"

After what seemed like a long time I said: "What the hell are you doing here, Homer?"

Then I thought of a better question: "You mean you *knew* it was me here?" The bastard had been shooting to kill, after all.

There was a pause. Then he called: "I'm sorry, sir! You put me in a slightly difficult position. I certainly didn't expect it to be you, sir. But I gave my word to Mr Hartmann to give him protection on this mission—and down on the beach you did seem to be threatening him!"

"Threaten him?" I yelled. "I'm going to blow his head off!"

Not the brightest thing to say, in the circumstances.

I saw Hartmann's point, all right. If he could recruit Homer and bring him over as a bodyguard, he'd have collected a very useful man. And he must have met him down on my lake, when Oskar was pinching my petrol.

But I couldn't see how Homer had got himself in the market for being recruited.

"All right!" I said. "All right! But Hartmann's just a cheap crook. He killed the two people who brought you here—sabotaged their plane. He's the one who killed the German pilot down in the lake. So let's just forget the whole damn thing and get home before the Russians catch us all!"

From down on the beach, Hartmann shouted: "You kill him, Homer! He'll kill me as soon as he gets the chance!"

I rolled over and let go both barrels at the beach. I'd forgotten they'd be able to hear every word we said up there. They weren't more than fifty yards away.

I boke open the gun and dumped the empty cartridges.

"Homer!" I called. "Are you ready to pack up and go home?"

He said: "I'm sorry, sir. I gave my word!"

"You're crazy!" I shouted.

A bullet smashed into the undergrowth a few inches from the edge of my rock.

I knew it then. He *was* crazy; barmy as a box of birds. Maybe every full-time big-game hunter is a bit eleven-to-the-dozen; maybe you have to be to spend your life getting close to dangerous animals just to prove you can kill them before they kill you. He'd said *The whole sport with dangerous game is in getting up close.* And he'd practically given me the rest of the story on a plate. He'd worked his way through all the dangerous game, making his point with each one. Not tried to get the record score with any one: just proved he could face it and kill it. Now he'd finished his list: after the European brown bear, there was nothing.

Except the most dangerous game of all: another man with a gun.

That was why he'd come with Hartmann—he'd probably asked to come, once he knew what was going on. And all that fancy shooting had simply been an invitation to come up and shoot it out in the forest. And I'd gone.

His sister must have known all about him. The estate could have waited weeks or months, but she'd wanted to get him home *now*. Maybe she had the same list that he had, ticking off the ones he shot, one by one, and knowing as well as he did—probably well before he did—what was the last one on the list.

Me.

He was sorry it had to be me, of course—but he'd given his word like a Virginia gentleman, and that was that. And now we could get on with a good clean sportin' contest; him with his stalking skill and experience with a rifle—me with my military training and experience under fire. Perfectly matched. May the best man win.

I was getting angry now, with a cold, hard anger. The
forest had stopped having eyes; that was for the fairy tales.
It was just a piece of fighting country, a mass of good or bad
cover, good firing lines and bad ones.

*All right, Homer. A man with a gun IS the most dangerous
game you can meet—and I'm that man. Not a set of big
teeth twenty yards away, but a bullet that can take off the
top of your head before you can blink. Think about that,
chum; let it sink right in. Forget all about spoors and keeping
down-wind and sticking to the code. Tigers and bears don't
stick to a code, Homer; they just do the best they can. Had
you thought of that? Now you're going to find out what a
man can do. Now you're up against the real killer. Think
about getting shot, Homer; let's see if I can MAKE you think
of it.*

I snapped the gun shut on two solid rounds, crawled to
the other side of the rock, fired one at where I thought he
was, reloaded, fired again. Reloaded and fired again. He'd
wanted to know what he'd be like under fire; now he could
find out. It's worse than you expect.

I reloaded and fired another. If I could panic him into
doing something, I wanted to have a second shot in reserve.

It didn't work. If he was still there, he didn't move and he
didn't fire.

Finally I reloaded, fired off both barrels so that he'd know
the shotgun was empty—and then grabbed up the pistol. He
wouldn't be expecting that.

That didn't work, either.

Now I had to think up something else.

I wanted him to fire before I made a move: then I'd know
where he was, and he'd have deafened himself. By now I
was so deaf myself that he could be singing Lapp bear-
hunting songs up there and I wouldn't know.

I reloaded both barrels with birdshot; if he liked to think
he was in more danger from solid rounds, I'd been happy to
oblige him. But for real work on a misty night I wanted the
spread of birdshot. I wasn't trying for the clean kill that the
code demands. Any sort of hit would suit me.

Now I wanted to move left. Which way would he move?
He'd been moving to my right the last time. Now he knew I
knew that, would be change, or was there such good cover
to the right that he couldn't resist it? And what did he think
I was going to do?

You can think yourself into paralysis like that. In the end, the only thing to do is move the way you want to. I wanted to move left, and then ahead, to try and get level with him or above. His advantage of high ground gave him too many odds.

But first I wanted him to shoot. There was a four-foot gap between two clumps of bracken just a few feet left of my rock, and he'd see me pass that. I reckoned it would take him four seconds to work the bolt and take a good aim again, and I'd be past the gap in that time.

I stood up, trod on a dead branch—deliberately—and threw myself flat to the right. He didn't fire—but I hadn't expected him to, that time. He would the next.

I jumped up and back to my left, into the shelter of the rock. The rifle flashed and banged somewhere left and ahead —he'd moved again—as I went down. Then I was scrambling on hands and knees across the gap and down behind the bracken.

He fired again, into the bracken, and I took off again, moving fast. He couldn't hear me now. The snag was, he'd hit me.

I didn't yet know how badly. His last shot had thumped me just above my right hip, and it was still numb. The pain would come later; then I might be screaming for help, or just quietly bleeding to death. Meanwhile, I had to keep moving. Luckily a .300 Magnum is far too powerful to have much stopping power. A slower, heavier bullet would have knocked me on my back.

I smashed through a screen of small bushes and bracken, headed uphill for a couple of yards in the shelter of another big rock, then turned left again and fell into a gulley. And that was as far as I felt like going.

It was about two feet deep and a bit wider than I was, and the bottom was wet sand. It ran diagonal to the lake shore, from somewhere up on my right to somewhere down on my left. More important, it was the best bit of cover from both view and fire that I'd met since the last rock.

I eased over on my left side and felt down along my right ribs. The leather jacket was torn just above the hip, and— thank God—torn in two places. That meant I hadn't still got a bullet in me—although I hadn't really expected a .300 Magnum to stay in my body. I unzipped the jacket and felt carefully along just above my belt. The shirt was ripped and wet and sticky. I probed carefully—and suddenly that hurt, all right. I shoved my left sleeve into my mouth and went on probing.

A sudden gush of water coming down the gulley splashed in my face. I managed not to cough and went on picking torn bits of shirt out of a four-inch gash just below my ribs. I wasn't going to die of it, but I wasn't going to throw any right-hand punches, either. When I tried to lift my right shoulder it felt like a hot iron along my ribs. I rammed a fairly clean handkerchief into the gash but couldn't do anything to keep it in place except zip up my jacket again.

But now, with all the attention I'd been giving myself, I hadn't an idea where Homer was. Except that he was still above me somewhere.

Another gush of water hit me under the nose, and stayed in a pool in front of my face. I realised I was acting as a dam, and leant over on my left elbow. The water drained away— the little bit that didn't soak into my trousers and boots, anyway.

I wondered dully what the water was doing coming down in gushes; it should be a steady trickle. Something blocking it and then getting out of the way. Animal of some sort . . .

Then I knew where Homer was. Parked higher up in the same gulley and doing the same as me: letting the water build up against him, then rolling aside to let it flow past.

I rolled carefully on my left side and started working my way up the gulley. It was slow work: left elbow, right foot, reach with my elbow, shove with my foot. Holding the gun by the barrels in my left hand and letting my right hand ride as a passenger. Even so, I managed to get it wrong every other move and collected the red-hot feeling again. I hadn't moved five yards before I was sweating cold all over except on my right hip, where I seemed to be sweating hot. I knew I was losing blood.

But for the first time I knew where Homer was, and was moving towards him silently. The wet sand in the gulley made no sound.

More gushes of water bounced in my face. I worked on up, reach with the elbow, shove with the foot. There were rocks sticking out into the gulley and I had to ease round them smooth and quiet like a young lizard. Except that I was a tired, lame old dinosaur. I kept my head down and watched the coarse, gritty sand creep past my nose. I just didn't want to look at anything that needed effort. There was a pulsing in my ears that was nothing to do with the last shot I'd fired. Just my heart, pumping blood out over my hip.

Why should that worry Bill Cary? He can climb cliffs with his teeth, and him shot full of holes like a colander. The original iron man, he used to be, back in the old SIS days. Give him a Sten gun and a course to fly and he'd roll back with the plans of the fort in the morning. Good old Bill Cary. He'd fly an aeroplane with one hand and the other tucked away in his pocket for the surgeon to sew on again.

That stopped me. The noise in my ears was the tramping of a Guards battalion and my wound wasn't hurting enough. My whole body was getting numb. I hadn't even looked up for yards. I'd just crawled, looking no more than one elbow reach ahead. And after all this, I still had to fly the Beaver out of Russia.

I lay gently down in the gulley and pressed my face against the hard, wet sand. I didn't know whether I'd gone fifteen, twenty or twenty-five yards in all. I knew I'd gone far enough. Maybe too far. Now all I wanted to do was sleep.

The water woke me. It splashed and flooded over my face. I lay there and drank it, let it flow into my mouth and then swallowed. It was ice in the desert sun. The battalion in my ears marched on and away. I knew about the gulley and the forest around me. I was ready again. But I also knew I couldn't go on. Whatever I did, it had to be done from here. I twisted up the right side of my body to try and shut the wound, and was happy when it hurt again. I had lost the numbness. I lifted my head slowly and looked and listened around.

Then I realised that not all the noise had been in my head. Far off to my left there was the throbbing of the helicopter —searching the long, thin lake, probably. We'd be next. There wasn't anything more I could do about it.

I was just a few feet before a small step in the gulley, made by a ledge of rock. Beyond it, the gulley bent to my left, then—I thought—bent back again. Seven or eight yards beyond it, there was a jumble of big rocks.

I studied them carefully. They stuck up eight or ten feet and were split and weathered into big ramparts facing slightly off to my right. And they weren't just a line, but a clump; I could see a couple more pinnacles sticking up behind them. It was a square or circle or just jumble of rocks about thirty feet across.

The gulley flowed probably through the middle of it, and out on my left. And that was where Homer had to be.

He'd known enough not to get up in the ramparts where he might get outlined against the sky and where there was rock on both sides to ricochet any solid rounds I fired. He must have stayed down at the near corner of the rocks, with a rock wall to give him cover on one side, and in the gulley to give him cover from the other. He was vulnerable from behind—but he knew I couldn't be behind him yet. And he was trusting his eyes and rifle in front.

Not a misplaced trust.

Now, either I crawled left or right to work round behind him, with all the din that fifty yards crawling through that undergrowth involved—or I crawled on ahead and straight up his gun barrel. Only I wasn't going to crawl anywhere. I couldn't. We were going to have to shoot it out here.

I could manage the ledge of rock in front of me. I reached with an elbow, shoved with a foot—and got a scream of pain from my wound. I felt the blood start to flow again. But I reached the ledge.

I leant the shotgun across it, the muzzles as high as I dared to keep them away from the gushes of water, and hauled the Smith and Wesson into my left hand. As far as I could remember, it had had a light, easy action. It should have: anyone who'd gone to the trouble of filing off the trigger guard would also have done some tuning on the trigger. The factories send them out with a very stiff pull.

I just hoped they'd tuned it enough. The shrouded hammer had only a knurled knob showing. I stuffed the gun inside my jacket and thumbed the hammer back onto full cock. It went back with a click that sounded to me like the Bell of Doom but probably couldn't be heard three feet away. I rolled onto my right side, waited until the pain had died down, and then threw the pistol, over-arm like a hand grenade, into the middle of the rocks. Then I grabbed the shotgun.

The pistol went off. With a clatter and a bang and a flash that lit the whole fort of rocks. And because it had been behind him, Homer jumped.

He'd been further back than I'd guessed, just behind the edge of the first rock, and he leapt clear out and twisted as he leapt, ending sitting on the edge of the gulley with his rifle pointing at the pistol flash and his back almost to me.

So I shot him in the back, twice.

The ages passed. The sound rang and echoed and faded in my head. The flash dwindled to a misty red flare on my eyes. I lifted my head off the cool metal of the gun barrels and looked towards the rocks.

There was nothing to see, nothing to hear except the *whut-whut-whut* of the helicopter, closer now. So now I should reload and crawl up cautiously, just like the book says. But I was past that, and I knew it was all over anyway. I used the gun as a catch to get myself upright. The forest went dizzy, then settled down. I walked stiffly up the gulley to the rocks.

He was lying with his knees in the gulley and his face flat on the ground by the rock on the far side. Between his shoulders, his hunting jacket was a mass of small punctures, some of them growing stained. I sat down beside him, reached and twisted him over. He rolled and fell on his back in the gulley. The water trickled down past him, trailing out his hair.

After a while he opened his eyes and asked huskily: "You threw a pistol, did you, sir?"

I nodded, then realised he probably couldn't see, and said: "Yes."

He said: "Ah. I wasn't expecting that from—you, sir."

"There aren't any rules," I said. "Not in this game."

He closed his eyes again and just lay there. Then he asked: "Did I—hit you—at all?"

"Your last shot, after I crossed the gap. Got me just above the hip."

"I thought—so." His voice was tired and thick. "I hope— you'll be all right, sir."

"Sure to be." Gradually I was getting dragged into his polite, crazy dream.

"I managed—under fire—I think, sir."

"You did fine."

He paused.

Then: "Without the—the pistol—would I—have killed you?" His baby face fought the words out.

I said: "Yes." And for all I know, it was true.

He tried to smile, and, in the middle of trying, died. Perhaps, by his rules, he'd won.

The helicopter throbbed beyond the trees.

CHAPTER 27

IT TOOK me ten minutes to cover the sixty yards back to the beach, using the shotgun as a walking stick in my right hand, and carrying the pistol in my left. It had two rounds left in it, and nothing had got broken when it hit the rocks.

The mist was thinning slightly; there must be a wind getting up. It had to wait until now, of course. Still, it would making landing back at my private lake easier—if it didn't thin so much as to give us away to the helicopter. At the moment, he could only see us from directly overhead.

The shape of the Beaver hardened by the shore, then two figures beside it. I waved the pistol at them.

Hartmann said: "So you got him. I didn't think you could do it."

"You're always making mistakes about me," I said.

Judd said impatiently: "We've got to get going; the helicopter'll be back any minute."

I leant on the shotgun and bent an ear towards the fast heartbeat in the sky. If anything, it seemed to be fading.

"He's doing that long lake we came over," I said. "He's come down one side, now he's going back up the other."

"He'll be down again in a minute. We've got to move."

From somewhere, they'd raked up a couple of old metal cases that looked like big deed boxes. By now they were battered and streaked with rust and with some of the corners eaten away.

Suddenly I felt cold and wet and shivery. I sat down heavily on one of the boxes.

Judd said: "He hit you."

"That's right." I waved the pistol. "Go back the way I came. You'll come across a gulley; go up it. He's in it, near some big rocks. Bring him down here. I'm taking him home."

Judd said: "Look, you don't need to do . . ." Then he saw the way me and the pistol were looking at him, and went away.

I laid the pistol back along my knee. I was limp and a bit distant; the shock of the wound was wearing on as the shock of the gunfight wore off. The mist was a quiet, cosy cave to hide in. The helicopter had faded. Behind me was just the gentle gnawing of the lake on the beach.

Hartmann asked gently: "Can I help? Is there a first-aid kit in the plane?"

Sure he could help. I couldn't stop him helping. He took a tentative step towards me and his face was twisted in true concern for my pain. He took another step. Let him. I was too tired. I was giving up. Let somebody else take the decisions.

He took another step. I lifted the pistol and leered at him through the mist. "How were you thinking of helping, chum? Grabbing the gun and putting me out of my misery?"

He had stopped, just out of reach. "You won't last the night," he said coldly.

"Don't rush your luck. You may not last it yourself."

"I never tried to kill you, Bill," he said quietly. "You won't kill me just in cold blood."

"What d'you think I was doing up in the forest?"

"He was shooting at you. That makes a difference."

"I'll lend you the shotgun. You can walk away, turn and fire when you like. I'll keep the pistol by my side until you turn. How's that?"

He thought the idea over carefully, studying me, then the shotgun by my feet.

He said suddenly: "The gun isn't loaded."

I nodded. "That's right."

He relaxed a little. "You weren't going to do it."

"Perhaps not. But *you* were."

He pulled the other box a few feet away and sat down on it. Then he said: "You're going to make me walk home?"

"Something like that."

He leaned forward. "Look, Bill—I know I've caused a lot of trouble for you in the past. But there was a reason. Now I'm in a position to help you. I'll buy a passage on the plane. I mean real money—big money."

I seemed to have played this scene before. "What d'you call big money?" I asked.

"Ten thousand pounds."

"You haven't got ten thousand."

"I have now."

I stood up. "Get up and open that box," I told him.

"Don't be crazy, Bill. Get your plane started."

"Open it up."

He was on his feet now. "You're mad, Bill."

"Open it!"

He spread his arms in a hopeless gesture, then stab-kicked

at the lid of the box. At the second kick the lid jerked loose.

I walked across and lifted the lid of the box with my toe;
it grated, then flopped over and came away at one hinge.

Inside was a mixture of bits of rock, some with smudged
old labels wired to them, bundles of mouldering papers,
small tins and jars and a few Lapp ornaments. Keeping half
an eye on Hartmann, I bent down and picked one up.

It was a rough circle about three inches across, punched
with a few holes, dents and scratches in a simple pattern.
It belonged hanging down the side of a Lapp *shaman's* magic
drum. So?

Stones clinked behind my back. It was Judd, carrying
Homer's body slung across his shoulder: a huge, shapeless
figure trudging heavily through the mist. He turned and laid
Homer down carefully a few yards away, then came over.
He was breathing heavily, but nothing more.

"Throw me your lighter," I said.

He looked surprised, but brought it out and tossed it across.
I picked it up and flicked it and held it near the drum ornament. The metal was rough and greyish, with a few streaks
of rust. I turned it over. The back had a series of fine
scratches on it. After a moment I realised they were Cyrillic
letters.

From Mountain of the Ulda it said in Russian: *Fe, Cu,
Ni.   1910*

I shut the lighter.

"Well, well, well," I said. "So now the SIS goes on treasure
hunts."

Judd said sharply: "What d'you mean?"

I tapped the box with my foot. "Take a look in there. Tell
me if it's what you expected him to bring back."

Judd peered at it, then leant down and fumbled around.
Then he stood up. "No," he said. "I don't think it is what we
expected." He looked at Hartmann, then me. "Just what is it?"

I said: "I rather think it's the Volkof treasure."

Judd said: "I thought that was just a legend."

"So did I. I used to say it was impossible because Volkof
was an engineer—a bourgeois—who wouldn't *have* a treasure: jewels and gold and so on. But nobody bothered to find
out what *sort* of engineer he was. Answer: he was a mining
engineer. This would be his treasure: rock samples."

Judd looked into the box again. "Would it be worth anything?"

"Hartmann thinks so: it's what he's been looking for all these years. I get the reason for it now—why he made the deal with the Germans to get in here in 1944, then scuppered them to go off on a private treasure hunt. But he must have missed it then. So now, when he's got better information, he gets you to send him back. He must be pretty grateful for all the SIS help he's had over this time.

"But I'd still like to know how he knew it had never come into Finland, even," I added.

Judd said: "That's easy. His real name's Volkof."

I said slowly: "Well, I'm damned."

Judd said: "I suppose it was never in the legend that there was a child with her when she got out. He was it."

"Well, I'm damned," I said again.

Judd looked at Hartmann. "No, not quite what we'd expected," he said. Then he turned back to me. "We'd still better be getting out of here. Shall I get Homer on board?"

"Yes," I said. "Yes—you do that."

He trudged off.

After a moment, Hartmann-Volkof said quietly: "You see what I was talking about, Bill? There's some good stuff in those boxes. My father lived in Lapland—in Kuolojärvi and Ivalo—for twenty-five years while it was a Russian province. He surveyed the whole of Eastern Lapland—he must have found a lot of deposits that haven't been found since."

I nodded. I was remembering the Kaaja company telling me of the mining engineer who'd explored south-east Lapland "many years ago" and most of whose reports were lost, but the one saying nickel near the Kemijoki valley.

Volkof-Hartmann said: "We'll halve whatever you can get for this stuff from the mining companies. Okay?"

I shook my head slowly. "What about Oskar Adler, or Mikko Eskola, or the boy who got killed coming to pick you up in 1944? What do we pay them for their help?"

He waved a hand. "Don't be childish, Bill. Are you on?"

"No," I said.

A rifle banged behind me. I wrenched around and went to my knees with the pistol up.

Judd said: "No, not you," and lowered the rifle and walked past me to where Hartmann-Volkof was lying spread out. He leant down and peered carefully, then turned back to me. "You forgot about this. You ought to have thrown it away." Then he just handed me Homer's .300 Magnum.

I took it with my right, leaving my mouth open for the mist to walk in.

Then I asked: "You get a sudden attack of personal justice?"

"No." He sounded surprised. "No—he'd been cheating the Firm. It would be very bad for us to let him get away with that. I think London will back me up."

"Probably they will."

The beat of the helicopter sounded through the mist, coming fast now, with a new sense of purpose. Running down the middle of the thin lake to start searching our one.

Judd said: "Now all we have to do is get out of here. Can you out-run a helicopter?"

"What's his top speed?"

"About 130 miles an hour."

"I can beat it." Not by much; the margin would be only about 12 knots. And that meant he could tag along, keeping me in sight for quite a distance—and shouing out my position and heading the whole time over the radio. Without him I could dodge the radar until we were within a few minutes of the frontier.

"Get the treasure in," I said, "and we'll get off." I stuffed the pistol in my pocket and picked up the shotgun.

"We've wasted enough time."

"Get it on board, Judd." I waded out to the Beaver, threw the guns in the back, and hauled myself on board. Homer was lying huddled on the floor by the drop hatch.

I sat down, then changed my mind and moved over into the right-hand seat, where my left hand could do all the work with the throttles and pitch and flap levers.

Judd splashed out with the first box, dumped it through the passenger door, and started to say something. Then the helicopter noise changed suddenly. A deep *thud* as the rotor blades hit the air on a changed angle, then a quicker, nervous beat as it slowed to start searching.

Judd dropped into the water and galloped at the beach.

I unpinned the control yoke, swung it over to the right-hand seat, pinned it solid again. Master switch *on*. I positioned the throttle and pitch.

Judd slammed the second box down on the floor, then hauled himself in. The Beaver swayed. The beating of the helicopter seemed to shiver the mist around us.

"I cast us off," he gasped. "Get going."

"Let's hold on a minute."

He bounced down into his seat. "Get started!"

"I've been thinking, Judd. He's going to see us now, anyway—"

"Then what? Are you planning to buy your way out by giving them me? Maybe I shot the wrong man, after all." He started to scramble aft and I knew he was going for the rifle.

"Sit down, Judd." The dark shape of the helicopter slid overhead and the rotors speeded up as it slowed to a hover. The mist boiled around us in the downwash.

"He's seen us now!" Judd shouted.

"I know. I just don't want him following me, giving away our course."

The thin muzzle of Homer's rifle poked over my shoulder. "Get her *started*!" Judd said in my ear.

I said: "He'll drop a rope ladder and send people down. When they're halfway down—off we go. He'll be paralysed."

For a while there was nothing but the pounding of the helicopter above us and waves of mist whisking away and back.

"And if he starts shooting instead?" Judd asked grimly.

"Then I'll have been wrong. But he thinks the plane's still empty. Our propeller isn't turning."

"I noticed." Then the muzzle lifted away. "Do you *often* get ideas like this?"

The helicopter slid away a few yards to stand over the beach. I leant across with my left hand and put on the booster pump and boost coil.

Judd said: "There's a ladder. There's somebody climbing out."

I pressed down the starter switch. The propeller jerked, the engine hiccuped, fired, missed, fired again and caught. The water flickered with blue flame from the exhaust.

As gently as I could manage I pushed the throttle up to full, then jabbed on left rudder and swung slowly south. She hated going from cold to full power and I wasn't getting the best she could do. But fifteen seconds later we climbed out of the mist, flattened out on top of it, swung round a clump of gaunt pines and headed north-west with the speed building up.

After a couple of minutes Judd said: "I can't see him at all." He settled back in his seat. "I'm sorry I got worked up back then. I suppose in the war you got quite used to cutting things close."

"You don't get used it to. What about Hartmann?—they'll find him."

"That won't tell them anything. He wouldn't have anything on him to identify him as one of us. He was a very competent man, you know."

I said: "Yes, I know."

They probably put fighters up, but I went out on a different route. I kept going north-west for just over twenty miles, until we hit the railway I'd avoided on the way in. Then I turned gradually west, running along beside high ground, with the third radar station—the one that hadn't seen us at all on the way in—hitting us every time round but not knowing we were there. Finally there was high ground that I had to climb over and he caught us. But by then we were on the frontier, thirty miles north of where we'd crossed it on the way in.

I reached my private lake at half past two.

CHAPTER 28

I TOOK a noisy swing over the cabin before I landed. Then I ran the Beaver up onto the beach and supervised Judd pouring the last of the petrol into the tanks.

Then I sat down on one of the floats and just waited.

After a while, Judd asked: "Where are you going now?"

"Norway or Sweden."

He thought about something for a moment, then said: "When we thought we'd be using the Auster, we arranged to end up in Norway. NATO power, and all that; we thought it would be better. We never cancelled it. Some friends should have been waiting for us in Kirkenes since about midnight. Would you accept our hospitality?"

I remembered how I'd thought of trying the NATO line for myself in Kirkenes, and smiled. And now, just by committing a few more crimes, I'd made myself a lot safer from extradition.

"I'll take it," I said. "We'll get off before it's light."

"Do you feel fit enough?"

"I can make it." My right side was one big ache, shot through with sharp pains whenever I stretched it, but I was hardly losing any more blood.

Judd said: "I give you my word: I had no idea Homer was going to be there."

I nodded. Mrs Beekman hurried out onto the beach.

I watched her come towards me: a small, white hurrying figure. Then I could see her face and her smile and I wanted to reach out for her. But she was further away than she knew.

I stood up and said quietly to Judd: "Stay out of this. This is my problem."

She stopped a few feet away and waited for me to come to her. I stayed where I was.

Her smile became a grin. "So you made it. I guessed you could. Are you all right?"

Judd said: "He got a bit shot."

She lost the grin and took a step towards me.

I said fiercely: "Shut up, Judd." Then, to her: "I got slightly wounded. By your brother. I killed him."

She was stone and ice. She just stood, and looked at me, and her face said nothing. It was the way she'd have to take it. For her, there couldn't be any other way. And for me, there was nothing.

Then she lifted her chin and asked quietly: "Did you know he was going to be there?"

"No. He'd got taken over as bodyguard by the man we were supposed to pick up. The whole thing turned out a mess, and I had to shoot it out with him. I brought him back."

She said: "I guess he'd have taken it on. You know why I wanted him back now. Maybe I should have told you before."

"It wouldn't have done much good. Not by then."

"There wasn't anything else you could have . . . ?" Her voice had a sudden desperate edge as she grabbed for the might-have-been. Then she shook her head. "No," she said quietly. "I guess it was inevitable."

"In a way. Because he wanted to shoot it out with someone. Because I was there. Because I was good with a gun. That sort of inevitable. None of it need have happened."

"I'm sorry it had to be you, Bill."

"If it hadn't been me, he'd probably still be alive."

She stared at me. "He was the gifted amateur," she said softly, "and you were the old pro. Was that it?"

Judd started to say something. I said: "Yes. That was it."

After a moment she asked: "Why did you bring him back?"

"Because . . . I just didn't want to leave him there."

"Can you bury him here?"

"Of course." I waited but she didn't say anything more, so I went back to the Beaver to find something to dig with.

We buried him in a patch of mossy ground on the far side of the lake. When we were ready to start shovelling earth in on him, I turned round to suggest she needn't watch. Instead, she handed me the .300 Magnum.

"Give him this. He'd—he'd want it."

I took it, then opened it and checked the magazine. There were only three in it. I knelt and dug two more rounds out of his pocket, put them in, then laid it down beside him fully loaded.

He'd got us living his dream right to the end and then a bit beyond it, out into the happy hunting grounds themselves. But I'd still liked him a lot more than a lot of people who hadn't tried to kill me nearly so carefully.

She said: "Thank you."

When I looked round again, she was standing there with her chin up and tears moving slowly down her face. And nothing I could do for her any more than for her brother now. I watched her cry silently in the quiet, lonely forest.

We flew out at just after half past four, and there was a smokey yellow light in the east when I ran up onto a beach on Lake Inari, just south of Inari itself. Mrs Beekman climbed down without my help.

"There's a tourist hotel just left of the main road, this side of the river," I told her. "They'll give you breakfast and fix a taxi back to Ivalo."

She looked up at me; I was still sitting in the co-pilot's seat. "What d'you want me to tell Nikkanen?" she asked.

"Anything you want to. I don't suppose he'll ever see me again."

She said steadily: "Officially, you'll be the last person who saw my brother. When it comes out he's vanished, you'll be suspected."

I nodded. I hadn't quite got around to thinking out that end of it.

She said: "You took me there, and I saw him. He told us he was going on a hunting trip. In a few days' time, when I go back, he won't be there. Nobody'll know until then—and I saw him as late as you did."

"You don't have to go back," I said angrily. "We can think up something else."

She shook her head. "This is the only way. They'll decide a bear got him."

They would, too—with her word behind it. Without it, Nikkanen could keep a suspicion of murder on the files for years, ready for a fast draw whenever I got in range.

She smiled gently. "I know how it was, Bill. If it hadn't been you, it would have been somebody else—and the somebody would have got killed. And after that, somebody else. And so on—until he met somebody like you. It had to happen."

"Somebody like us," I said slowly. "Of course. It had to happen."

"You said it wouldn't work—anyway. And I still don't hate anything." Her chin was still up. "Good-bye, Bill."

I nodded. I'd said it wouldn't work—and if I'd been right then, I was right now. I started the engine and swung the Beaver back into the water.

I looked round and she was a lonely small figure on the beach, just a few yards and a million dollars and one small killing away.

CHAPTER 29

WE HAD about sixty miles to go to the Norwegian frontier. I kept low over the lake because we were still in the prohibited zone. Instinct, more than anything. Another infringement didn't matter much now.

"What'll the Russians do now?" I asked Judd.

"Not much, I should think. They'll be a bit embarrassed at complaining, since they didn't catch us. And in case your chap Nikkanen doesn't know about the sovereign run by now, we can always make sure he finds out. That'll give him something to bargain with the Russians about. I don't think anything will be said officially." He looked across at me. "What'll happen to you?"

"Same thing. If nothing happens officially, I don't think they'll jump on me for fear I'll blow the story open. I'll have lost my work permit, but I think that would have happened anyway."

"I'm sorry about that." He was twiddling a cigar container,

wondering whether it was too late or too early to start smoking, or perhaps whether the smell would make me faint. I must have looked a bit worn.

He said: "Our friends in the trailer—Koenig and company. Do you think they'll be angry at you?"

I shrugged my left shoulder. "Doesn't much matter. They aren't good enough to worry me."

"A bit amateur," he agreed.

After a while I asked: "And what'll you report?"

He sighed and twiddled the cigar. "Mostly failure, I'm afraid. We've brought Koenig into the open, and I'm glad we've found out about Hartmann, but . . ." He shrugged.

"Was it the sovereign run itself or the forgeries you were after?"

"The forgeries. Strictly between ourselves, we aren't really trying to stop the Russians getting genuine sovereigns. Actually, we make a profit out of it, as long as we keep minting them. Koenig sells them to the Russians, but we sell them to Swiss currency dealers like Koenig—at a percentage. Besides, the sovereign runs are a good clue to who the Russians are dealing with in the West.

"And even if we did stop the runs, the Russians would just start forging their own—in the right gold purity, of course. No," he shook his head, "it's the forgeries with the low gold content that we're after. That ruins everybody. We still use them a lot ourselves. And I dare say the Russians were just as worried. In fact, if Hartmann had proved the forger was on their side of the frontier, we'd probably have slipped the evidence to Moscow and let them deal with it."

I stared at him. "D'you mean *that* was how Hartmann got you to send him across? He pretended the forgeries were being done by the man who picked them up from Adler on *their* side?"

"Oh, I'm sure he was right. He just didn't try to find the man Adler was delivering them to, that's all."

"You still don't know Veikko was doing it?"

He smiled knowingly. "Well, I'd thought so myself at one time—but he wasn't."

"You just didn't find it," I said slowly. "I searched the house, too. It was in the back of the stove: the press, blank discs, melting pots—everything."

His face went very still in the cold, slow dawn light.

I said: "And you thought you'd killed Veikko for nothing."

He struggled to keep two sorts of surprise on his face. Then he said: "Not me, Mr Cary."

I found the Smith and Wesson in my pocket and weighed it in my hand. "So I turned this in to Nikkanen to match up with the bullets in Veikko, it wouldn't matter?" I grinned at him. "It *had* to be you, Judd. Veikko was a fool, but at least he knew what Koenig and Claude were up there for: he wouldn't have let them in the house. And that house isn't easy to break into. But he didn't know you. You could have walked in. Then, when he knew who you were, he'd have pulled that old French cannon. Even *that* shows how much he relied on the house as defence: it probably wouldn't even have fired."

After a little time Judd said: "I couldn't be sure of that."

"You were carrying a gun, Judd."

He nodded. "Well, thank you for telling me. That makes the report rather better. I was wondering if I *had* been a little hasty with Veikko."

I stared at him. "But now you feel better about it—now you know he was forging sovereigns?"

"Well—as I said, it does rather ruin everybody."

"Just your Firm. And the Russian Firm. And a few people like Koenig. But that's all. It still isn't much of a crime outside the spy trade; it was only your world he was wrecking, not the real one."

He sighed. "But a necessary trade, I'm afraid, Mr Cary. And you do know it can't always be fair."

"Yes—I know. Forgive me if I still prefer people who kill people because they think it's right, not necessary."

"You know, we do think we were in the right in this."

"I'm sure you do. But you'd have done the same if you thought you'd been in the wrong." I looked at the pistol in my hand, then slid open the window at my shoulder and dropped it through.

"Maybe," I said, "I just don't like hired killers."

His face went very white and still. Then he fought a smile back onto it, a small and not very real one. "That's just your sense of personal—" Then he shook his head.

"I'm sorry," he said. "It's stopped sounding funny."

We were off the lake now and ahead across the grey empty tundra there ran a thin straight line: the frontier fence.

Judd said: "I shall be saying some nice things about you in my report, quite apart from clearing up the old Hartmann business." He spoke fast and without expression, as if he were reading from the report already. "I think you can take it that you'll be invited to join the Firm again, if you want to."

"Tell them not to bother asking me."

He turned to me, and his face was tired and slumped. "We seem to have messed up your life on two occasions now. We must owe you something. I mean—what have you got out of all of this?"

I touched the *shaman's* drum ornament in my pocket. *From Mountain of the Ulda,* it read. *Fe, Cu, Ni.* Iron, copper, nickel. The mountain of the *Ulda*—the good spirits who look after bears in the winter—lay just south of my survey area. The iron wouldn't be worth working; the copper just maybe. But it was the *Ni* that interested me.

"Just rich," I said. "Just rich."

The frontier fence slid underneath and Finland was behind me.